MECCA PIMP

A NOVEL OF LOVE AND HUMAN TRAFFICKING

BERNARD RADFAR

THIS IS A GENUINE BARNACLE BOOK

A Barnacle Book | Rare Bird Books
453 South Spring Street, Suite 531
Los Angeles, CA 90013
abarnaclebook.com
rarebirdbooks.com

FIRST TRADE PAPERBACK ORIGINAL EDITION

Printed in the United States
Set in Goudy Old Style
Distributed in the U.S. by Publishers Group West

10 9 8 7 6 5 4 3 2 1

Publisher's Cataloging-in-Publication data

Radfar, Bernard.
    Mecca pimp : a novel of love and human trafficking / by Bernard Radfar.
    p. cm.
    ISBN 9780988745605

1. Human trafficking—Fiction. 2. Stalking—Fiction. 3. New York (N.Y.)—Fiction.
4. Saudi Arabia—Fiction. 5. Investigations—Fiction. 6. Marriage—Fiction. 7. Sex—
Fiction. I. Title.

PS3618.A3488 M43 2013
813.6—dc23

To the four families that are more than family to me:
Eradat, Navasky, Shaheen, and Radfar.

And T.C., partner in crime, and so much more.

May those who are born after me
Never travel such roads of love.
                                    —Hitomaro

Thank you, dear Winder, a most gracious stranger in my life,
for helping set this adventure in motion.

This Preface is Also the Opening
by Mary K. Black

M<small>E?</small> It has been said that no individual is an island and so I ask myself why anyone would bother telling a story as if it were the story of an island. My concept of truth accepts all that is colorful and gray, not black and white.

Nothing about me fits in, not even my way of revealing a story. The one I want the world to hear, because it is both like no other and like everyone's.

I've asked myself to describe myself, so you can locate me somewhere inside you. Contrary to my preference for a mature appearance, I look younger than my years and am told that mine is the otherworldly sort of face that belongs on the poster of an old French movie. Some good that does me. Born in the wrong era, in other words, and the wrong place. But nothing is wrong in this world because it is how it should be. We deserve it as is and make it so. We act our parts. And if a bread truck hits you, then you were supposed to get hit by a bread truck. A Croque-Monsieur has to have both ham and Gruyere; it must be served that way, or it isn't a Croque-Monsieur. You get the point.

The source of all our suffering lies in our ignorance.

There are so many elements to even one measly individual. We will get to my history and some explanation of how I got here, I promise. That we have a past in itself isn't the accomplishment. Our duty is to make something of it.

Mine involves a man and our love, and how it unfolds.

We embrace the heavy burden of loving too much where one can't.

Beginning with a disillusionment with my successful career was the truth I could no longer ignore: I, a wife of twenty-two years, was lost, most of all, as a woman. It had to be made different, and it is this fate that I beg to share.

INTRODUCTION

Mary, A New Life
by Cyrus Kahn, The Mary Black Foundation

I say that, from that time forward, love governed my soul.

—Dante Alighieri, *Vita Nova*

MOST OF US HAVE a place within where we savor the idea of a new life. But every time we contemplate what it would entail, we find ourselves in the same one we were trying to escape.

How new can we become? It is the question of science, of how anything is, and it was the heart of Mary Black's life.

The fall of 2010 marked the end of a pivotal transitional period for her. Mark Black had left for the Middle East, to run the lucrative businesses they'd started together. This time it signified the end of their turbulent marriage. She'd retired from everything having to do with him, but it was wrenching for Mary.

As her biographer, and the Honorary President of the Mary Black Foundation, I believe it is safe to say that it was at this stage in her dangerous and restless life when Mary withdrew from the world on a manic mission to invent herself.

According to trusted sources, it was on one night with a cold wind that Mary went upstairs to her bath. That was it. A decision had been made to start again. Optimistic about the possibility of a new life, she seemed desperate to leave as soon as possible. I found this revealing cry buried deep in her papers, not long before she would march out of the Bronx on horseback:

Dear Professor Winder McConnell,

I read with great interest that you are a teacher of chivalry. Though I grew up in the city, I have always considered myself to be a knight. I am about to embark on a journey in armor and would like to know if you've any suggestions for me. I am at a point that I am disgruntled with life. The future is a nightmare from which I am trying to wake. What then would you say to a wandering knight who will leave Manhattan to travel upstate and then cross-country in this day and age?

Mary K. Black

Dear Mary Black,

Thank you for your note, the first of its sort I have ever received. At the risk of being labeled "retrograde," I'm afraid there is a problem to begin with. If you are, as I surmise, of the "fairer sex," you have no business being a knight at all, at least historically. Joan of Arc was a remarkable exception to the rule that only males engage in combat, at least in the Middle Ages.

Today's warriors have that in common with their knightly predecessors. The weapons have changed, but the code of knightly virtues has not, with respect to one of its three components: honestum (worldly honor), adherence to prudentia ('wisdom'), along with fortitudo ('courage'), temperantia ('moderation'), and iustitia ('justice') would be just as much expected, I imagine, of today's warriors as it was of knights of the thirteenth century.

Mary, I would say that adherence to the concept of honestum, along with a healthy constellation of honor and loyalty, would be the best advice I could give to any contemporary knight. These are virtues that have withstood the test of time.

I am sorry to hear you are disgruntled. The trick, my dear Mary, is to fit into the world without losing one's sovereignty. That may take you a lifetime, but it is, as I have found, quite possible.

All the best,
Winder McConnell
Professor of German, University of California

ALL THIS WAS MORE than sufficient for her to begin her journey, and, as one of her greatest admirers, I salute her for it. Engraved on the platinum ring she wore at all times was the knight's oath, *We freely set ourselves upon this course, binding ourselves to the light as strongly as we are capable of.*

Cyrus Kahn
The Mary Black Foundation
Hillsdale, New York

PROLOGUE

by Mark Black

M Y MONIKER HAD BECOME The Worst Man.
I, Mark Black, lover, husband of many years and brother spirit to Mary, confess that it was now impossible for us to coexist at our picket-fenced home. What was once a blissful union had morphed into its opposite.

Call it a war.

Following our dramatic fall, I became possessed with such grief that, separating myself from everyone, all that remained was a feeling of total ruin. Once you are tied to someone, let alone someone as unique and heartful as Mary, you never part.

Go, pretend that's possible, but then you haven't loved.

Love is the madness that is shared by two.

For me, being with someone else is not comparable to my Mary. So if I want a day like a day with her, hearing a voice that touches the depths of me the way Mary's does, there's no option but to find her. So much of the rest of life lumps together.

On paper, we are still one. She won't answer the lawyers I send her way. It isn't normal for a person not to fear, but Mary doesn't. Never has. Anyhow, they provide me with her accurate status now, so I needn't listen to her tales any longer. Once upon a time that is how it was; I wouldn't know something, and she would tell me her *I'm Going to Turn Your Mind Inside Out* version. That's why it is essential to stay away, realizing in my soul that her goal had become destroying everything we'd made and all that's left of me in her.

If only we could go back to all that was.

We must keep apart. You there, I here.

Meanwhile, I will protect Mary, even when she won't accept what I offer, in my own quiet way, from above. What she feels as she goes about her life is precious to me. Each time we tried to salvage our unity, the torment had been overwhelming.

We were once tender and beautiful.

Weep, lovers, for all that is now lost.

CHAPTER ONE

From an Officer, About Four Minutes and Thirty-Three Seconds of Awkward Silences

FROM THE DESK OF OFFICER JACKIE CANAL
NEW YORK POLICE DEPARTMENT

It may have been that his knife went into her as she drove her knife into him. Being one of the first to enter on that humid summer morning, I found an ear-piercing Nina Simone playing off an iPod clock radio, a half-gallon of dried blood spread out in splatters across the pale gray walls and the couple's modernist zebra-hide rug, where unconscious he and she lay, woman on man, body on body, sworn to one another in silence, it seems, in a bond the likes of which few of us can attest to comprehending.

This was love at its worst.

Rarely are things as they seem between two lovers.

And here they were as I found them, in the middle of things.

A few days before this scene of carnage I'd been sent to the Black's home. The two of them hand in hand on the couch trying to convince me, after several uncomfortable pauses, that there was no cause for concern. They looked remarkably similar, had the same laugh. I suppose that happens in love.

There were fresh white roses on the end table.

After an hour of routine questioning, and bearing witness to two foot massages, I checked each of them for physical abuse. Mark Black was hiding a major posterior intramuscular bruise but insisted that it was not something that concerned him. Their explanation: passions escalated, and they assured me that this too passed. Mary Black expressed regrets about having struck him, which seemed reasonable, a sign that they were restoring matters to peaceful ones.

The systemic abuser often justifies his or her actions and puts the blame on the spouse.

When it comes to love, a certain amount of violence is expected, so I typed up my warning and left it with our sergeant, where it would be filed for three months and then moved to an archive upstate.

On the tragic and bloody day that followed later that week, ambulances arrived just after me, as I happened to be nearby wrapping up another house call for domestic violence. This is the Bronx, and, in the heat of summer, we're doing overtime.

It was up to our team of specialists to unravel what had occurred at the property. I say property because hair, blood and fresh semen were found outside, after their maimed bodies were rushed to the trauma center.

Mark had been the one to call, with terror in his voice. The emergency operator asked about his condition and all he could manage to get out was, *She says she is going to cut it off.* Doctors found three gashes along his inner leg, as if an attempt was made to castrate him, but it was impossible, from a criminological perspective, to determine whether Mary had been aiming there or for his innards. By the time the lawyers would mettle, the intention to castrate wouldn't be enough to go on, unless we had a case of premeditated castration, which didn't seem likely.

Male spousal abuse by females and wives is a serious matter, one that has informed much of my academic research. For me it is no laughing matter, as it is far more commonplace than we realize; men are routinely raped and attacked and killed.

On a deeper level, what we professionals are discovering is that the biological man, the one with the penis (or both or neither in homosexual relationships), is not necessarily the man at all times in the relationship. Think of it as a gender spectrum, and at any time we exist somewhere along the arc, so that the wife or girlfriend can just as easily fulfill the male role. We refer to this as a fantasy, as the two try to form a unity.

The *mise en scène* of these fantasies is the bedroom.

You can imagine how complicated that can become, over time. It is the reason I have a job, because this type of violence, I'm sorry to say, will occur. Lovers keep on loving and hating.

This is because desire and attraction aren't love, though we pretend and believe they are.

The flip side underlying the intoxicating state of romance is composed of enmity and violence. The extent of the physical damage due to the hate can, in some relationships, occur with the same intensity as the feeling of attraction. That said, the fact that Mark had been the one to make the call also raised our suspicions that he might be manipulating the facts. In my initial interview with Mary, while Mark was detained in the other room, she complained that he was a chronic liar. The same occurred when I met alone with Mark. We have techniques to deal with the truth, such as having the story told backwards, but as far as I could surmise, each was forthright and honest.

Based on the physical evidence in the house, we were left with a long list of questions. Fingerprint analysis, for example, often tells multiple stories. The primary answer we sought was which party set the trail of violence in motion. Samples were taken from around the house and all was documented while we waited for the couple to come to.

After an initial meeting, with each of the investigators present, we decided that the couple's testimonies would determine our course of action.

That evening Mark woke before her and the first words out of his mouth were questions about Mary's condition, whether she'd survived. He wept, stating that it had all come down to a misunderstanding, and begged nurses to house them in one room. "Our love is deeper than any ocean," he told me. The same basic testimony occurred the following day, once Mary woke up after her reparative surgeries. Both were under arrest, however, and their respective locations were to be kept confidential.

Once the doctors permitted us full access to the subjects, we found ourselves in a deeper mess, as neither would press charges. The last thing I wanted, given the extent of the physical damage, was to dismiss it as a routine case of mutual domestic violence. Mary and Mark claimed that the first blows had been dealt simultaneously, each with their own knife. There was no issue of self-defense and, since both of them were trained in martial arts, to some extent they knew what they were doing to one another. Plus, the stories matched up, down to each minuscule detail. Lawyers arrived wanting to throw the whole case away, dismissing it as a crime of passion.

One curious mystery that we were never ever able to solve was how the two met. Each of their lawyers forced us to stop questioning along those lines. My sergeant was desperate to get one of them to admit some wrongdoing, or, at the very least, press charges. But at some point he had to close the file.

My destiny? I was taken off the case, and a year later we stopped investigating the Blacks, after routine visits to the house determined that no further violence had been inflicted. I set aside the file with the eerie feeling that these two were not done with one another. They pay penalty and retribution to each other for their injustice in accordance with the ordering of time.

Jackie Canal
Domestic Violence Unit, NYPD
April 13, 2006

CHAPTER TWO

Which Retains the Fleeting Forms of Things, When Things Themselves Are Gone

Mary Black
December 18, 2010

I may not be prepared for the hostility that will greet me when I leave the open stretches between towns and enter forth as a stranger. The need to keep moving, moving all the time. I wish I could be sure of myself, but in a world that requires slaves, I realize I might never fit in. There will be so much more to fear, including Mark.

It isn't in him to leave me alone. Adorable, yes, charming beyond belief even, but that's only the half of it.

There were people out there to help with these incapacitating feelings:

Dear Rick Cluchey as Samuel Beckett,

It has come to my attention that my beloved playwright was your dear friend, and that you are performing a play about the two of you. I'm in a bind, struggling with a question that I'll need you to answer as Sam, if you don't mind; I hope that you aren't insulted, as I know that it is you speaking. So here we go:

Dear Sam, I am at an end that is a beginning. I didn't say the end and I know that to you the two are more similar than mortals ever care to admit. It has come time to put on the old armor suit and head out into the world with few possessions but a sack of coin, a book of Persian poetry, and one of your plays.

Have any words of advice for me as I wander through this country, hoping to remake myself? I am starting to fear, the closer I get to leaving. Really scared. Please answer soon.

Regards,
Mary K. Black

Mary K.,

Be careful wandering about. Wise if you took along a jug (I found Bushmills a sound companion) and a big old dog for the hard road. Mine was German, as in shepherd, long hair, sharp teeth, a mean bastard as well. If you find a good dog, be a gentle owner and please don't name it after me.

My plays, sadly out of fashion lately, were meant to inspire the dead. I'm happy to learn you formed a connection with the deceased in your ample imagination.

Good luck,
Samuel Beckett

COURAGE FROM THE DEAD, what better? It was a warm evening for this time of year and I could hear people on the street gabbing about trivial things late into the night, when most were already home, long asleep. I went back to my kitchen and heated up three biscuits, buttered them. Delicate food for delicate times. My nerves were getting the best of me.

That's when a knock started on the side door. The plan—not to answer it, but the person persisted twice more, louder each time.

I stood up and went to answer. You have to confront fear.

"Mary? Mary, you can't hide forever."

A friend's voice. I get it, this is what they do, they drop in. I've been known to visit too, but not lately. That mood hasn't hit.

I opened the door with reluctance.

"At least you're alive." Guy wore a tan cashmere overcoat and matching tan leather gloves, the cheapest sort one might buy from a Vietnamese lady on Canal. "You know, you could pick up the phone once in a while."

Guy seemed fragile at that moment, as if he didn't know where he stood with me. *I've been ignoring you, and we both know it.* No, I couldn't say that. Not yet.

How did we connect with Guy in the first place? I knew him from an evening seminar on modern South American novelists, where we sat in the back row. In case we fell asleep we had a place for our heads.

Even then Guy didn't seem to care that I was already married.

He lived downtown, in a cramped railroad apartment above a Tibetan shop where they always burned foul incense that wafted its way into his place. He put up with it because of the rock-bottom rent. Guy is also my only friend with a car, a Mazda that most people would have demolished. Sometimes we leave the city together, sharing books by Sebald, Cortazar, and clippings from the week's New Yorker. One morning he picked me up to visit several apple orchards, on a hunt for Russets. Describing it now, I can see how this could be construed as romantic, but it wasn't. That was the sort of thing we did together this fall, before I decided to stay home, all the time.

I know what you're thinking, that this sounds like the beginnings of the blues. It was more than that.

"I've been busy here," I said. "We all need alone time."

Guy filled the kettle to the rim with water from the filter tap. He knew his way around the kitchen. If I were to bring home a new Darjeeling or jar of honey, Guy would spot it and open it without asking. The first Sunday of the month was risotto night over here, and he was in charge. Inexplicably, Mark let him use his knives, and no one else. "Where's your husband?"

Even though I recognized that he was trying to be clever, it annoyed me that Guy didn't call Mark by his name. I let it slide. "He marched off and left the country again."

"That's it?"

Guy picked the wrong evening to mess with me.

"How long's it been this time?" he added.

It should've been obvious that I was grieving and didn't want to talk about it. "I don't know, two or three months, maybe." I could tell that he wanted to hear more, but wouldn't oblige. "You want a biscuit? I made them from scratch this morning."

"Why not?" Guy took off his jacket, something he'd probably snagged from his father's closet. He looked silly wearing it, in that hand-me-down kind of hipster rebellious way. "Mom asked me if you'd come over for Christmas. We're doing it in the country this year."

She wasn't my mom. Mine died a long time ago. He should be thoughtful and add the possessive. People's presumptions get to me. As for the invite, somewhere within he must've known that this wasn't my year for celebrating holidays. "I'll let you know. That's sweet of your mother."

"No, I'm not letting you stay home," Guy said. "Come on. It won't be the same without you."

"No one ever discovers the depths of his own loneliness."

"You and your quotes. Who said that?"

"Georges Bernanos."

"Did I ever tell you how cool beyond belief you are?"

Maybe he thought I'd given him a green light to flirt, but I hadn't. When someone has been alone long enough, they see through intentions, even when they don't want to.

To some people it feels good to be wanted. Not me. I was head deep in my study of classical epic poetry at this point, fine preparation for what was ahead in my life. And then there were long, steamy baths. Nina Simone on the turntable, Offenbach's Orpheus in my bedroom. "I'm borrowing a horse and leaving soon. This life I've been living, it's over."

"You're kidding," he said.

It seemed to me that it was dawning on him that this threat of going away was genuine.

Guy continued. "You must love your husband deeply."

His sarcasm hurt. "He's your friend. You know his name, so use it. And yeah, there's a lot of pain right now."

"May I ask you something personal?"

He must know I won't answer that question with a no.

Guy tilted his head my direction, as if to express curiosity. "Why did you fall for Mark in the beginning? Out with it."

"He was born charming. Mark has that special kind of beautiful where you only want to be with him. He could be ordering a coffee, but the way he does it has so much conviction and grace, you end up wanting to be with him all the time. And though you may not know it now, at one time he didn't have a mean bone in his body."

"Time changed him?"

"I suppose much did." It wasn't something that could be explained. Sure, now my life is resetting itself, but there's history with this man I chose as my companion in life. "Besides, even when he talks tough, he doesn't have what it takes to back it. They're words. Cheap words. Behind it all is a warm, funny man who is playing with the world."

"Yeah, I've seen him avoid stepping on ants when he walks."

"Kids called him Chocolate, because of his kindness and peacefulness."

"That's amazing."

Ah, that word. I needed to change the topic, because of the pain, and divulged how I had been contacting realtors about selling the house. "This is about going away for good. I have to start over."

"What about Pastis, our morning coffees sitting outside?" Guy asked. "I don't believe this." That's when he scratched the area just above his ear and smelled his finger.

"Why did you do that?" I had to comment on it.

He looked at me all confused.

"What are you sniffing?" It wasn't as if I thought he didn't understand me.

"Nothing," he said, and did it again.

How we lie, I thought. We fool ourselves into believing other people aren't perceptive. I knew what he was doing but wanted to hear him describe it. He shrunk instead. "Sometimes I sniff my finger after I haven't bathed for a few days. In case you can't figure it out, that's to check what I smell like down there." I pointed at my privates. After I said it, I was hoping he wouldn't think that I was now suggesting something more with him. That would be a mistake. Making mistakes with men is a no no.

"Oh really. You do?"

"You mean Mark never told you that? He liked it when I smelled strong." I knew how close he was to my husband. They shared everything, or at least more than I wanted them to. It was hard to believe this hadn't come up between them.

"Hell no," Guy answered, on the defensive. "We don't talk about these kinds of things." Guy was smiling the way someone smiles when they want to believe you want them.

"You're saying Mark hasn't called you since he left?"

"Nope. Emailed, but he doesn't answer," Guy said. "Guess he's like you."

He was so at ease it was starting to bother me. Besides, I know Mark better than Mark knows himself, and he answers every email within minutes, on that iPhone he's so smug about owning.

"I think you should leave." I said it and started putting away the wood bowls that were drying on the countertop. "I'm so damn tired. It isn't about you."

Guy looked put out nevertheless, and I couldn't blame him. He had too much pride to deny my request. A final sip of tea and he came over to hug me. "Fine. I'll swing by one of these days. You look like you're going to fall down from exhaustion."

I wasn't that tired. He was making himself feel better by saying so.

Once he was out of here I knew I'd be up most of the night arranging things to leave. I felt almost free again.

There was one problem: Mark hadn't been on my mind at all in recent days, but seeing Guy changed that. At one time Mark and I had been so close that together we were better than being one person. Now, how different it was. Thoughts shouldn't have wandered to him right then, but they wouldn't stop. *He was once Chocolate.* I had to keep from tormenting myself with destructive emotions, and stay on my path. The new life, at least I'd the promise of that. It was night, and I needed it to remain peaceful.

CHAPTER THREE

Nothing is Beautiful From Every Angle

Mark Black
December 19, 2010

What a louse Guy is. I should be thankful that's the case. For a little help with the rent, or a mediocre sushi meal, he'll do anything I tell him.

It is inconceivable that Mary divulges as much as she does about herself. I imagine she foretells that he will relay me his findings. That's how cunning she is.

When dealing with a person as selfish as Guy, it is necessary to be on the ball; he's always had his eyes on her. One can feel these things. There was a little too much attention and wonder showered upon her, even if I was the one speaking. You've been there, I'm sure, with a similar weasel. He tried to merge with each of us, befriending me, while offering her massages. Guy is someone that fell into my life because of someone important to me. I have no friends, not these days. I'm not that type, and my conclusion is that we've to accept that this is often a friendless world.

Truth be told, Mary was my only friend. That's why I can be so forthright.

The following is a record of our chat from the other night, after Guy left Mary:

ME: Finally!

GUY: What? It hasn't been that long.

ME: Well?

GUY: She's gone crazy. She's selling the house and says she is leaving everything.

ME: Nothing too new about that.

GUY: Well, this time it is for real. There's a for sale sign out front.

ME: Because she's going where?

GUY: She won't say.

ME: Then find out. How difficult is that?

GUY: Trying.

ME: I'm worried about her. What's she been doing all day?

GUY: Same old. She stays home. I got the feeling she's writing again.

ME: Watch out. Did she have any books out?

GUY: I saw some Montaigne on the kitchen table.

ME: Figures. She acts like she has that kind of mind. Writes in her journal all the time.

GUY: I'm trying to get on her computer.

ME: Good. So try and figure out her email password.

GUY: I know. You told me that already.

ME: And I won't see one cent from the sale of the house.

GUY: Why?

ME: She owns it, not me.

GUY: It sounds like she's not going to work with you any more. She's done.

ME: So what?

GUY: I thought you were partners. But she told me how much she hates everything to do with this business.

ME: I'll run it without her. I have plenty of women now. We got a shipment this week from Brazil.

GUY: I'm jealous. Hot ones?

ME: The best.

GUY: Any virgins? I know how much you like virgins.

ME: Yes, a few.

GUY: Save one for me, man.

ME: Yeah right. They're already working anyway. The Arabs can't get enough. BTW, how did Mary look?

GUY: A little pale. She looks like she never goes out.

ME: Make sure she doesn't get sick. That's the last thing I want.

GUY: Will do.

ME: I need you to find out where she is going. This chat is all fine and dandy, but I have to know a lot more. I feel sick with worry.

GUY: Okay, I'll check into it all.

ME: I mean, like I would die for her. Guard her from all suffering.

GUY: I get it. Also, please send me your recipe for beef Bourguignon. It was the best one I ever had.

ME: Sure thing. I learned it from my mother, bless her soul.

GUY: Awesome. And Mark?

ME: What?

GUY: Can I get some cash?

ME: I'm still here in Mecca. But I'll wire some to you.

GUY: Cool.

GUY DIDN'T KNOW HOW helpful he'd been, but far better for him not to have a clue. Mary and I had great success with keeping people in the dark about these sorts of things. Keep them hungry and scrounging. I do the same with the women who work for me, in a way. They have plenty, but there's always that hook of the promise of more that brings them back. Money kills them. Otherwise they'd take their big tips and disappear. I believe in granting them all the freedom in the world, in other words. It is important for these women to adore me. And I will protect them with everything I have.

Between the lines I'd have to figure out how she was playing Guy. Yes, she's different from me and befriends people, even if it is to satisfy a weird idea of life she happens to be working on. It has become an agony to imagine myself without her. I suppose you could assert at this point that she is powerful because, although I meant to be talking about myself, I ended up on the subject of Mary Black, my wife, and the person in this world I fear I hate more than anyone, because of all this love inside.

CHAPTER FOUR

Aggression in So Many Guises, With the Help of My Professor, Winder

Mary Black
December 20, 2010

If so many around were willing to lead bitter, unsatisfying lives, then I knew I had to hurry out of here before I would become like them. The stars clustered in evil signs. Everything was coming together, meanwhile. My sister's friend, Qishon, delivered my Arabian horse in the morning and said she didn't mind me calling him Beckett. So what if he didn't look anything like Samuel Beckett. This one was well-fed, impressed upon others the aura of exercise and continuous grooming, his chocolate coat gleamed even on this cloudy day.

The garage was empty enough that I felt assured Beckett would be comfortable sleeping there, next to the cardboard box full of my ready-to-wear armor. That's all the time I was giving myself. Something told me that hesitating to depart wouldn't prove wise.

Guy returned, again uninvited, as he hinted he would. I was upstairs in bed and was thinking about masturbating when he knocked.

So it was natural to consider him an interruption.

I put on my trendy pink panties and spa robe and went downstairs to open the door. On the way I realized that for the foreseeable future I might not be sleeping naked. That's depressing. I would do what I could to make the wild luxurious. A knapsack filled with biltong was ready, at least. My iPad in the waterproof case was charged and I'd downloaded plenty of productivity apps to keep me busy. There are travel purists that would take issue with me for this, but they're not the ones snowshoeing in the woods in search of somewhere to sleep, as I will be.

So Guy asked me about the horse. *Damn he's annoying sometimes.* He must have been poking around. "I told you the other day that I got it from someone."

"Someone." It came out of him all skeptical. "Who?"

"Qishon."

"You never mentioned anyone named Qishon before."

"I know her through my sister, from way back." That's about all I had to say. I went back inside, and he followed me.

"Thalia?"

"Yes."

"I haven't heard you mention her in ages," he said. "Since when do you talk to her?"

Guy was full of questions. "I don't."

"Fine. But I'm anxious to hear where you're going with this horse."

"That's a secret." I dropped some espresso beans into my new portable grinder. Another toy for the road; please don't dismiss me as a yuppie. "You can't take it personally just because you're another person."

"What's that supposed to mean?" he asked.

"You're another person, so I can't share it with you." It seemed like Guy wanted me to feel sorry for him, pushing this tale about how he was losing a friend. "My mistake was telling you anything."

"You can talk to one person," Guy answered, "and it would still be your secret. A secret is a secret until you share it with a bunch of people. Once many know, it becomes something public."

Clever. But annoying. I'm more of a member of the *A word is dead when it is said* school of things. I wasn't going for his sales pitch. Little shivers meandered up my spine that felt like fear. My body was telling me something. *Why the interrogation,* I wondered.

"I'll tell you where I'm going if you promise to leave me alone about it," I said. "Don't ask me anything afterward, you hear."

"You're being so uptight," he said.

"Then forget it."

"Okay, deal," Guy said. "I'll try not to ask more."

"I'm flying to Florida next week." I said it as though I was telling him that I craved his body, so that he couldn't help but be tricked by the lie. Flirting blinds men. They'll believe anything that much more this way. "But that's it. Not another word."

"You're so not Florida." Guy grabbed a banana from the counter and started peeling it. "No fair. You have to tell me more than that."

At times like these my tendency would be to leave him with a book and go upstairs to my bath. But I didn't trust him not to follow, or rustle through my drawers. If there's one thing I have as a gift, it is intuition. A conscious decision was made to make myself boring and give him zero attention, so much so that he drank his coffee and left.

Time for some immediate help from a trusted source. Back to the computer:

Dear Professor Winder McConnell,

I am preparing to leave, now that most of what I own is packed away and the horse is ready. Waiting on some decent weather in the Northeast, more or less. I've a question about what you know about how knights handle the matter of departing. I've one friend who has been poking around more than I like, asking about where I'm going. I've told him that it is none of his business and even ended up lying to him about what's next. It seems to me that I have the right to embark without telling those that know me. Supposing they end up on my trail, I'm not sure whether I will be able to treat them as friends. This will seem like an act of aggression, to be handled as such.

I look forward to hearing your thoughts, as you have a knack for bringing wisdom to my life.

Warm regards,
Mary

An hour later this appeared in my Inbox:

Dear Mary,

One has to be careful here. Parzival leaves his mother, Arthur's court, and the Grail Castle without much ado—as long as he remains a bit of a fool, having spent his earlier years in a forest. Knights may have individual quests (Parzival, Erec, etc.), but they are, at heart, "social animals." The loner, in the way we experience him in many of Clint Eastwood's Italian and post-1966 American westerns, "the solitary hero," is not a concept that one would associate with medieval knight-heroes. I think I would adopt a "softer" tone: "I have something that I must do; please do not ask me to elaborate at this time…" and not alienate. Erec, of course, at least in the German version, takes an unceremonious leave of his home after he has been admonished by his wife, Enite, for his idleness, and tells her to keep her mouth shut or suffer consequences, as he sets out on his own "quest." Gachmuret, father of Parzival, leaves the prospect of a domesticated existence—thanks to the generosity of his brother and the love shown him by their vassals—to set out and make his own way, dismaying the latter.

This may give you something to work with.

Best,
Winder McConnell

WINDER WAS RIGHT, BUT I couldn't trust Guy with something this precious. I opened my browser and bought a refundable ticket to Miami, making sure to leave it out for Guy to find. Knights utilize any number of decoys, so why shouldn't I?

It was high time to pull the trigger. People will ask how I can afford to leave. Mark and I hid a stash abroad, accrued from our business. Sex is lucrative. Frank Bauer at Swiss Bank International answered me that morning with great news: "It will be a little expensive, but we can arrange a debit card where there will be no trail and no name on it, with a number identifiable by you. Your peace of mind will not come cheap, however." My duffel bags were packed, and I had not much left to think about.

All I needed was to leave.

This is it, wake up and do it, Mar. You hand a realtor your keys, tell a Swiss banker you're on the loose, and nothing in the world can stop you.

CHAPTER FIVE

In Which the Equipment and Torment of Mary, and Mark, and Others is Treated

ME: Guy?

GUY: What, Mark?

ME: I need you to get serious. If she's leaving, you gotta follow her.

GUY: I can't. I've a job.

ME: F your job.

GUY: Why? Like you're going to pay me.

ME: That's what I implied.

GUY: I want it up front.

ME: Half.

GUY: Good enough.

ME: Florida is expensive. You'll be on a budget.

GUY: I'll be careful.

ME: Don't go opening Michelin guides to figure out where to eat.

GUY: I get it, Mark.

ME: There's a steak place I want you to try, but other than that it'll be diners and delis.

GUY: Cool.

ME: Investigate everything. Notice, find clues. Stay near the house, most of all at night.

GUY: I will. Have you contacted her?

ME: I won't, no. Fuck her.

GUY: You should.

ME: No advice please. I'm hiring you. Don't mess this one up. You have to be perfect.

GUY: I know. Perfect like you.

ME: What's that supposed to mean? Being a smart ass?

GUY: You have it all. Brains, looks that make women blush. And now on top of it you have tons of money. You must know your effect on people.

ME: You forgot about my modesty.

GUY: Oh yeah, that's your defining quality.

ME: But if you want the other half, you'll have to figure out WTF is up. You have to make sure that I can protect her. That's my duty. Nothing can happen to her. Got it?

GUY: Yeah. Roger wilco.

YOU GET WHAT YOU pay for, in other words. I don't trust Guy with my wife, but I can't spend my days troubling myself with her. At one time that was the case, and I was a better man for it. At this point I've a business to run, and other women to attend to. They can't be left alone.

Without me, anything can happen to these women, and it is my duty to guarantee their safety.

Mary hid much. I promise that—even if it is the last thing I do—I will unearth it. It isn't clear what sort of thing it might be. She's got passwords on everything she owns, for example, so I could never get into her computer. I once knew everything about her, and now I can't let go. Every first Friday of the month she would go to one of the bank safes in the city that she pays for. It is my duty to know what is in there. Or she'd take the phone to the bathroom and turn on the fan. I can't connect the dots. Never was a more mysterious woman to walk this planet.

I can play the role of the cheat, if need be, but at least I admit it. Others are the same and they deny it about themselves, which is a whole lot worse in my mind. Hypocrisy. So maybe I have a hard time trusting other people, like she used to repeat ad infinitum. So what? You want the gullible type, go be with the gullible type.

I'm tired of nice.

She made me this way. Before all went sour, I was an innocent person who believed in people, compassionate to a fault. Maybe I am a broken man, jaded and embittered. Even so, I make sure my women are always treated with complete respect. No client can damage them, no matter what fantasy they're hoping to create. I am prepared to destroy men.

For years, Mary affirmed my faith in love, but then she figured out a way to open up the deepest miseries in me.

Now, it was essential to follow her in case she was leaving for good. While Mary schemed, my plan of attack would be devised. Since we are equal in number, man vs. wife, I would have to gain my advantage in some other way. She's more cunning, but I am closer to savage, so it is anyone's game. What worries me is that she will be alone, and when you are alone, even though you risk weakness, you can hide from your enemy. That's figuratively speaking, I guess. Mary is not my enemy.

We ran our tiny kingdom together.

For this reason, Guy's crazy if he thinks I'm not going to spy on my spy:

Dear HPI Private Investigation,

I need your services as soon as possible. My wife is going to Florida next week and I am in possession of her flight information. What she will be up to afterward is anyone's guess. I don't like to guess.

Mary and I are no longer on speaking terms. But I am one step ahead of her, thanks to Guy, this person who thinks he's my friend. You know the kind of jerk I'm talking about: yoga every day, wears big headphones, long sideburns.

Warn your officers that she's seductive. Mary's beautiful and luminescent when she wants to be, cracking jokes on Latin sayings and discoursing on the psychology of 16th century samurai while making you the best bouillabaisse you ever had in your life.

Tell me that's not every man's dream.

You've figured out by now that she is rather perceptive. Her IQ is off the charts and she is self-educated to the max. There isn't a La Rochefoucauld aphorism that she doesn't know by heart. She and I have taken our share of anti-surveillance seminars on top of it. Although Mary is a believer in nonviolence, I wouldn't be surprised if she is armed. We have done sniper training together in rural Arizona.

I don't care about Guy; he is bound to mess up.

I understand that hiring you for a lengthy project such as this will be pricey, and ask that you consider my sanity when you begin quoting me for your time and expertise.

Sincerely,
Mark Black

Hi Mark,

Thank you for your inquiry with us. I am convinced that we can cover all your concerns, but it is very difficult to locate people at the airport, let alone follow them from the airport to see where they are going. Our surveillance investigations begin at $1300 per day.

Unlike your friend Guy, we are professionals and have retired federal agents, police officers, seasoned investigators, and a vast array of connections at our disposal. Above all, we are here to provide you with the truth and facts—there will be no ulterior motives when hiring an outside source like an investigator vs. hiring your friend. Try and find out where she will be staying.

Thanks,
Alison Garbo

IF I COULD JUST get over the sticker shock of what they charge, I think I could get somewhere. Something tells me it will never be easy. Because when it comes to Mary, nothing ever is. The bond is one that can't be broken, no matter how great the separation.

She's the blood of my existence.

CHAPTER SIX

Which Treats of the Character and Pursuits of Her Getting a Life

Mary Black
December 23, 2010

Regarding leaving, I can't say it was easy, but nothing great is. It has been recorded that Sir Parry had no complaints on his way to the Arctic, aside from parting with Lady Parry, so I took his words to heart when I showered and came downstairs for what would be the last time. Up Broadway in the wee hours of the morning so nobody would see me is how I decided to do it, like any sound of mind knight who lives in the Bronx would.

The occasional sanitary truck passed, but my guess is that they weren't in the state of mind to look around.

Beckett moved at a full tilt, as if he were desperate to get out of the city, too. It was like war: you need to go unnoticed, you move as fast as you can. From Yonkers I pointed his crest towards the Old Croton Trailway and continued north, stopping for sips from a bota bag that was filled to capacity with a new crop of Sencha tea. Brewing it was the last thing I did before hanging the keys on a low branch of a maple tree for Maximilian, who would get rid of everything. It was like surviving a flood. Only me, the horse, little else.

I knew I was in the clear when we trotted past Sleepy Hollow Cemetery, meters past the Amoco station. Daylight was just starting to appear so it couldn't have been better timing to be standing before all the forests ahead. Forty-two minutes after departure the gateway to my disappearance stood before me, a world of trees and valleys, paved pathways between for the lazy in us. I'd figure out a way to cross highways, one way or another. There was no rush to be anywhere. I had, after all, no intention of having anything like a destination. It would get easier the further I got from the suburbs, with all their golf courses and fenced estates, owned by the kinds of people who wanted to live free from the likes of me. In Scarborough, the yellow M peaked out above the trees, the smell of exhaust emerged again. For some reason it was many legal practices and nursing homes that littered the towns. A few minutes in the relative wild and I'd grown accustomed to it. It was my turn to play Thoreau in some weird way. He explored the sea of Concord and I would begin with the dry sea of Westchester, the flat remains of a glacier. I hurried out of there, in no small thanks to Bear Mountain Bridge Road, where I crossed the Hudson, keeping east of the military academy.

There was always so much to avoid in life. It starts when you're a kid and you're told to look both ways before you cross the street and not to talk to strangers. By the time you've become me, it is more like a philosophy of existence.

CHAPTER SEVEN

The Individual Thinks That Harm is Occurring, or is Going to Occur, Skip Tracer

Dear Erik Soderbergh,

We come to a certain point in life when we realize it is time to leave everything. I understand that you are the foremost expert on people who disappear, whatever their reasons might be. I can imagine why fugitives or people escaping family do this, but I am contacting you today about my beloved wife. Mary, a woman so unique and wonderful I can't bear the thought that she has been planning her escape from our cherished life together and starting anew. Our mutual friend informed me of this, on the condition that I keep it private. I have been sleepless ever since. My days and nights are full of heartache and misery. I write to ask what you suggest that I do. I can't bear to lose her.

Yours,
Mark Black

LIKE I SAID, I will stretch the truth if I have to. I know when I'm lying, and that's what matters. He doesn't have to know any more than that to tell me what I need to know. The truth would confuse things. In a society that pretends it is truthful, it is advantageous to lie.

Fifteen minutes later Erik Soderbergh answered from his Droid with a simple hello, some pricing information, and the transcript of a talk he delivered to an assembly of detectives:

Tracing The Patterns of Your Existence: Erik Soderbergh

Twentieth century man is a painfully self-conscious creature, but he has lost that pride of consciousness which, in centuries past, was so magnificent. We live in an age of deliberate choice about who to be, our identities constantly in flux, according to a consumer culture that designs itself around each of our respective desires. Ever since Moses vanished in the desert to die, never to be found, modern society has wondered about what it means to leave everything, including who we have been before.

I know many of you aren't here to explore the philosophical implications of your work. You want devastating techniques so that you can get home to your children at a reasonable hour. I understand that. Now, I'm not that kind of person. I am a singular man that has nothing else to live for.

There are patterns to the kinds of people who disappear. You must first analyze how the person spends or gathers his funds. If he finds work, your life has been made easier. Everything you've ever spent on a credit card is on file. That's a pattern. Your service provider stores what you look up on the Internet. Such a person cannot have left information about himself in any way. The local library records what books you've borrowed. Your passport shows when you went where, if you left the country. Your digital camera will reveal the location of every photograph you take. The more modern the person, the easier to track, in some respects. These are the kinds of leads you need to follow, knowing full well that the skilled person will pile the information thick with deceptive leads. The person who abandons his past must never contact anyone he has ever contacted before. That isn't easy when it is your mother's birthday. But people like this are struggling for their survival, and they can go to extremes to do so. Your task is a most challenging one, as a result. But the beauty of existence is that it implies something that is. Existence implies effect. It is Newtonian in essence, every action creates an opposite reaction. You've to find the ripples. I hope that I have been helpful in clarifying in this limited time some flavor to the nature of the kind of pursuit we need to follow to discover who is hidden and concealed. Given the privacy abuses of the public sector in gathering information about our country's citizens, doing anything mysterious without being recognized will prove more difficult, making your tasks even easier, if you know how to execute them.

Mary Black
December 24, 2010
2:30 AM

The dreamer is the idiot. Or it could be that this isn't the case, and I'm delirious. Some days that's how it feels. This is one of those times. Call it an acceptance of my suffering for having made queer decisions, martyring my life to chase an elusive sense of satisfaction. I wanted to bang my head against the rock because that is about all I had to bang it against tonight. Maybe it could be seen as expressing a peaceful feeling, this silence that surrounds me. I knew there was no going back. Nothing was lacking from this day, one of the most exhilarating I've ever had. Ending it with crème fraiche and farm-raised caviar by candlelight with Beckett looking happier than I've seen him should leave me feeling exhilarated. I've always wanted to end up living in a cave, and now that I'm here for a night, I can't believe I didn't choose a more opulent path. My apologies to those that think it, but you'll need to get your heads examined if you think pain and pleasure are the same thing.

STATE OF NEW YORK

VS.   Case No. 08-CF-5094

MARK BLACK

    TRANSCRIPTION OF TAPED CONTROLLED

        PHONE CALL

       TRANSCRIBED BY:

       Will Shaheen

       LAURA SIMON REPORTING GROUP

APPEARANCES:

GUY PERSONS

MARK BLACK

CONTENTS:

MARK: Hey Guy, how goes it? I'm not asking you how you are, by the way.

GUY: Good. So I just, ah, left them. I'm going to give you the short version of the story.

MARK: Don't go leaving anything out.

GUY: Of course. Bottom line, it's a lie. There is no Florida plan.

MARK: The horse was a giveaway.

GUY: I guess you're right. Anyway, let me tell you it was lucky that you had me stay nearby, because lo and behold Mary left the house in the middle of the night. I heard the garage door open.

MARK: See. I told you.

GUY: I thought I was fucking dreaming when I looked outside and saw her standing there in full armor. Bingo, there was Mary. Wicked cool. I got into the rental car and stayed after her. It wasn't easy keeping up, man. She avoids big roads sometimes.

MARK: She doesn't know you're following her.

GUY: I keep my distance. I have to because like last night we were the only people out there. She would disappear for long stretches of time and I'd get all anxious, 'cause I knew you'd kill me if I lost her. But I had this feeling she was hugging the river, and I was right. She would always turn up.

MARK: I don't need to know about how hard your job is. That's your goddamn problem. Where the hell is she?

GUY: We're both here near Sundown. This little town is like the end of the earth, far from everything. There's nothing here.

MARK: I don't understand. I'm asking you where she is right now.

GUY: That's it. I spent three hours in the woods looking all over the place and I couldn't find her. Then it started snowing real hard. I was going back downhill to my car, but then I spotted the horse tracks. I ended up following them, freezing my ass off the whole way. About an hour later the tracks disappeared. That's how I figured out she was inside this cave.

MARK: What are you pausing for? Go on.

GUY: By the time I got there it was dark, but since it was a full moon, I could see. Otherwise I would've given up. So anyway I stood at the edge of this enormous mass of rock thinking about what I should do. It was freezing. I waited out there for something like two hours. My testicles shrunk to nothing. I was glad I had some food on me.

MARK: Then?

GUY: I went into this thing, this cave. It went pretty far back. It took me a minute to find her, but she was in there with this huge man. It was the weirdest thing I've ever seen. They were sleeping next to each other, he was holding her. I think he's Asian.

MARK: She didn't notice you?

GUY: I got out of there. I was worried about the horse waking them up. He just kept looking at me as if I did something wrong.

MARK: So she'll see your tracks when she gets up.

GUY: Except that it is still snowing like crazy.

MARK: She's never mentioned another lover to you?

GUY: Never. He's enormous, Mark.

MARK: Weird. Keep discreet, like you're doing already. It could get ugly, you know.

GUY: True.

MARK: You're prepared.

GUY: I've got the knife you gave me.

MARK: Threaten them if you have to. But don't kill her. She is the love of my life.

GUY: I know.

MARK: Keep me posted. I'm in Jerusalem now, but you can call me anytime.

GUY: What's in Jerusalem?

MARK: Same thing. Christmas pilgrims who need my services.

GUY: Right. I forgot. I'll call you soon.

(THE CALL ENDED.)

I, Will Shaheen, certify that I was authorized to and did transcribe the foregoing proceedings, and that the transcript is a true and complete record of the tape recording thereof.

CHAPTER NINE

The Ordeal of the Unknown Man and Oprah on the iPad

Mary Black
December 24, 2010
3:30 AM

More cold, more loneliness. *In a world of one color, the sound of wind.* Desperate, I needed someone to talk to, so I grabbed my iPad and turned to a person I would never meet, but could pretend I knew, hoping to feel consoled:

Winfrey: So, this is the first time we've met.

Mary: Yes, it is.

Winfrey: And my producers tell me that your real name is Mary. All this time I thought you were someone else.

Mary: You aren't the first one to be confused by how I do things.

Winfrey: I need to know something, because I'm surprised to find you here, in this cave. This is my first cave interview. I've done this show a million times, but this is a new one for me.

Mary: I'm honored that you came.

Winfrey: How'd you end up here? I assume you thought that it would be stimulating to your creative process.

Mary: Hardly. I guess it was my destiny to end up in a cave. It has something to do with my character. My horse and I were lost in the woods when the snow started and this was the first bit of shelter I could find. It is anything but inspiring.

Winfrey: I don't know about that. I can imagine that being here would feel quite peaceful.

Mary: It is one big unknown.

Winfrey: We have a lot of things in common. First of all you know that I'm no longer running the Oprah Show. I will go on and do other things. And you, when you decided to start your life over again, I cannot imagine what that was like, since you were attached to that house. It was your whole world.

Mary: It was huge.

Winfrey: I can't imagine. How did you feel?

Mary: Well, at first I was elated, but then there came a point where I cried as I've cried once before, and that was when my mother died. It was uncontrollable, and I'm not a big crier.

Winfrey: But isn't it interesting that you told Mark that one day every person in the world would know your name?

Mary: I didn't know.

Winfrey: Wasn't there part of your subconscious that knew?

Mary: Well, the thing is you've got to believe, haven't you?

Winfrey: Yes. And love wins. Do you think you'll ever make peace with him?

Mary: I don't know. That's something I will have to discover, in time.

"CALYPSO?"

I jumped up from my sleeping bag and shone the iPad every which way. Nowhere I'd ever been was so dark as deep within the cave. Whoever this was had a gentle voice, but that wouldn't prevent me from being ready to defend myself.

"What?" I think that's what I said. I was too frightened to remember.

"C-A-R-Y-P-S-O." He spelled out the letters.

I shone the light on his face and he didn't flinch. *What the hell is happening?* He held a carved walking stick. "Who are you?"

"I'm Aki," he said, pausing for a moment. "Aki Taraka."

He came over to me and bowed. Before I say any more, I think you should know that by then I'd already decided that Aki was the most unusual man in the world. I don't mean to exaggerate the point, but he stood over me like a mountain, a giant of a man, the widest creature I ever did see. I could have presumed myself cuckoo, there in the snow in some unknown place with this misfit of a person.

I asked him to sit down.

He wore a white, glossy full-body snowsuit and a black bandana and had what looked like the softest skin I'd ever seen on a man.

The effect was tremendous. I started gathering my thoughts.

"Are you a sumo wrestler?"

"Almost," Aki said. He came even closer and removed a small cloth from his pocket and spread it on the floor to sit on, at a breath's distance.

I wanted to tell him that I wasn't whom he thought I was, but this was all too magical to blow it. "Yeah, I'm her." He was so peaceful that I knew I had nothing to worry about. Having a stranger meet you this way would signal a nightmare ahead, but I can't emphasize enough how unique Aki seemed.

"Good. I was looking for you." He pointed in the direction of Beckett. "This is your horse."

"Yes. He's Beckett, like the author."

"Is that right? Calypso and her horse." He slapped me on my upper thigh as if to say he couldn't be happier. He couldn't contain his innocent joyfulness, or that's how it seemed.

It was a little strange, being touched in this location, but I wasn't offended. The flashlight went across his eyes and I saw that he wasn't affected. He hadn't made eye contact with me, I realized.

"Aki, are you blind?"

"Yes." He smiled in my general direction. "From birth."

In the snow, at this hour? The randomness of it filled me with a feeling of indescribable love for this man. I hope you understand what I mean when I express this; a few times in life one's destiny is so perfect that emotion fills you with some kind of realization that transcends so much of the mundane meaninglessness. It didn't matter if I was Calypso or not. Here we were on this revolving gaseous saucer of a planet, far removed from everyone, and nothing in the world could take away the total beauty of it.

"If you are blind, how did you ever find this place?" The steep old logging roads and narrow deer paths in these parts are nothing but uneven ground and rocks. It didn't make any sense.

"I have blindsight," Aki said. "Eyes see, but brain not, so I am blind."

I went to Wikipedia and looked this up. Indeed, blindsight. He was one of those rare people who could wander through the world as if he weren't blind. "So you know I'm moving my hands right now even though you can't see it."

"Exactly. And I sense things other people can't express." Aki held up his hand. "I feel that there is a ceiling eleven feet above us. Right?"

I said that seemed about right.

"You can feel it, too, but you don't need to know that you feel it," he said. "I can tell from your hands that you've been crying tonight. From here I smell your breath when you speak and I know you had seafood for dinner. That's how I am. When I knew you were here, at first I was afraid, but when you answered me, I knew you were gentle. I knew you wouldn't hurt me."

Who could hurt you? I wanted to ask.

There was something so endearing about hearing that this giant of a person could've been worried that I would harm him. In some intangible way he was what I had always been looking for. I wanted to be honest with him in a manner that I hadn't been with anyone in a long time. I would do things for Aki that I wouldn't for others. I knew I could be alone with him, and he would feel what I needed. "I still don't understand what you're doing here, Aki. You must be from somewhere else."

"I lived in Japan, but I came here for vacation. But now I stayed over a year. I started walking last night, and I got lost."

I'd always wanted to get to Japan, and he had deserted it.

"Where are your belongings?"

Aki took off his snow gear. He looked even bigger without it. "I left them at my uncle's house," he said. "He has a hunting lodge here. But he lives outside Hiroshima. He is married now. He told me he was going to sell the place, because he couldn't use it anymore. I visited here once when I was a boy and I wanted to come back once more in my life. I have peaceful feelings here."

I remembered that there was still some green tea in my thermos and offered it to him. He took a sip, gave a nod of approval, and asked me to show him the tea. I had to dig it out of my duffel bag. He put the tin close to his face and touched the leaves. "From Uji. Very good, Calypso." He put his hands on my upper thigh again, but it wasn't something that seemed like a sexual advance. "You're so lovable."

When you're alone with someone, no rule in the world exists to tell you what is right for that moment. Convention and habit have us bound to certain excruciating limits that prevent us from behaving naturally. We have become awkward as a species. Lost. If I was going to be free, I had to act it and say what I felt, give myself the luxury of expressing whatever I wanted. "Are you tired at all?" I asked him.

"Yes, I am."

"Then I'd love it if you came over and held me. Would you?" I longed to get lost in his embrace. *Touch me with your naked hand or touch me with your glove.*

I needed this from him, this man.

No other would do.

Love is when you can not substitute another.

Aki came to his knees and brought his huge body around me from behind, nuzzling his head on my shoulder. I think it was four times the size of mine. All of me felt minuscule in his embrace.

That's what I remembered from the night, closing my eyes in total peace. A sleep so peaceful there was nothing to dream.

But when I woke Aki wasn't there.

Here was one of the most touching experiences in my life, and I thought I had made it up. Beckett was where he'd been the last time I checked. It was a sickening feeling, as if I'd lost something great and mysterious.

Think of it as something akin to suffocation.

CHAPTER TEN

There Must Be Some Way Out of Here

Dear HPI Private Investigators,

My wife is no longer coming to Florida, as far as I can tell, although her ticket still isn't for another few days. She is in a cave (with a Chinese man) somewhere in the hills above Sundown, New York. I've spent the last twenty minutes on Google trying to find something out about this town and I know next to zilch.

I have no idea if she is armed. They were both asleep when Guy found them in a cave. Also, she's never mentioned an Asian man to either of us before.

Meanwhile, I have been informed that a crew of men has been hired to empty Mary's house. I'm hoping that somewhere in her belongings is a clue as to where she is headed, and why. I expect to reach some kind of financial arrangement with the crew by the afternoon and am in the process of figuring out who will be in charge of that investigation, once we are in possession of her belongings.

Sincerely,
Mark Black

Dear Mark,

We've canceled our Florida staff and have someone based out of Newburgh, New York on his way to Sundown. I will be waiting for your call with specific coordinates on the location of the cave. I have a feeling Guy is in over his head. He needed to figure out why they were in the cave and whether they're armed. Hans Hansen is our local investigator and he's experienced with fugitives. He can't be on duty around the clock, so after twelve hours Jan Buehler will be taking over.

Our company stands behind our work and we will do everything we can to ascertain what your wife is doing there. I hope you're holding up all right, given the circumstances.

I'm expecting your call.

Alison Garbo, HPI

Mary Black

I lost Aki and with him went a very special feeling. It was cruel, and I was alone and glum again. It took several minutes for me to rise, weighed down by misery, thinking about pretending to speak to my crutch, Ms. Winfrey, again. It wouldn't be right to rely on her so much already. So I walked the twenty feet or so to the opening of the cave and looked out at the hill of pines. Just when all seemed dreadful and I was back to another day alone came the great discovery: Aki was out there tending a fire. I came closer to him, filled with an overwhelming happiness, and saw a small carcass being grilled on a stick. "What is that?"

"Squirrel. I killed it this morning. Calypso loves fire."

Yes, fire is passion.

How a blind man can catch a squirrel is beyond me, but I figured if anyone could, it was Aki. He had this special way about him, even how he had stacked the rocks so that the animal would be easy to cook. Nothing seemed to escape his attention.

I went over and kneeled beside Aki. "When did you wake up?" I asked. We felt like children out there, far from our pasts.

"Me? I don't sleep a lot."

I could tell Aki had an erection when I happened to look at that spot. There was a part of me that wanted to get him off right then, for no other reason than to make him happy. I wanted to see his pleasure in full. It wasn't something that came over me so soon after meeting someone. But I decided to wait, even though I didn't want to. I wondered if he could sense me looking at him and decided he must have.

"And I don't sleep too much either, at least not like other people do," I said. I rubbed my hands over the fire, unsure of what to make of the bony carcass in front of me. "You like eating squirrels?"

"I want to try. I like to try everything," he said. "Funny. You didn't wake up when the man came into the cave."

It was all so confusing. *How much more remote than this bit of rock in the middle of nowhere could we be?* I would've bet my life that no one was within miles of us. "What man?"

"He came in and stood over us. Then he ran away," he said. He flipped the squirrel on its back to char its belly. "I wanted to attack him, but he was in a superior position. Trust me, and don't worry. He had wrong life." Aki snipped a bit of burnt skin with a small pair of scissors. "I know how to find him."

He pulled at the measly creature and tried handing me a tiny piece of very rare meat from the thigh. I turned it down.

Aki shrugged his shoulders and put the meat in his mouth.

I asked him how it tasted.

"It is like tiny bird mixed with bit of snake. You try?"

There was no way I was going to eat that. But I felt some joy watching him devour this strange creature, as if the pleasure was my own.

Pleasure would be our bond.

"Not yet." I was still feeling unsettled and edgy about this intruder. "You said you could tell from my voice that I'm peaceful. So I'm wondering if this stranger in the cave seemed dangerous."

"Maybe dangerous," Aki said. "He was frantic and afraid, a lost man. I could feel him looking at me."

I didn't have a clue how he achieved it but I already had an innate feeling of faith in Aki. He wasn't exaggerating when he said that he sensed things in his own way. He was like a flower to me, that innocent. Still, there's no point in asking a blind man what someone looks like. I had to assume the worst and figure a way out of there, my beautiful cave.

CHAPTER ELEVEN

All Our Privacies Are Open

THE NEIGHBOR'S LETTER

Dear Mark,

I have done everything I can to help you with your unusual request. The fact that you are a tidy couple and put away the many books you have, rather than leaving them scattered, helped me to deduce which books Mary was reading. I have racked my brain trying to figure out what this has to do with her leaving on a horse, but that's not the part you're paying me for.

Now, my report: Mary, if I were to guess, was in the middle of four books at the same time. The first was a play by Shakespeare called *Henry VI*. I don't know how much of the book she read, but what I can say is that she highlighted and underlined the hell out of a commentary in the back by one Professor Brockbank. There is no point in telling you what she highlighted because the whole essay is more or less marked up. It is called "The Frame of Disorder" and it seems to be the part of the book that she's read. There is one note in the beginning in her handwriting: *Do what he is saying if you want to be Henry. Don't be weak.* The other marking in the book is in the Second Part. On three occasions she has underlined the word strength, as in *And tugg'd for life and was by* <u>STRENGTH</u> *subdued.*

Moving right along with your request, the next spot was in the master bathroom. I must mention that she hadn't flushed when she left. I thought you would want to know that.

This second book is called *Surveillance Countermeasures: A Serious Guide to Detecting, Evading and Eluding Threats to Personal Privacy.*

On page 37 is an explanation of how important altering hair is as a disguising technique. She underlined the sentences about the removal of body hair. Later in the chapter there are additional notes she wrote with crayon about tracking someone at night. Mentioned are techniques for adapting your eyes to the darkness. I wouldn't be surprised if she read this when she decided to leave in the middle of the night. Her bookmark was in chapter 8, regarding active vehicular surveillance detection. From what I could understand, it was about analyzing a person's travel patterns and enhancing your ability to conduct an investigation with that knowledge. She put a star next to a diagram regarding the standard reaction of surveillance vehicles to a U-turn. Later in the book she underlined much of a section about foot anti-surveillance, including a discussion about transitioning from vehicular surveillance to foot surveillance. Being able to anticipate the person you are following based on your understanding of their patterns seems to be a fundamental this book is trying to instruct. If you need to know more about this let me know, but I think I should move on to the next book.

On the steps leading upstairs I found a short treatise about teaching, by Jacques Lacan. There was a bookmark on page 21 and a star next to this sentence: *Sexuality is precisely the domain, if I can put it that way, where no one knows what to do about what is true.* Otherwise it was unmarked. I don't know what to make of that. As the man of the house, you must.

Excuse me but I went into your bedroom, and the first thing I had to figure out was who slept on which side because there was one book on each nightstand. On the east side of the bed was a history of tennis, and I remembered that you play tennis so I assumed that this was your book. The book on the other stand is by a Portuguese writer whom I've never heard of, Fernando Pessoa.

1a. Pessoa wrote: *If I imagine, I see. What more do I do when I travel? Only extreme poverty of imagination justifies having to travel to feel.*

1b. Mary's note: FP is right, but I am in on his little secret: he lived a rather miserable life. Be careful, Mary. Love the book, but hold on to yourself. Make Oprah joyous.

2a. Pessoa wrote: *I compare them because they are two instances of the very same phenomenon—an inability to adapt to real life—motivated by the very same causes.*

2b. Mary's note: Allow yourself to expand into something more. Being one person is simplistic.

3a. Pessoa wrote: *I don't want you to be upset. I want you to be happy, the way you are by nature. Will you promise not to get upset, or to try your best not to?*

3b. Mary's note: FP is so much kinder than Mark. (I am sorry, Mark)

4a. Excuse me, but Pessoa wrote: *A man who masturbates himself is not a strong man, and no man is a man who is not a lover. Many men make many mates. You are a moral child many times over. You are a man who masturbates himself and who dreams of women in a masturbator's manner.*

4b, Mary's note: I wish FP was a woman because I need to know what he would say as a woman. But he was always men. Think hard about that, along with what he said in this paragraph. It is a revelation.

As a side note, I must mention that I spoke to Maximilian, the mover, for the fifth time. He signed legal documents with Mary that go beyond the scope of any job he has ever worked on. She warned him that you might be contacting him and admitted that she paid him plenty so that he would not cooperate with you, should you turn up.

That's it!!! Let me know what else I can do. I'm not working these days, and would love to be helpful. I feel bad for you. I always felt closer to you than that strange bird of a wife of yours. I'll never forget the time you brought over the matzah ball soup when I was sick. It was the best one I ever had.

Eileen Friedmann

CHAPTER TWELVE

Pass on the Expertise in Fraud From the Leaders of the Region

TIMES OF ALBANY, March 15, 2010, pp. 24-25. "Private Investigator's Report Was All Made Up, Court Hears," by Raja Mansur.

Evasive answers given by a private investigator during questioning turned him from witness to prime suspect, an assistant police commissioner said yesterday. P. Nicholas Fenjves said that when Guy Persons was called in for questioning regarding a report alleging irregularities in the financial documents of Mary Black, he refused to reveal the identity of informers who he claimed had hard evidence in hand, as he would not breach professional secrecy. Persons, the officer explained, was interviewed as a witness, but when he remained evasive in answering questions put to him, the interview turned into an interrogation. He was testifying before Magistrate James Lahey in the compilation of evidence against Black, who is pleading not guilty to filing a police report against people she knew to be innocent and spreading false news that could alarm the public. The assistant commissioner explained how on November 15 State Comptroller Daniel Yamshen asked the police to investigate allegations made in a report drawn up by Black. In the report, Black claimed that Maxine Oswald, managing director of Alert Communications Ltd., and the son of the Director of Contracts, Juan Bastor, had met representatives of Global Strategic Exports and spoken with former Foreign Affairs Minister Dick Harrison. On July 13, the police started investigating the case and exchanged information with several people, including Gideon Levy, the legal representative of Mark Black International.

The legal adviser explained that their company, Global Strategic Exports, suspected corruption regarding the tender which had been awarded to Mary Black and, consequently, commissioned Levy to look into the matter. The lawyer also told the police that Black had contacts within the Saudi secret service and knew of telephone conversations between Armand S. Armand and Guy Persons. Attempts to gain access to those conversations have gone nowhere, according to the State Comptroller. Raising suspicions were documents showing over forty visits to Saudi Arabia by Mark Black (her husband). No explanation was given by Levy, Black's attorney. The police also spoke to Global Strategic Exports's local representative, Francis Spinelli, who said he had met Mary Black when he handed over a report on July 13, 2008. After this report, Global Strategic Exports's representatives and Mary Black did not meet until December 29, 2009, when the company contacted him to investigate the matter again after the tender was awarded to Black and irregularities were suspected. The assistant police commissioner went on to explain how the police had approached Black as a witness in the case, and he released a statement in which he confirmed carrying out investigations into the tender and compiling two reports after having been commissioned by Global Strategic Exports.

Mary Black insisted she did not have any evidence in hand, as it was in the possession of third parties whose identity she refused to reveal since she was bound by professional secrecy.

Mark Black told the police that if they wanted evidence, they would have to investigate without him. Black confessed that he had gone to Latvia to meet Tatiana K. Campbell, a Brazilian model, for business reasons. He claimed that he was to get thirty percent of the value of her income if it were to be awarded to Global Strategic Exports. Black said Lahey insisted on the hard evidence of the irregularities alleged in the report. Black had told others to go to the police, as they had the legal means of getting hold of such evidence. The witness explained that although he had been offered witness protection, Black remained evasive, and he was cautioned. Black said that the whole matter had gone over his head. He admitted that the facts in the report had been invented. Asked why he had made up such serious allegations, he replied it had all been the result of Mary Black's insistence on the evidence, and he needed to justify the fact that he had been paid for his services. Mary Black could not be found to discuss the last claim. At the end of yesterday's sitting, the magistrate ruled there were enough reasons for Mark Black to be indicted.

CHAPTER FOURTEEN

Love at its Worst, The Brochure

MARY AND MARK

THE MARY BLACK FOUNDATION
564 Broadway, Suite 6104
New York, NY 10012
info@maryblacktrust.org

They pay penalty and retribution to each other for their injustice in accordance with the ordering of time

LOVE AT ITS WORST

Given the amount of mail we've received from people who have been unable to see the permanent display of The Mary and Mark Exhibit, we decided to make this brochure available, showing several of the highlights. It is in no way meant to be a substitute for visiting. For group tours and hours of operation, please contact us.

MARY'S BECKETT $249.00

A full-size reproduction of Beckett, signed and dated by our President, Cyrus Kahn, in a limited edition of 30 copies.

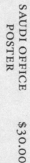

A sketch of Beckett found in Mary's suitcase

Mary's rendering of Sundown, NY

THE BEDROOM $2449.00

A doll-house size reproduction of the mid-century bedroom where Mary and Mark consummated their relationship. With painstaking detail, these handmade pieces are available for a limited time only. *Made in Switzerland*

NYPD Detectives discussing findings

Mary and Mark's master bedroom

SAUDI OFFICE POSTER $30.00

For the first time now available, an exterior shot of where Mark Black ran his operations in Riyadh. We don't know for how much longer we can sell these, so order while supplies last.

Mark's offices in Saudi Arabia

Protestors against human trafficking

CHAPTER FIFTEEN

Findings on the Scattering of Three and the Praline from Troy

CASE DETAIL REPORT
Hans Hansen, HPI Private Investigation For Mark Black
Case Number: Black297.3
Hire Date: December 29, 2010
Date Filed: December 30, 2010

ACTIVITY REPORT:

Followed the subject one day during the week of December 29, 2010. We file such reports after several days, but due to the client's insistence, the following is being submitted before reaching any full conclusions. All times are for a 24-hour period starting the date of December 29, 2010 at 11:25 and ending the date of December 30 at 11:00.

11:25—Guy Persons stood outside the post office in Sundown, New York. He seemed to be trying to make a call on his cellular, but wasn't getting reception. Sundown is a remote place and the Post Office is someone's house. The postal worker had a sign on the door saying he'd be back in fifteen minutes. Guy left after ten minutes and drove his vehicle a quarter mile down the road and parked by the side of a stream. He rolled and smoked a cigarette then returned to the post office house holding a manila envelope. CF. attached photograph, diagram 1. I was able to make out that the letter was made out to someone in Saudi Arabia, Fatima something. The door was open. I ran out and attached a tracking device to his vehicle. He came out after three minutes without the envelope.

11:50—Guy drove six miles east and parked again. He switched to hiking boots. He wore a yellow balaclava and started walking towards the path. I was able to stay some distance behind because I'd brought my dog. Posing as a hiker, in case he noticed me, I wore a large hat and goggles; my face couldn't be seen.

12:30—One mile in, and at a higher elevation, Persons climbed an oak tree and found a perch about twenty feet above ground. CF. attached photograph, diagram 2. I pretended I didn't see him as we continued on the trail. The area was dense with trees and rocks so I figured I would be able to conceal myself without too much trouble. Thirty feet ahead I came across an abandoned fire. I could tell that someone had been there, and recently. I was pretty sure this was Mary's fire. Given the description of her being in a cave, I figured she wasn't far away.

13:30—From behind a large boulder I kept my eyes on Persons, who hadn't yet moved. The temperature dropped.

14:15—Subject exited an opening in the rocks, which I assume was the cave described. Subject walked five minutes and urinated in the bushes. CF. attached photograph, diagram 3. Subject rubbed hands on the snow and walked back into the cave. She is dressed in black Spandex. Persons stayed in the tree.

15:10—Persons urinates from up in the tree. CF. attached photograph, diagram 4. Notice that he looks both uncomfortable and agitated.

17:00—No activity yet, and it is past sunset. The opening to the cave is twelve feet wide by perhaps ten feet high. CF. attached photograph, diagram 5. Persons fidgets from branch to branch. Nevertheless I don't suppose that the Subject noticed him.

20:00—Relative darkness, but the moon approached full. Visibility was excellent as a result. Persons came down from the tree and urinated again. He ate a candy bar and was careful to pick up a bit that he dropped in the snow. He had no gloves and was looking like he couldn't tolerate much more. He sat down on a rock and kept his eyes on the cave. He often paces.

22:00—Nearing the end of my shift I called Jan Buehler and told him to wait. I would have to work overtime, given our location.

01:00—Subject exited the cave with a horse. She paused and looked around. She left the horse outside and remained inside.

01:15—Subject left the cave with a very large man. He was in snow gear and she was now in armor. Anyway, I must assume that it was she under the armor, that is. CF. attached photograph, diagram 6. The man is too large to ride the horse so they begin walking back downhill, towards Sundown.

02:15—Subject and the very large man reached the main road and began traveling east. Persons emerged two minutes later and got in his car. Soon he followed them. I waited and continued in my vehicle also, five minutes behind. The GPS I placed on his car allowed me that luxury.

04:45—Persons seems to have reached Boiceville, New York. This is a larger town than Sundown and offers a number of new options for our Subject. I drove by the intersection of County Road 42 and saw the Subject standing by a deer crossing sign. Further off the main road was the Subject's companion, an Asian man, age 25-45. Difficult to say his age, but he was enormous, at least 400 lbs., if I were to guess.

There are few vehicles on the road and I saw Persons turn around and drive the opposite direction, passing me. He seemed to be trying to avoid being spotted by our Subject.

04:53—A white Audi station wagon with a New York license plate of ADD 2597 pulled up. There was a U-haul attached behind. A slim African American woman, age 35, height 5'5", exited the Audi and began loading the horse in back. CF. attached photograph, diagram 7. The huge man bowed in front of the African American woman and went into the back seat, and our Subject loaded her belongings into the hatchback. They drove away and Persons showed up driving a few hundred feet behind them. Despite the U-haul, they drove like maniacs (at least 80 mph).

05:15—Subject crossed the bridge to Rhinecliff, New York. Persons is still just behind them.

05:30—Entered Taconic Parkway northbound. Approached speeds of 100 mph.

05:55—Exited on Route 23 East towards Hillsdale. Continued on Route 23.

06:15—After traveling at dangerous speeds the driver pulls into Dad's Restaurant, a small diner near Copake, New York. They continue and stop at Mom's Country Cafe, in Egremont. They park the vehicle near the back. CF. attached photograph, diagram 8. Subject, the Asian man, and the African American woman all enter and have breakfast. Each of them orders a lot, especially our Subject. They seem to be enjoying themselves, but I see no obvious signs of affection between Subject and large Asian man. Persons is parked down the street by the Riverside Cemetery.

07:15—Subject leaves with large Asian man and the African American woman. CF. attached photograph, diagram 9. They get into the Audi and drive again. We enter Massachusetts.

08:15—Audi pulls into the campus of Bennington College in Vermont. They stop in front of the Crossett library, and Subject runs towards the front door of the library. She signals to the others that the library is closed. She is upset. CF. attached photograph, diagram 10. Persons is watching them from the other side of the

street. I don't know why they are at the library. They drive through
the town of Bennington, Vermont, following the speed limit.

08:30—Audi pulls up to the Hannaford Grocery Store on
Bennington Road. Audi is parked in the handicapped spot. Asian
man in snowsuit exits the vehicle and goes inside alone. He has a
blind man's walking stick. But he walks as if he sees. I suspect that
he is posing as a blind man. Persons is parked at the far end of the
lot. I call Jan Buehler and tell him that he needs to take over soon.
He leaves Albany, NY, for Vermont.

08:40—Asian man comes out of the Hannaford with a long item in
a grocery bag. CF. attached photograph, diagram 11. I make out a
fish head and realize that he's carrying what seems to be a whole
salmon. The Asian man bows when he sees our Subject, opens the
door, and sits in the back seat with the bag on his lap. They pull
away.

8:55—Audi drives through the campus of South Vermont College,
but they don't leave the vehicle this time.

9:10—Audi drives by the William H. Morse State Airport, outside
of Bennington. Subject gets out of the car and looks around, then
returns to the car and they drive away. They head to Route 7 and
race westbound. I warn Jan Buehler that we are headed away from
Vermont.

9:50—Audi stops in front of the Dunkin' Donuts in Troy, New
York. CF. attached photograph, diagram 12. Subject runs inside
and comes out with a large box of donuts. Jan Buehler shows up in
his own vehicle. We communicate on the phone.

10:00—Audi driving at high speed enters Albany Intl. Airport. Audi
goes to the departure area. Subject and the large Asian man leave
the car and walk towards the Air Canada booth. They have two
duffel bags and the bag with the fish. The African American lady
pulls away with the horse still in the U-haul. I park my car and chase
after the Subject and the large Asian man. Jan Buehler follows

U-haul. Persons sits in his car looking like he doesn't know what to do. CF. attached photograph, diagram 13.

10:05—Subject and large Asian man check in their luggage and are handed tickets by the person at the Air Canada counter. They walk arm in arm together. But the Asian man is still carrying the walking stick. They go towards security and hand the security official there the tickets. The Asian man shows his Japanese passport and bows. They pass through security and disappear.

10:10—I go to the agent who sold them their tickets and tell her that I need to know where they are going. She refused to cooperate with me. My being a former officer wasn't good enough for her. I looked up at the board and saw that the only flight for several hours on Air Canada was headed to Toronto.

10:15—I called HPI headquarters and Alison Garbo suggested I fly to Toronto, that we needed to stay on the Subject. Alison Garbo reminded me that our client, Mr. Black, was demanding notes every 24 hours on what had occurred. Otherwise he would not pay for the time. She needed me to send my report.

10:30—I purchased a ticket to Toronto on the same flight as the large Japanese man and the Subject.

11:00—Sent this report to Alison Garbo and our headquarters for our client's immediate review, as per his request.

INVESTIGATION FINDINGS:

It is not possible to determine that the subject is involved in an extramarital affair. All direct evidence suggests that Subject and the large Japanese man have a friendship at the very least, and extra-marital activity cannot be discounted. Additionally, the furtive nature of the Subject's contacts with the large Japanese man suggest that she was ill-at-ease with being seen in public. Also, the Subject seemed withdrawn and agitated, based on visual observation.

It is not possible to determine that the Subject is planning the murder of her husband. The large Japanese man could be a hired man, but so far it is not knowable.

Hans Hansen, HPI Private Investigation

CHAPTER SIXTEEN

A Doctor, Osama, and the Parrot Who'd Set Me Free

Mary Black
December 29, 2010

The whole time we drove around I kept telling Aki that he had to try the crab here before asserting that the best in the world were being served in hot pots all over coastal Japan. Like I said, his happiness meant more to me than my own at this point. I was feeding off his innocence in some level of my being. He was positive and encouraging, a lot like what I would imagine a mother would be. We were enjoying ourselves so much in the car, playing Name That Tune and singing a Japanese children's song about two beetles battling loneliness. In the spirit of meeting him in a cave, I whispered in Qishon's ear to take us to the airport, which she did, and I went straight to the ticket booth and bought business class seats to Vancouver for Aki and myself. By the end of the day I wanted to find some crab for him. That became my temporary mission in life. Call me crazy, but pleasure was my goal again.

"I'll call you with information on where to send Beckett," I told Qishon. "We could end up anywhere at this point."

Beckett got me out of my old life. It took a horse.

ﻉﻝ

DEAREST READER, WITH THE boarding of the plane my whole inner being changed in the deepest way, as you will see. It occurred to me that this journey had taken me somewhere else, and the story of how my life was to be a new one had taken a turn for the better. Mark was now several steps away from me; I had shed myself of so much of my past and felt lucky not to be anywhere else. This was my realization as I clutched Aki's hand during takeoff and looked out the window at all the snow-covered forests that had given me so much in so short a time.

Accept me, dear reader, as I continue our next adventure, across this continent of highways, mountains and deserts.

Close in on this image of us, the row to ourselves, Aki wearing a thin silver necklace around his massive neck that gave him a certain indescribable elegance.

"Why were you crying?" he whispered to me, somewhere above central Pennsylvania.

I understood what he meant so I didn't need to ask him if he was referring to the time before he arrived in the cave. "I was too alone, and I felt stupid," I said. That answer made sense to me. "Do you understand that?"

He laughed. "I feel stupid every day. And I feel alone most of the time, too." He lowered the shade on the window. "When I was a boy I cried a lot. I would go to my room and all the tears would start. It could have been anything. It could have been something said in school or from a newspaper that upset me about the world."

"We're all sensitive when we're kids."

"But listen. I had a parrot back then. It became mine after my grandfather died. He spent the last years of his life training it." Aki shifted to the side so that he could face me straight on. "He knew it would end up being mine. One night I was going to sleep and the tears started, like many nights. At school they showed us a sweater from back when we received the bomb in Hiroshima. It was a little girl's sweater. We were told how her whole elementary school exploded in a millisecond, but this little hand-knit sweater survived. You're not going to believe it, and I don't expect you to, but the parrot in the cage spoke to me."

He was right, I'm not the kind of person who wants to hear about anything bordering on the delusional. My critical powers won't let me to go anywhere near there. Yet sometimes it is about the messenger, not the message. Aki wasn't Shirley MacLaine ranting to the other world on an infomercial at midnight. He wasn't your average Tibetan or Indian guru coming to town looking for bohemian cronies.

"This was my grandfather's bird, you see. And my grandfather wasn't like other people. Special bird, special man. One day I will tell you about him, too."

"We have plenty of time," I said. "Time growing old teaches all things, wrote one of the Greeks." It was almost a test, to see if he agreed with my sense that neither of us was going anywhere. He smiled, as if to say, *Of course we did.* Images of his naked body came to the front of my mind, but what I felt wasn't erotic.

I desired him, not him to desire me. Note the difference, and decide whether you have felt this.

"So, are you going to tell me what your parrot said?"

"He called me Osama, like my Grandfather used to. Because I was born like this, so big. People and animals can be afraid of me, until they get to know what kind of person I am. Osama means King in Japanese." Aki paused for a long minute, as if the words weren't coming out. "So he said to me while I was there in that bed, '*One day Osama will see that he holds the suffering of all women.*'"

"Those were the parrot's exact words?"

"I am translating it in the right way. He used the word see." Aki looked like he was still haunted by it, as if it was something he was still trying to understand. "You are the first person I told this to."

"Maybe the parrot's spirit is flying this airplane?" I meant it as a joke and Aki understood it as a joke, and laughed, but here we were in flight and a secret about a parrot was told for the first time. "That's incredible."

"Until I met you I carried this sentence with me as my hidden treasure," Aki said. "I would forget it for years at a time and then out of the blue something would trigger some acknowledgement of its existence. We all have precious objects we put away in a drawer, rather than carrying them everywhere. That's how this was for me, this special moment. But since I met you, I haven't stopped thinking about it. And forgive me for asking you why you were crying."

❧

August 26, 2008

The United Men Foundation
356 West 34th Street
New York, NY 10001

Dear Mark Black,

We here at UM have received and thank you for your generous tax-deductible donation of $2800.

Hating men is seeing a revival across the globe. Many forces would like to see our masculist voice squashed. At some point the misandry culture will adapt to our wishes, as it is what every person in this world desires, the right to fairness.

Our goal is to form a United Nations Initiative and Charter to protect the rights of men worldwide by the end of the decade, as is provided for women. As you know, violence against men by women is on the rise everywhere, and the more armed our nations become, the more likely it will be that some men will suffer under the hands of abusive spouses. The great majority of soldiers killed are male, despite the fact that women make up a significant percentage of the armed forces. We are seeing rising numbers of men committing suicide and the death rate is higher for men worldwide, and we die earlier. Sentences for female criminals are 20% shorter than for males. Yet, the government has no task force to address the issue of the worldwide maltreatment of men.

While circumcision of girls is forbidden here in our country, it is routine to inflict this on men. Our children go to the mothers in the majority of divorce cases, with sole custody granted with great regularity.

We have no choice when it comes to reproductive rights. It is her body, her choice. We stand resolved never to forget John Bobbitt, who was castrated by his wife.

Over 40% of domestic abuse involves cases of women hurting men. Much needs to be done so that violence against men in the movies is no longer tolerated. The bias against men is reaching intolerable proportions. If you kick a woman onscreen, it is a crime, but if you do so to a man it is considered funny. Not to us.

You've my personal vow to do all I can to turn this around, so that men and women can live together with justice.

Sincerely,
Ian Brown
President, United Men International

CHAPTER SEVENTEEN

Concerning Human Understanding
and Prelapsarian Suffering

International Freudian Psychoanalysis Conference, Symposium on the Reinterpretation of the Pairing of Autoerotic Egos: Lugano, February 23, 2009. Cited from pp. 297.

Professor Parenti: Still you have to ask why she considered it her prerogative to stop psychoanalysis after the eleventh week, since there seemed to be so much progress. When she complained about headaches every day for three years straight, you must consider it something to address, what the reasons were for them to disappear. To deny the success in each patient under treatment is to question everything we stand to achieve.

Dr. Adrienne: That is correct. That is my intention.

Professor Parenti: The ego that you considered in your last paper was demonstrated to be in a state of decay, due to the overwhelming evidence of your patient's obsession towards autoandraphilia. She didn't dream of an androgynous body, but one that was male. Are we wrong to assume that this was the case?

Dr. Adrienne: From the beginning, I have expressed my wish that colleagues recognize that my subject thrives on being aroused by nothing more than imagining herself as a man. The real man doesn't satisfy her. She has to become one. Now, on the fourth week, she brought in her husband, as I've stated. I hadn't met him before, and was stunned at first by the resemblance to my patient. Matching her obsession for andraphilia in perfect proportion was his autogynephilia. Neither of my subjects have ever been transsexual. Bringing that up in week five, neither of them flinched. It wasn't an issue for them, as we've seen before in other individuals. But that doesn't mean anything commonplace was occuring. When the husband masturbated, he imagined himself to be a nude woman in bed. He imagined that he had her vagina and her breasts and the more he did this the more he came to believe this was the case. He believed he had no penis and he went to great lengths to describe the quality of the pubic hair he had on his vagina. His nipples were erect. What struck me most about this case, not only for its vagina envy, was that she had told me that she would lie in bed and stroke herself imagining that she possessed his penis. Not any penis, after all, but her husband's. Exacerbating the problem was that what often took place when she aroused herself was that she complained about her erection. Now, in the meeting of these two, once they were in bed together, neither was able to satisfy the other after they realized each was a perfect mirror of the other. Their relationship had taken on a certain kind of sexual paralysis.

Professor Parenti: And yet you distinguish this from a man and a woman each being involved in autoerotic activities. In every human being a vacillation from one sex to the other takes place, and often it is the clothes that keep the male or female likeness, while underneath the sex is the very opposite of what it is above. We've seen the same thing in tribadism, where vulva to vulva stimulation is the norm.

Dr. Adrienne: The symmetry between the vagina envy and the penis envy can't be ignored if we are to speak of this as autoerotic. I'm relieved that you used this term and distinguish it from masturbation, since that is one form of autoeroticism. To complicate the case of this couple, they described to me that they would *masturbate one another*. When asked about why they called it masturbation of the other, they told me in session after session that in fact that is what it was: it wasn't gratifying the other, it was masturbation. What I discovered in time—and you must remember that we had daily sessions that allowed us to get quite detailed—was that each of them had once read Robert Baden-Powell as a child, who outlined the dangers of masturbation. The two went so far as to have Dr. Jocelyn Elders, the former Surgeon General, for dinner to discuss, in the middle of our sessions, her positive views on masturbation, for which she was chastised.

Professor Parenti: So you're saying your sessions led them to research their personal history relating to autoeroticism?

Dr. Adrienne: That was one of the results, but it wasn't my intention. They are rather intellectual people, so they became familiar with all the research they could get their hands on. That's just how they are. As their counselor, I was focused on the gender issues because to a large extent neither was functioning in the world as their birth gender. There is nothing extraordinary about this. We see role reversals all the time in marriages. The more I asked, the more odd patterns I discovered that they both shared, such as always masturbating face down, on their stomachs.

Professor Parenti: What fascinates me most about these two is that despite their process of discovery, much of what occurs is still unconscious. No matter how conscious they become, the unconscious remains a creative force, as it does in childhood.

Francis Mauceri: May I interject something here?

Professor Parenti: Of course.

Francis Mauceri: When I gave testimony in the courts regarding what I'd seen between these subjects, the issue of personal violation was paramount. I think that if we are going to talk about this case in detail, we can't ignore the actual issue of violence between these two. The simultaneous destruction of one another while maintaining a sexual innocence has been, to put it bluntly, mind-boggling. I can't tell you how difficult it was to decipher which rape plea had validity, if not both. After much court time and psychological counseling, both of them dropped their cases. I still don't know what happened, but I worry for them.

Dr. Adrienne: I'm glad you spoke up about the other aspect of all this, because the courts aren't involved in speculation in quite the same way we are. They are trying to reconstruct what happened. As far as I am concerned, the reasons are irrelevant. Our whole purpose, besides working towards creating some harmony for people, is to reveal what may be happening and why. I worked hard with this couple, and believed I was making progress. Then they disappeared. It wasn't until a few months later that Francis called me and told me about the criminal cases each had made against the other. I was stunned. Francis told me all about the double rape charges, and I couldn't help but feel like I was wrapped up in this. These two are still out there. As far as I know they're still married. It is our task to try and make something of all they have given us. That is why I published my case study about them and that is why I will continue to try, however I can, to get to the bottom of this.

I, MARY BLACK, KNIGHT AND wanderer, alone and free, am going to do what I want and not what I am supposed to, since that is what it means to be free. That sets me up as your worst nightmare of a woman, perhaps.

Love knows no single source, and all of it is the same.

I put my hand on him where I knew that he would not expect it. He moved his head over and stared at me, and it looked like he was looking at me, but I knew he couldn't see me. I pushed my right hand down through the top of his pants and left my hand there across most of him without moving it. I felt his warmth and it filled me with positivity. There was nothing to say. It was a form of worship, and the divinity flowed both ways. We were communicating. I don't know how it is possible, but he became even warmer. I put the airline's itchy blue blanket over him and pushed his pants down all the way to his ankles so that he could be free. I didn't care if anyone noticed, but there was one man (probably an air marshal) that could, and he was deep asleep. I stroked Aki and held him until I needed more of him. Outside me wasn't enough. There comes a time when the exchange of desire requires more than hands. It was chemical and tangible and fulfilling to the point where the purpose of existence made sense again. I decided to put him in my mouth. I was craving that. Aki was precious to me. I had a feeling that I already knew the way he would taste, reminiscent of salty vanilla donuts, for some reason, and this is how he tasted. I peeked out the window for a moment and was wishing Mark was there to see me doing this. Yes, this too is possible: I can put my mouth on another man. These are the same teeth I will bite him with, and you should see it. Yes, he's invited to watch. And as I wrapped my tongue around Aki, a flood of thoughts came over me. They were like visions, the faces of people I've never known. There were children in school uniforms near a wooden house by a wild river with a bridge, and an old lady with a painted fan watched over them. There was a wood staircase with the figure of a body impressed upon a body. I felt like maybe these were all Aki's memories. A petite woman wearing dark blue walked through an alley in the rain. And he was hot in my mouth as I thought about fire, which made me go crazy on him. I took him like he was my own. The way he touched and grabbed my hair told me about his happiness. He was worshiping me back. It was tangible and I didn't want it to end, but I could tell he was there. I swallowed his orgasm with joy, something I haven't done for someone since I can't remember. I took all of Aki into my mouth on that plane and nothing in the world at that moment could have been more perfect.

The Japan Times, July 27th, 1980. "The Death of Dr. Akito Hara," section 2, page 11.

Dr. Akito Hara, a local World War II hero in Okinawa, died of old age at his home in Tomonoura Sunday, his family said Monday. He was 86.

Dr. Hara was born in Fukuyama and graduated as valedictorian from the Kumamoto University School of Medicine in 1936. He was awarded the highest honor of the Red Ribbon by the Government of Japan for his humanitarian work protecting citizens, culminating with the Battle of Okinawa.

There is much mystery surrounding his humanistic contribution, because Dr. Hara was a most private man. After the war, the people that knew him informed the public about what he had done. In 1943, he led a group of local men into an abandoned warehouse in Yokohama, where hundreds of Chinese and Korean women were being held. They came to be known as Comfort Women, forced sex workers. A great number of these women had already committed suicide. Dr. Hara cared for these women himself.

Japanese poet Yoko Yamaki contacted us to say that many women would never have survived without his actions.

Hearing reports about war crimes against women and children, in 1945, during the Battle of Okinawa, Dr. Hara traveled south to the Motobu Peninsula. Dr. Hara led escape efforts for local girls raped by American soldiers during the battle. During fighting with these soldiers, Dr. Hara lost his left arm. Nevertheless, Dr. Hara was able to organize medical help for locals hidden in the caves above Okinawa, where at least 200,000 people were killed during the fighting. According to the Military Intelligence Service Research Center, he was instrumental in convincing the American troops to curb the unnecessary killing of the local people and transfer them to internment camps instead.

In 1978, he was given a Lifetime Commitment Award by the Faculty of Medical Professionals at Hiroshima University, where he'd worked for three decades.

Dr. Hara married Moon Kim, a Korean national whom he had met in Yokohama. Moon Kim Hara passed away in 1976. Hara is survived by one daughter, Sachi, and one grandson.

CHAPTER NINETEEN

On Praising Shadows, Brains, and the Stratagems of Those Who Claim to Be Prophets

Dear Guy,

Because you don't seem to honor what I have offered to do for you, it is incumbent upon me to articulate my position one more time.

There is a box and you can't live in that box. You have to work outside of it. That way you can understand what is in that box, you shithead. That box, right now, since you're working for me, is you becoming my eyes and ears. You become my brain. You hunt like Mark would hunt, think like Mark would think.

For me this is a matter of life and death. I know you are proud of living with a sense of moral relativism. You're guilty of thinking the day more or less turns out the same no matter what you do. It is an average view of life that leads to the kind of person you are, more or less average. If you want to look squarely at it, you'll have to decide whether you might be a little less than average. Sure, you've read your share of classics, but that's not what I judge men by, if you know what I mean.

Allow yourself to be judged for a moment.

Desire is at the root of all human experience, giving the world a foundation in irrationality. There is no better force to describe the continuous creation of all existence than this ubiquitous place called love. I call it a place because it is material, just like the rock you piss on. You can be destroyed by it. Where love is a rock, hate is indefinable. It is a perfect hatred.

That is because it is an illusion, and it is the shadow love casts on everything.

I have always sensed a degree of jealousy towards me, given that I am a successful person, and given that I have been with the person you have not been able to be with. Excuse me for being so forthright, but down the road I trust you'll appreciate this gesture of honesty. It is the thing that will allow us to succeed in our partnership, instead of behaving as though we are friends. If you were a friend, you would have been in the airport figuring out what the hell was going on.

Meanwhile, the following confidential letter is from a doctor I visited the last time I was in the United Kingdom:

Dear Mark Black,

I am glad you visited our center on your way to Saudi Arabia, and hope that you're having a successful visit there. The results of your neurological analysis have come in and I believe I can say with authority that though you have negative feelings towards your wife, it is not my professional opinion that you hate her. We have done a full study of your medial frontal gyrus, right putamen, media insula, and frontal poles after showing you hateful images. The patterns of neural activity that are associated with hate did not correspond to the patterns we witnessed in your brain when we a) showed you pictures of Mary, b) played audio recordings of Mary, c) showed you video footage of Mary.

The results of each were consistent, precise, and, I would add, predictable. What I will say is that they were much closer to those we see in subjects in love.

I have attached the results for your review, as well as a recent study we published on revengeful feelings. Please feel free to contact me to discuss the matter further.

Dr. Marc Gallagher, Laboratory of Neurobiology
Department of Cell and Developmental Biology
University of Nottingham, Nottingham, United Kingdom

Therefore, Guy, I don't sit on my behind and wait for understanding to come to me. There is active living and passive living, and the latter occurs when the triune reptilian lazy brain takes over and fools the person into thinking that what he is doing is living. We've spoken about this mediocrity before, but how we go about transcending the offensive, boring, and sheepish to actually knowing what to do about it is something few of us will ever have an inkling about. Now this doctor may reach his conclusions about my brain, but I can smell hatred from the other side of the planet, let alone in myself.

Which brings us back to our nemesis. Mary deserves each and every one of my feelings towards her. That may sound harsh. I am also going to add, in fairness, that I deserve her sentiments towards me. Love has torn us apart again. If I were to guess, I'd say she's an enigma to you, but to me she isn't. I've fucked her three thousand five hundred plus times, so I know what is up. A husband has a right to tell someone that. You have to submit to me as a result, because that is how it is when someone has what you don't.

So, I insist of you, get back on your feet and figure out what the hell is going on, for heaven's sake. That said, you'll have to stop thinking about yourself as a mediocre human being if you're going to come on my adventure.

Remember, dissolve into me, my boy.

Mark, from Riyadh

P.S. Attached you'll find my mother's recipe for the beef stew. Enjoy. And do tell how it comes out.

CASE DETAIL REPORT
Hans Hansen, HPI Private Investigation For Mark Black
Case Number: Black297.3
Hire Date: December 30, 2010
Date Filed: December 31, 2010

ACTIVITY REPORT:

Followed the Subject a second day during the week of December 30, 2010. We file such reports after several days, but due to the client's insistence the following is being submitted before reaching any full conclusions. All times are for a 24 hour period starting the date of December 30, 2010 at 22:15 and ending the date of December 31 at 17:15. Activity is based on observations following Air Canada Flight 7397 Albany to Toronto and Flight 34 Toronto to Vancouver. The Subject slept the whole way. Given that I was seated in their row, I chose to remain quiet and stay in disguise. No activity to report.

22:15—Subject and large Japanese man leave airplane.

22:20—Large Japanese man goes to the restroom and Subject waits for him outside. He uses the handicapped stall.

22:30—Subject and large Japanese man take two duffel bags and place them on a rented cart. They exit the airport and head towards the taxi area.

22:45—Subject and large Japanese man receive a ticket from the taxi administrator and board a taxi. I approach the taxi administrator and hand him a few bills. He informs me that they are going to the Pan Pacific Hotel. I request a car as well.

23:15—I arrive at the Pan Pacific Hotel, a glass structure on the waterfront. Subject pays the taxi driver and a bellhop takes their duffel bags and leads them to the reservation area. Large Japanese man hands his credit card to the hotel clerk. They take their room keys and go upstairs.

23:25—I proceed to the hotel clerk and leave some cash on the counter. She obliges and gives me a room down the hall from the Subject. I learn the name of the Japanese man: Aki Taraka. The clerk wrote it down for me since it was a bit much for my brain. I was unable to find anything out about him on the Internet. From here forward I shall be referring to him as Aki. The hotel clerk informed me that Aki had requested a late check-out and would be spending one night. She gave me a room that was between the Subject's and the elevators.

23:40—I place a wireless microphone above the door of their hotel room. While an imperfect device, at least this will allow me to know when they exit the room.

00:30—I hear the door open and I rush to leave my room, pretending to get ice. Subject had ordered room service.

01:30—I hear the door open again, but this time it closes soon after. I leave my room, pretending to get ice. Subject leaves room service tray outside the room. Note: it was a tremendous amount of food. I looked at the bill. Four hamburgers, a bottle of wine, a Wagyu steak, three Caesar salads, a side of barramundi, three dozen Hama Hama oysters, a red pepper soup, chili, and three unknown desserts, but I saw some chocolate smears on one of the plates.

03:00—I heard nothing for all this time so I go to sleep with the speaker next to me.

10:20—I wake up and order room service. I take a very quick shower with the speaker connected to the wireless microphone at full volume. I get dressed once again. I go get ice and I see the DO NOT DISTURB sign on their door. There is no noise inside.

11:45—I hear the door to Subject's room open. Through my door eye hole I see Subject and Aki pass in the hallway. I get my jacket and head downstairs.

11:50—Subject and Aki go to a coffee shop in the lobby. They stand around holding their coffees admiring the view of the waterfront. I sit down and pretend to read a newspaper.

11:53—Subject starts running over towards the bar area. I wait and watch. She confronts a man sitting at the bar and hits him hard on the back. He is very skinny, wears an old vest and colorful pants. He looks like a hipster. I go around the other side of the bar and sit behind the Subject so I am out of her vision. I realize that the stranger is Guy Persons. They don't look at me, as the Subject and Persons are deep in argument. Aki touches Persons and comes close to him. He tells him he knows that he came to the cave. Aki stands behind Subject and holds her back, as she's infuriated. Mary grabs a glass and threatens him with it. Persons calls the bartender over. Persons, at this point, looks desperate. He stands up as if to leave and Aki blocks his way. Two hotel security men hurry over and restrain Persons. The stranger admits that he is not a hotel guest. Subject approaches and kicks Persons in the groin. I deduce that she is trained in martial arts. A bellhop holds her back. Security takes Guy Persons away. NOTE: Security later turned Persons into the Vancouver Police and he was still being held for questioning at 22:15, to the best of my knowledge. He was not seen again on this day.

12:10—Bellhop hails a larger taxi vehicle for Subject and Aki. I hurry to fetch a taxi and follow after them.

12:25—Subject and Aki arrive at Sun Sui Wah Seafood Restaurant. They are seated in the middle of the room and they begin eating dim sum, off the carts. They seem to be enjoying themselves more than most people enjoy themselves. Aki orders a bottle of cold Ginjo-shu sake and the waiter brings a platter with a six-pound specimen of king crab on it, as well as one steamed Dungeness with ginger. I also notice that they have ordered many oysters and mussels. Several minutes later a very dark whole squab (with the head on) is brought to them. I had to ask the waiter what that gamey creature was. A plate of deep fried crab claws with chiles arrives next. They order more sake, but I don't know what kind. The waiter brings the carapace stuffed with a seafood infused rice. Now and then Mary and Aki slap hands, but for the most part they crack away at the crabs. I can't emphasize enough how pleased they seem with their meal.

14:45—Subject and Aki hail a taxi after their meal so I do the same.

15:05—Arrival once again at the Pan Pacific Hotel. Subject and Aki discuss something with security and go to the elevators. I stand back, take the next elevator. Note: I stopped at the desk and checked again with the hotel clerk from the day before and she informed me that the Subject had not extended her room reservation. I go to my room and wait by the speaker.

15:55—I hear activity and return to the door eyehole. Subject and Aki pass by my room with their luggage. At this point I am packed, so I head down to the lobby. By the time I go downstairs they are nowhere to be seen. I ask at the front desk and am informed that they had checked out from the room. I was relieved to spot the Subject and Aki walking towards the Port Authority, having already crossed Waterfront Road W. I stood fifty feet behind them to see where they were going with their luggage. A large cruise ship was docked on the Port.

16:10—Subject and Aki enter ticket area for the Silver Sea cruise ship. They show their passports and board the ship. I run over and speak to the same ticket agent. He tells me the boat isn't leaving for three hours. I ask where they are headed and the ticket agent accepts my bribe and tells me that the couple is scheduled to get off the boat in Tokyo.

16:15—I phone Alison Garbo to find out what I should do. She has me wait on the line while she phones Mark Black. She was unable to reach him for one hour.

17:15—A decision is made by Mr. Black, for practical purposes, to continue the investigation from the other end, in Tokyo, where they will arrive in sixteen days. I return to the ticket agent and find the precise time of arrival of the boat into Tokyo Port, as well as any stops along the way. I return to the airport and fly home on the redeye.

INVESTIGATION FINDINGS:

It is not possible to determine that the subject is involved in an extramarital affair. All direct evidence suggests that Subject and Aki are living it up, but other than that I have not witnessed any obvious physical contact to suggest that it is not platonic.

The purpose of this voyage to Japan is unclear to me, as an observer.

It is still possible to imagine that Aki could be a hired man, but I am beginning to doubt it.

Hans Hansen, HPI Private Investigation

CHAPTER TWENTY-ONE

What Happens on Oceans Stays on Oceans, and the Future of Giants

Dear Tokyo Private Investigators,

I have quite a situation in my hands. Although I am fully committed here in Riyadh with my luxury consultancy business, my wife is believed to be on a cruise ship to Tokyo, with someone who may be a former sumo wrestler. I have been told that he is an enormous Japanese man and I'm not certain whether he is a lover or a friend or a bodyguard. I can't determine what it is they are doing together, as they seem to be on some kind of journey. I have a feeling they met somewhere in New York and went camping and hunting, but I haven't been able to piece it all together, although I have a private investigator, as well as a friend, following her.

My wife is trained (by me) in anti-surveillance countermeasures. I believe that is why she was able to uncover my friend who had been following her across North America. He is somewhat out of the picture. His name is Guy Persons and he will be coming to Japan to assist with the investigation; he is a very cheap addition to the surveillance staff. My wife and this Japanese man are alone on the cruise ship together. I have not been able to find anything out about this person she is with. I have searched through her belongings and books and am still not certain what her intentions are. My feeling is that she thinks that she is fulfilling some destiny in Japan. She is a learned and cultured person, an avid reader of philosophy, including the poetics of your country.

I would love it if you could provide me with some inkling of who this giant man named Aki Taraka is.

My hope is that you can suggest a method to track her and her mysterious companion. I've never been to Japan so I am all ears. My area of expertise is the feminine market in countries like Brazil, Saudi Arabia, and Latvia. Perhaps I can share some of my knowledge with you, to lower the cost of the proposal you will make me.

Sincerely yours,
Mark Black
Riyadh, Saudi Arabia

ॐ

Mary Black
Prime Meridian
Pacific Ocean, 23:15

"It is a different kind of happiness I articulate when I feel this much loneliness. Here, in the middle of all this darkness and ocean, as we are rocked to sleep, I feel like I belong to you. That's why I experience such happiness when I'm lonely with you."

Aki was almost asleep when I said it, if I had to guess from his breathing.

It was my nature to say more than him, to try to keep him awake when he couldn't. I wanted more of Aki than the day was long. He reached over and patted me on my butt. He said it reminded him of a ripe piece of fruit that you pick from the grass.

Maybe I wasn't talking to him anyway. It had been so long since I wanted anyone to listen to me. Before I left I could feel myself dying, and now I have this tangible sense that there is no other way that I should be living, even if I'm headed on a path towards death. Maybe it was obnoxious and spoiled of me to find this much solace in escaping. Now that I am here and the storm won't stop pounding, I am scared of the ocean around me. There is much too much of it to drown in. But I am ready to disappear into it. "I will never tire of looking at you," I want to tell Aki but can't bring myself to, even if he's sleeping. I once said that to Mark when he was most hurtful to me, and that is part of the reason I have to go so far to keep myself from killing him.

"Have you ever killed someone?" Aki asked me while I flossed my teeth in the wicker chair, not realizing he was also up.

The storm had me tossing about all night. Killing was in the air.

That's Aki for you. You are lucky when you meet someone who takes you so far into himself. "Why do you say that?" After I said it, I realized that the question was a stupid one. He already knew that I hadn't killed anyone. He understood more about me than he would ever verbalize.

"Last night, at dinner, while you were at the bar making your salad, an Indian woman came over and sat down at the booth," Aki said. He sat up in bed and faced me, giant face in my face. "You didn't see her?"

"No, I had to go far away from our table."

"She said to me that she noticed you from the first day. This woman, you understand, was improper, correct?"

I got the feeling that Aki was offended by whatever the woman told him. "This isn't Japan, Aki."

He laughed a bit. "I always forget that. People butt in over here," he said. "Now, this woman was insistent to speak. I didn't know what she wanted from me in the first place, but she started speaking right away. She said you had wild eyes. Gray eyes. She said that if I could see your eyes, I would be afraid. I told her that even though I am blind I see your eyes. Even though I am blind I need to see the world. I was speaking and she interrupted me and she told me that I should be careful. I guess she saw you coming back to our table. She held my hand and begged me to take her words to heart. She called you a person like a devil."

I would be the first to admit that the eyes tell who we are. Having such an impact on a stranger gave me bragging rights, but not for something like this. Yeah, I've been told to act in horror movies, but I thought it was because of a certain intensity to my gaze, rather than an evil essence. There were several Indian families on board so there would be no way to know who this presumptuous person was and confront her. "Does what she said worry you?"

"When we slept next to each other that first night in the cave, I had many dreams," Aki said. "I felt like I woke up a hundred times, but it was only my mind playing tricks with me. I didn't tell you this, but I was walking as lonely as a cloud when I found you. I was wandering around for a couple days, further and further from my uncle's cabin. I couldn't go back, even though I knew I should." Aki turned his head my direction. "You remember how I asked if I could call you Calypso?"

"Of course." Who could forget that moment?

"I knew you weren't really her. She died a long time ago, like Odysseus. But who each of these people is as forces of being is something immortal. We are all gods in some way," he said. "Now, regarding my dream, I promised to tell you that. I was surrounded by fire, and you were there and I had decided to tell you everything that happened to me. But the fire kept stopping me. I said I'm not the simple man you think I am, and when I would try to say more, I couldn't, and I'd wake up. There was so much to share with you, and yet it wouldn't come out."

"So all of that turmoil and you got out of bed and killed a squirrel?" I asked.

Aki was logical when he wanted to be, but I liked him most when he blurred the boundaries in life, transcending it in some unique way.

"Something like that, yes," Aki said. "When I was kneeling there, roasting the animal, I made up my mind that you would be the one to hear my story." Aki paused and put his hands on his large belly. "It won't be easy to tell it, no. And I hope you don't end up hating me."

I could never feel that towards someone who was being honest, no matter what they'd done, within reason. *You, my giant friend, keep reminding me of the moon.* I wish I knew why. Was he going to tell me he stole cereal from the corner store when he was twelve? The more I thought about it, the clearer it was that I was meeting Aki in midstream and I didn't know anything about what came before. That's how it is with everyone, except often we don't care, at least not enough to do anything about it. Even the most basic things about someone we've spent much time with remain unknown.

"But first we must start with you. I'm not a child, Calypso," Aki continued. "You can be direct with me, tell me why you were crying. That's part of why we are together in the middle of the ocean. It isn't chance that we're here right now. It is as it is supposed to be, every detail."

Part of me didn't know what to tell him, so I just started talking, to an uncomfortable extent. It was as if Aki reached into my mouth and started pulling the words right out of me. "Who I am doesn't make sense to me anymore. I was turning myself into someone new. I even had a person in my life to do this with. But something changed in me, and I was no longer true to the person I wanted to be. I was a lie, a fraud even, and all I had done was seek the truth in everything. I couldn't work with him anymore. I became a riddle to myself, a ball of confusion, and I knew it. I could speak about every intricacy of my confusion, so maybe I'm not giving myself enough credit for what I knew. What I recognized deep in myself was that I was a failure."

"You're right," Aki said.

What the hell? He's agreeing with me?

He turned the light on, which I didn't understand, since he couldn't see. "Until you realize that the whole thing is a big lie, you're lost," Aki said. "We are bred lost, and after that, if you're not confused, there is something wrong with you. That's why I trust you even more now." He put his large face into mine. It reminded me of being a child and having my cat come over on top of me. "That's why I'm going to trust you with what is left of my life."

Did this mean he was dying? It wasn't fair. I would need to know more. If it was his weight, we could fix that.

"Were you ever raped?" Now Aki wasn't giving me a chance to say anything. I was thinking about everything he was telling me. "You don't have to answer me. I want you to know that I understand. Everything is always present."

In some ways, as masculine as he was, I felt like I was with a woman. The way that he understood me turned me on. I was already wet, and impatient. I wanted Aki inside me, the way a man probably feels when he doesn't want anything but to get it inside. Hoping he wouldn't resist me, I pulled his black underwear down (so big they looked like a lampshade) and then couldn't even wait to take my own off. I pulled my panties to the side and sat on top of him. He didn't have to move. I put his specimen inside and went crazy on him from the first moment. I wanted to see how I could bring him to the end and began moaning, letting my breath take over. I crashed up and down on him with roughness, as if I were trying to crush him. We shared no words. I smelled of sweat, but he didn't say anything. I came forward and licked his right nipple as I pushed into him at an angle, breathing even harder. I didn't know how he could take it. I was giving him every bit of woman I could. I knew I had it in me to be like this, but hadn't let myself. There was always something in the way. Aki pulled my breasts towards him and pinched my nipples as I bounced, bringing me to the edge of wildness as I howled through my orgasm, screaming *Osama, Osama.* I collapsed onto him and don't know what happened after that, but when I opened my eyes I could see a family on the opposite veranda already having lunch. I turned over in bed.

Aki wasn't there.

CHAPTER TWENTY-TWO

Human Kind Cannot Bear Too Much Reality

2006 Adult Leisure Conference, Bangkok, Thailand.

Panel on the Sustainability of World Tourism:

PANELISTS:

Dr. Kim Carter, Professor of Gender Studies, Loyola Marymount University.

Shlomo Bernstein, London, proprietor of Babylon's Club.

Anonymous, Global Strategic Exports, Riyadh, Saudi Arabia.

Moderator:

Awut Prapass, Journalist, Programmer at Radio Bangkok.

The following is an excerpt from the panel on The Sustainability of World Tourism. To purchase copies of the entire event, please contact Mr. Awut Prapass at: ALCBT212@ THAITOURISMNEWS.COM :

Awut Prapass: As far as I know, no one has determined whether people are having more or less sex in the modern world. What we can say is that the sex worker industry is booming. It isn't only here in Thailand. The issue of supply of women is crucial. I'd like to know what each of you thinks about how the adult service market will cope with this problem.

Shlomo Bernstein: A girl in our club can make several thousand dollars per night. That goes a long way towards paying your rent, or for your education. As an employer with a club of some repute, I am in a position where I am turning away many qualified candidates. I promise you that there are a limitless number of women to serve a high-end market.

Dr. Kim Carter: Exactly. A woman who charges $500 per hour might feel somewhat differently about what she is doing from the one who works the street and struggles to make twenty. The first might even feel glamorous doing it, for a while. In the end I think this line of work eats away at people, but that might be because of the extent of the social stigma attached to doing this. That's part of what I've researched, anyway.

Anonymous: Look, this is all rather obvious. There will always be women willing to whore themselves. When the economy is bad, they do it to pay the rent. When the economy is great, they do it to make beaucoup bucks. There are countries where women have no rights and they get roped into it. I realize that, and it disgusts me. Does my disgust make it go away? Will it ever go away? I doubt it, but I'm glad people are working on rectifying the issue. I'd love for that to fade out the way of polio, eradicated. If I could see trafficking come to an end in my lifetime, I would consider it progress. Even if I would lose a bunch of income.

Dr. Kim Carter: And yet you're known for working in unusual markets, where women sometimes have no rights.

Anonymous: My screening process for women interested in working as sacred prostitutes is thorough. The way I look at it, I am offering women an alternative to being enslaved wives. Or factory laborers. If there's one thing that defines me, it is the relentless seeking of pleasure for as many people as possible.

Dr. Kim Carter: I'd just like to say, for the record, that we are talking about women here. Children and forced slaves are a different discussion, and that's a crime against humanity. This is about adults choosing this way of life.

Awut Prapass: Exactly. I'm glad you raised that point. So would you say that your women experience pleasure when working?

Anonymous: First of all, it is work and few of us find our work pleasurable. Regarding whether they turn off and turn cold in order to do what they do, that's a complex question. People are always closing themselves off from the world. People are lost. They are hollow. They eat bad fast food and they don't believe in evolution. I don't mean that as a complete snapshot of the human landscape, but it is often the case. We all go through life acting our part. So I don't know. An academic can speak more about this, but I believe that your average whore is happier than most any husband or wife.

Awut Prapass: Are you serious?

Anonymous: Dead.

Dr. Kim Carter: One of the problems with happiness is that it is so difficult to measure. Plus, as soon as we ask people about happiness, they seem to get unhappy. The way you phrase it is jarring, but I believe that the relationship between marriage and sex work is something that we're now beginning to understand. The collapse of the marriage institution, all the divorces, is all new territory.

Awut Prapass: While this part of the sex industry booms.

Dr. Kim Carter: Maybe that's part of it, maybe not. It is also media agencies, modern day travel, the sexual revolution, or even the Internet. A lot has happened in the world. We've learned much in the last ten years regarding why some men choose to pay for sex when they can have it at home for free.

Anonymous: You pay for it one way or another.

Dr. Kim Carter: You know what I mean.

Awut Prapass: You're saying that this business will always exist.

Anonymous: Unless you kill all the women.

Dr. Kim Carter: Wait. You didn't just say that.

Anonymous: You heard me. Nowhere am I suggesting women should be compromised in any way.

Dr. Kim Carter: Then don't speak that way. This isn't something to joke about. If you continue on that level I will get up from this panel.

Anonymous: I said that for dramatic effect. It means so long as there are women and men, this sort of thing will go on, either in marriage or in brothels. And it works in thorny ways, where sometimes it is the women that are the oppressors. But there is no place for it when it comes to children. That is an abomination. We need to be practical when we talk about this tourist industry.

Shlomo Bernstein: What drew me to this business was the element of fantasy. It all comes down to that. Marriage is one fantasy, and there are millions of people selling that.

Anonymous: Good one. You're the first person I know of who's called it a fantasy. But you're correct in doing so.

Shlomo Bernstein: Everything that has to do with sex, from the beginning of our existence, operates on the level of our imagination, our perception of needs, the issue of projections, etc. The invention of clothing was the first step in our historical development, not fire. I would say that strip clubs and the like are the second step. We see it all. We have clients who want a new girl every night, clients who come in once in their lives, and others who develop a relationship with one girl over many years. Each one is trying to fulfill his needs in a different way. Some don't want the sex. Most of these men are what you'd call normal men. They run banks or they work in banks or they clean the floors of banks.

Awut Prapass: So you're saying your customers aren't a bunch of perverts?

Shlomo Bernstein: We're working beyond that model of looking at this in terms of victims and perverts. There is a lot more going on in the interaction.

Dr. Kim Carter: What do you say about the mass suicides of women in this field of work? You saw much of that in Japan, for example.

Anonymous: A tragic issue, I agree. It is everything we want to avoid. In the corporate world they refer to them as accidents, with insurance. But my heart is too big for that. I am not an investor. To me, that's another word for a criminal or parasite.

Awut Prapass: This anonymous panelist and I were talking last night about some of this. As we've seen, he is sensitive to the plight of women. But I think the audience would like it if you would share more about your specialty in serving people on religious pilgrimage.

Anonymous: First of all, I loved our discussion as well, Awut. As for me, I run a luxury consultancy company that does many things. It is true that one of the sectors I've been most involved with is serving devout people. Why? It came out of studying the legal papers associated with the Vatican child sex scandals. From the beginning I've been against all forms of child exploitation and pornography. (APPLAUSE) It had something to do with the loathing I developed for these priests. With time, I learned to understand the level of hypocrisy in human existence. I read my share of Nietzsche as well, thanks to a suggestion from my wife. I wish she were here right now, because she's much more articulate. After long discussions, she and I decided it would be better if there were hired sex workers for the priests, instead of children. Little did we know that the whole congregation would catch wind of us.

Dr. Kim Carter: There has always been a connection between the erotic and the divine.

Anonymous: Which all religious leaders have pretty much suppressed, while being leaders in the sexual exploitation of humanity. I love rare wines and caviar, and all of that takes money, a lot of money, in fact. While doing my research, I figured out a way to capitalize on all of this. I started on a small scale, but then it exploded, as word got out about us. Temple prostitution has existed since ancient times. Where did I think I'd find customers? I began in Italy, of course, setting up shop right next to the Vatican. The Italians don't care about God. The people in the world at this time that say they do care about God are in the Bible Belt. Yet I had so many born-again types from America coming to me, it was hard to keep up. This led to Jerusalem, but that is a smaller market. So I made my way to the king of them all, Mecca and Medina. Some of my women were there on pilgrimage, you know. They come from Nigeria to go to Mecca and they end up working for me. I think we might be the reason more and more people are going on pilgrimage.

Awut Prapass: So you're a pimp. And yet you're responsible for the religious revival in the world! Are we talking about large operations here, or a handful of people?

Shlomo Bernstein: Are you kidding?

Anonymous: We keep expanding every year. We started with women for men, then men for men, then men for women, then transvestites for either gender, and so forth.

Dr. Kim Carter: Tell me if I'm getting this right, during the day they fast and pray, and then after sundown they come find you.

Anonymous: Something like that. But they come during the day, too, don't worry. I profit on figuring out how to seduce them with their own sense of arousal. That's the whole thing. Arousal. Think about it.

Shlomo Bernstein: After a long day of devotion. I love it.

Anonymous: Because love and sex rule the world. Not God. We all know that. Fuck God.

CHAPTER TWENTY-THREE

I Want to Know Who He Is

Dear Mr. Black,

First of all, my apologies for the delay in responding, but we were looking into your matter. Thank you for considering us for your investigations here in Tokyo. What we can offer is surveillance of this sumo wrestler when he is out with your wife.

We did a quick search of the name (using different combinations) of the sumo wrestler provided but were unable to find any useful leads that matched. Once we can identify who this sumo wrestler is, we may be able to offer better surveillance. This will be the case after arrival in Japan.

We did, however, confirm with the cruise company that your wife and the sumo wrestler will be arriving in Tokyo, as you were thinking. They will be met by a limousine and they will be escorted to a suite at the reputable Conrad Hotel in Shiodome, as that was the package they purchased. They are in a first-class cabin. They bought their tickets the day before the ship departed from Vancouver. I do not have any other information about their activities on board, of course.

We would require a start location (address) and photographs or other identifiers to begin.

Our fees are from USD300/hour (depends on length of surveillance/availability, and excluding disbursements), but we can provide a more accurate quote once we know how you would like to proceed.

Best regards,
Yuichi Nozawa
Managing Director, Nippon P.I.

Dear Mr. Nozawa,

I'd always heard that Japan was expensive. My friend bought a pear there for twenty dollars, and when he told me about it I choked. He said it was floral and incredible, but come on, twenty dollars? That's obnoxious. Then he told me he bought one white strawberry for fifteen dollars. How'd it taste, I asked. *Like any other perfect red strawberry*, he said. He went and ate blowfish at a kaiseki place in Kyoto and that was over four hundred dollars. To make up for the cost of that meal he ended up eating ramen noodles for a week. He drinks some powdery green tea that costs thousands of dollars per pound. I ended up bailing him out by sending some cash to a Western Union near that busy crossing in Tokyo that you see in movies. So you're telling me all those people pay $300 per hour if they need to track their wives? Does money grow on persimmon trees over there or something? I think you won't mind if you offer me a little foreigner discount for the service because I can't digest that price. I live in Riyadh where for a dollar you can get a bowl of slow-cooked fava beans and an onion for breakfast.

I may need to hire you for a month, after all. That's a lot of blowfish.

I need you there from the first day, at the ship. They may not go to the hotel. I won't take the risk. We can discuss the rest of our arrangement in the coming week.

I have also sent you pictures of both the sumo wrestler and my wife. I warn you ahead of time that she is a master of disguise, as I trained her with a slew of sniper and anti-surveillance seminars. She thinks of herself as a martial artist, but any pro fighter could take her down without too much trouble.

I want to know if the man is her lover, who he is, who his family is, where he lives, how much money he has, what my wife is doing for money, how much money they are spending every day (itemized), what they do all day, how much time they spend in private, who they socialize with, etc.

Sincerely yours,
Mark Black

CHAPTER TWENTY-FOUR

Mary's Choice

IRST, I CHECKED FOR Aki by the pool and then at the café where we already established the routine of getting tea in the afternoon. There were people everywhere, but he's easy enough to spot. I walked the perimeter of the boat, checking all the public areas, in case he had decided to play shuffleboard or ride an exercise bike. I went back up to the cabin and waited while reading a book.

After an hour I called the front desk. "Did we stop anywhere today?"

She said we hadn't.

"That's weird," I said. "I can't seem to find my friend. He's disappeared."

The woman convinced me to page him over the intercom.

I waited, but hours into the night I began to get worked up. *After a storm comes a calm.* Yes, I repeated that to myself a thousand times. Once I couldn't take it any more I called the front desk again. A pair of French security officers with thick accents showed up within five minutes. I hadn't a picture of Aki, but he was easy to describe. They promised me they'd find him.

I went out again, too. Nothing I told myself made sense. At midnight I called security a second time. One of the two officers from earlier came upstairs. He seemed stressed, as if he'd had a long day. It didn't make sense to me. *What goes wrong on a ship?* I wondered. It wasn't as if there were people robbing each other.

He stank of bad cigarettes. He had the hoarse, mucus-filled voice of someone who gave up on taking care of himself.

"I don't mean to get personal, but we need to," he said, after telling me that his name was Jean Christoph. "Did you have an argument or anything?"

"Not at all, far from it."

"What about drug abuse? Even prescription drugs."

"No, no way," I said, and not without some annoyance. *We're talking about someone as pure as water.* "He's a normal man with no real issues at all."

"I understand. We have to rule out the possibilities," he answered. "Ms. Black, everything happens on this ship. We are vulnerable because we are in the ocean. People fight with one another, people sit in the sun for too long. People die, they have strokes, everything. As far as your friend, we have to take every last precaution. We may even have to turn the boat around."

"What do you mean? What would the other passengers do?"

"They won't make it to Asia when they expected to," Jean Christoph said. "We have searched this ship and there is no sign of him. He was last seen on deck in the late afternoon, around sunset."

That's when it hit me that this was much more serious than I had construed it.

He continued. "We are reviewing the video footage as we speak. Our Captain is aware of the situation and will soon be making the decision about turning around. So far we have spoken to many passengers who were in the area and no one mentioned anything extraordinary. If someone throws himself overboard and someone sees it, I'm sure they would have notified us."

"And no one has."

"I don't mean to worry you, but we need to consider the risk that he jumped," he said. "There are many missing people who end up in the ocean, whether by choice or pushed. It happens more often than people know."

"It doesn't make sense." Suicide was out of the question.

"I know, but this is how it is," he said. "People go hiking and they die. They send their children to go out for milk and someone abducts them. Or they get shot by a random bullet. It is the same here, in the middle of the ocean. People keep disappearing. I'm still hopeful that we can find him, but I do need to prepare you."

At 3:00 A.M. another security guard called to say they'd found video footage of Aki standing by the railing at 1:30 P.M., but added that he hadn't jumped overboard. They had discovered that at noon Aki had ordered the absinthe sampler. He had been talking to an older Dutch woman who had been identified and interviewed already. She reported talking to Aki about the weather. He was seen walking around. Jean Christoph apologized because the cameras were not everywhere; he could have gone overboard in another location. No one else had come forward with a sighting of Aki.

I spent most of the night walking around the ship and looking around, in a crazy state, along with a helpful pair of high school students who had asked me what I was doing, seeing me fall apart. Every now and then I'd go back to the room to see if there were any messages for me. I made the mistake of googling MISSING PERSONS CRUISE SHIPS on the iPad. Young and old, drunkards and children, never found again. Their pictures are online for all to see, along with details about the search for them, the presumed dead. Aki would soon be one of them.

7:00 A.M.: the Captain had made a decision to turn the ship around, assuming that Aki had gone overboard. The U.S. Coast Guard had been contacted and an international search was underway.

9:00 A.M.: there was pandemonium in the breakfast hall when it was announced that the ship needed to be rerouted, for emergency reasons.

I decided to tell Jean Christoph what the Indian woman had said about me. Then that forced me to explain how we had been followed by Guy, back in Vancouver, and that he'd been taken in by the police.

"It is possible that he wasn't working alone," the Frenchman said. "Nothing is beyond suspicion. We are treating this as a murder investigation."

I felt like I'd been robbed and wanted to die, too. I couldn't accept what was happening. Really, that's the complete feeling. Total resignation and misery filled me. I wasn't asking for too much, and we were going about our lives trying not to bother anyone.

Mark was, at turns, a cruel person, and I should have known that there was no limit to what he'd do to ruin me.

Jean Christoph asked me for Aki's passport. I had forgotten all about it and went into Aki's jacket and found it, along with a huge stack of yen in an envelope. It was the first time I'd seen his money. I showed it to Jean Christoph and he started counting.

"That's over sixty thousand dollars in yen."

I had no explanation.

"Please tell us about Aki, his work, his family," Jean Christoph said.

I couldn't tell him much. It all sounded fishy, and I knew it. There was nothing I could do. I had to tell him where we met and what we were doing, even though that was all I could say about Aki. The more I spoke, the less I knew and the stranger it all seemed. I was in love with a man about whom I didn't know anything basic, and I was already mourning his absence from my life. I'm sure they thought I might have killed him. If we hadn't been on a boat, I might have been handcuffed.

STATE OF NEW YORK

VS.   Case No. 08-CF-5094

MARK BLACK

  TRANSCRIPTION OF TAPED CONTROLLED

            PHONE CALL

      TRANSCRIBED BY:

      Will Shaheen

      LAURA SIMON REPORTING GROUP

APPEARANCES:

MARY BLACK

MARK BLACK

CONTENTS:

MARK: Hello.

MARY: Mark?

MARK: Mary, yeah, hi.

MARY: What the fuck is going on?

MARK: What? I'm home, making a Vongole. You should come over.

MARY: You won't get away with it.

MARK: Settle down a sec. Last night I had a dream with you in it. We had a kid together named Bint.

MARY: I don't care what you dreamt.

MARK: Come now.

MARY: You can't go around killing people. No. You've gotten away with more than your share, but not this time.

MARK: I didn't do anything. Where are you?

MARY: Don't play stupid. I don't believe you. I can't do this anymore. (Crying)

MARK: Look, this is a misunderstanding. I swear on my life, I have no idea what you're talking about. I've been having fond thoughts about you, remembering how you twirl your spaghetti on your fork.

MARY: Listen to me. We're over. If you won't accept that, then let me tell you something, I will hunt you down myself.

MARK: Honey?

MARY: Just keep to yourself. Run the business that I left for you. If that's not possible, if I were you, I'd start hiding now. If you're behind this, trust me, I will find you, and you know, this time I won't be letting you go. There won't even be a ride to the hospital.

(THE CALL ENDED.)

I, Will Shaheen, certify that I was authorized to and did transcribe the foregoing proceedings, and that the transcript is a true and complete record of the tape recording thereof.

ें▲

"On Spousal Murder, A Deeper Look at the Women," by Dr. Benjamin Kavian, Bureau of Crime Statistics, July 23, 2009, pp. 213.

Even in countries where women commit few crimes there is almost the same rate of murder of husbands by wives as husbands killing wives. We refer to both as SROK, the Spousal Rate of Killing. Some people are surprised to hear that the SROK are rather similar. Only the rarest of women is understood to be a killer. This underreported aspect of crime on a worldwide scale is due to our difficulty with identifying the feminine, the essence of creation, with destruction.

My particular field of criminological inquiry has involved putting my magnifying glass on female killers. This is a mysterious field, to say the least.

As a biographical note, my studies concerned Iran, where I was born. My dissertation was completed at the University of Hamburg, following the Islamic Revolution. Female crime has always been rare in Iran, but the female murder rate is on the level of the male murder rate. Ordinarily, it is a woman killing her husband, often for infidelity. These women tend to be married against their will at a young age. Recently, there have been more female Iranian murderers than ever before. A man in Iran is allowed to kill his wife if he catches her in the act with another man. Often he suspects what is occurring behind his back and carries out some form of an honor killing. A woman is not allowed to kill a man, however. She is often not even allowed to divorce.

In a society such as Iran's the laws do not protect women enough. They feel compelled to handle the matter on their own. Without legislative protection, they become damaged to the point of utter desperation. This led me to ask whether women become killers after abuse, or whether some of them were destined to kill. It is a hypothetical question, in the murky territories of history and our psyches. In societies with more advanced gender laws it is even trickier to understand the motivations behind these women.

Some women are attracted to men for the same reasons that they end up killing them. Any amorous intensity runs the risk of isolation and domination. Sexual chemistry is fully charged and those same elements that create so much pleasure for the man and woman can arouse the other passions. Many battered women see suicide as the way out. Male murderers are often under the influence of drugs while female murderers are sober, their acts premeditated.

Women abuse men. We have to know that this occurs, and that's why I state it in this simple manner. This isn't to say it is the norm, but it is something that happens. On an annual basis, tens of thousands of women are arrested for beating their husbands in the USA. Again, this is in no way to take away from the troubling statistics of males battering women.

It all comes down to motive. Why we humans do something is not always clear. Why you married this person and not the one you were involved with before, for example. Or the reason you chose X stranger to be your close friend, but not someone else, whom you might have liked even more. When lawyers enter the picture and all comments can be used against a person to discredit them, understanding a motive becomes even more difficult.

Women kill to avenge and in order to protect. Some are born evil, or so it seems. These creatures kill because they find pleasure in it. This picture of a woman is the most difficult for us all to digest.

"THE GIANT MAN IS here, in front of my eyes."

It was so wonderful to hear that it didn't make sense. "What?" I had been sitting in bed with my head under the blankets, hiding myself from the world when the call came in, awake with open eyes. It was a half-dream, but this was real. "Jean Christof?"

"Yes, Ms. Black, we found him walking in the upstairs hallway," he said. "I suggest you come here to the doctor's office."

I didn't give a hoot what I looked like in my robe. With my miserable, bloated face I hurried to the elevators.

I could feel the captain turning the ship back around on its original course.

I opened the door to the clinic and a pretty African assistant pointed me back to the first examination room where Aki reclined, hooked up to an IV drip. I grabbed Aki's big toe and yanked hard on it, went to his face and kissed his forehead several times. *I thought you were gone forever, my dream.* Yes, by then I thought of him as my dream.

He motioned me to sit down, then turned to the doctor and said, "She needs something, too. She isn't well. Some dry toast, maybe a steak." One of the three nurses left the room after whispering something to another nurse.

"Is anybody going to tell me where the hell you've been?"

"Have you ever tasted absinthe?" Aki asked.

"Of course."

"I wish I never drank it. I paid for two glasses, but the bartender saw how much I was enjoying it, so he started pouring shots. He wanted to stop, and I told him to take a look at me. I am like a whale. A baby whale drinks one hundred gallons of milk per day. Are you going to feed her a pint of chocolate milk for breakfast?"

"I didn't know you drank a lot." To tell you the truth, it was disappointing.

"Is that right? I think everyone escapes in one way or another," he said. "I must have had ten shots when the Indian lady came over. You remember her, don't you?"

Goodness gracious. Some people have a knack. "The one who thinks I'm a murderer."

"Exactly. We talked for a long time about everything. I told her how you and I met and what happened on the airplane."

"What do you mean?" I knew what he was referring to, but I couldn't believe what I was hearing.

"She wanted to know more about how you satisfy me."

What an idiot I am. This was a fool, an immature child, I had chosen as my journey's companion. I couldn't think of what to say, but all of a sudden I was glad he didn't die. I would have spent my whole life missing a man I had been overestimating by a long shot.

"She invited me to come see her room."

"Is this a joke?" I'd been through enough that day. *Woe is me.*

"Listen to the story," he said, reaching for his water.

Aki acted as though he was recounting to me something as mundane as a long breakfast as he went into tremendous detail about every little thing she did to him all night long. He told me way, way more than I wanted to hear, starting with the enemas they gave each other. Yes, enemas.

"But we were in bed together a moment earlier," I said. "I thought I made beautiful love to you."

"You did, but I am never satisfied," he said. "If I eat one fried octopus ball, does that mean I should stop? No. If there is another fried octopus ball, I'll eat it. I don't see, so I need to feel more than sighted people."

"Where do I fit into this picture of octopus balls?" It wasn't funny. The pain was tangible.

"That's easy," he said. "She is an ass woman and you are vagina and mouth."

At this point the doctor and the two nurses slipped out of the room without a word. Who could blame them?

"You treat me like I have a vagina," he said, while chomping on the ice left in his Styrofoam cup. Everything about him had become annoying. "She made love to my butt and I made love to her butt."

I could have killed him. I could have killed myself. "It isn't as though I own you, but I thought we had something different."

"We do."

"You didn't have the heart to call and tell me where you were."

"I was too drunk, and then I passed out. You have to believe me," Aki said. "As soon as I woke up, I hurried to come find you. Ask the man who spotted me on my way back." Tears fell from his blind eyes. "I am incapable of meaning to hurt you."

All human bonds are fragile. "And what is this crazy woman's name?"

"She's Poonah." Aki leaned over, grabbed his pants off the side chair, and reached into his left pocket. "She isn't crazy. This is her picture."

"Okay, she isn't crazy," I said, taking the small wallet photo of this woman with a red dot on her forehead. It's true, she had one in the photo. She must have been at least sixty. "Poonah gives blind men pictures of herself, that's all."

"I have blindsight, I told you that. That's different than if I were blind."

Aki didn't seem to understand what we he'd put me through. The whole issue was a little overwhelming. A few minutes earlier I'd been wondering whom Mark had hired that could have lifted Aki and thrown him overboard. Then I ended up listening to what happened to his rear end all night by an elderly woman who had it in for me. It was enough that I decided to go back to my room.

There's only so much a person can take.

CHAPTER TWENTY-SEVEN

The Memory of What Happened at Hiroshima, and Tomorrow Big Understanding

W E FOLLOW GUY PERSONS in Hiroshima after he gets off one of several hourly Nozomi bullet trains from Osaka, where his plane landed, three days ahead of the arrival of Mary Black and Aki T. at the Port of Tokyo. He would try to squeeze as much living in as he could before he would be stuck with the job of following. Hiroshima meant a great deal to Guy ever since he'd watched the Resnais Duras film at a revival house with an Austrian countess he was trying to impress. It was the universal love story, the one where something nearly perfect is happening, but the world stands in the way and separates the two. Though the film was a melancholic meditation on looking backwards at life, Guy had other plans for himself. Two nights at the Sheraton are all he had to work with. It was already late when he arrived at the main train station and hired a taxi to the hotel.

Four young Japanese women were standing behind the long reception counter, immersed in paperwork. The room smelled of a strange mix of fresh tulips and broiled mackerel, depending upon where you stood.

A young woman named Yoko was the one to check him into the hotel. Guy found her polite beyond measure, like many in this town.

He couldn't get his eyes off Yoko's mouth. No matter the number of times she put her lips together to dry them, they would seem wet again. It had the effect on Guy of being some kind of erotic magic trick.

He handed Yoko his credit card and passport and went through the usual check-in procedures, all the while imagining her upstairs with him, in the bath, her left breast in his mouth. It was usually the left breast that he thought about. The breasts were never that big.

"Mr. Persons, I will do whatever I can so you will enjoy your stay here in Hiroshima," she said, handing him his hotel key. "The elevators are over there."

As he walked towards the elevator he obsessed about her mouth and what she was implying about doing *whatever she could.*

Guy would hold on to so much about his first couple of hours in Japan. Even though he wore an old pair of blue jeans and a pea coat with holes, the taxi driver's professionalism and white gloves impressed him. So did the ticket agent on the train who bowed every time she left their car. He planned on altering himself to be like them.

The hotel room was adequate, with a view over the bay. He went straight to the bathroom. The electronic water-spraying toilet bugged him out, as did the low sink. "I'll stick to toilet paper." He fell asleep upstairs with the television on a rugby match, hoping Yoko would be working when he woke up.

Four hours later he opened his eyes and hurried back down to the lobby. Ah, heartbreak: she wasn't there.

This time it was all men. One of them printed out directions to the closest McDonald's. Guy pointed his iPhone compass westward and strolled down Naka Nishihakushimachiyo Avenue until he could smell the fast food that he loved most in the world. Besides, Guy hated plain rice, and he knew they didn't have anything with rice in it. He ordered his Big Mac meal with a root beer and sat down near three female university students hunched over anatomy textbooks. First, the fries, between six and ten at a time stuffed into his mouth with a dollop of ketchup, as he'd learned as a kid in various towns in central Indiana. Then, the burger was finished in nine bites, the same taste as the last one he had in Chelsea a week earlier. But Guy was more fixated on the students seated nearby than the burger. Each wore skirts, with bare legs from well above the knees. He had to say something. It was overwhelming.

"You speak English?"

The girls giggled. "A little," said the tallest, replacing the L with an R. She pinched her thumb and forefinger together to indicate how little. "I am Suki," she added, stiff in manner as she extended her hand to shake his, as if she learned the Western greeting from a how-to book.

He sat in the fourth unmovable chair and started putting on the charm, what little of it he had. Guy was on high alert to figure out which one of them showed any signs of being attracted. Two kept their books open. Suki closed hers and worked hard to complete a full sentence, speaking one word at a time. But another one of the girls blushed every time she looked up at him, then pretty much hid her face under her hair.

"You make visit Peace Museum?" Suki asked him. It was the reason most foreigners came to Hiroshima. Every day new ones arrive, they cry. Some buy flowers, lay them on memorials, eat seafood, and leave.

Guy had enough tact to tell her that he was visiting for that reason, even though he didn't care about the memorial. On some abstract level he felt bad for the Japanese, but other priorities needed attending to. Five years earlier, a black man on the uptown F train told him that *if you don't get laid in Korea, you may as well give up*, and Guy believed it, even though he wasn't in Korea. He'd packed plenty of condoms as well. "Hell yeah. I was thinking of going to the museum today." This was meant to be an invitation to her. He regretted saying hell yeah.

"Excellent idea," Suki said.

Guy asked her about what she was studying and where she lived. He told her that he was in Japan for a film project and how much he loved Hiroshima. He'd read somewhere that the Japanese had an overwhelming amount of civic pride. It was time for a story. He went into detail about his mother's recent death, a trick he learned from a friend, to win sympathy. Death triggered a woman's desire to please a man, supposedly. Suki seemed to be going for it, he thought. The animated manner he'd chosen and the stories he told led him to believe he seemed like someone more worth knowing than his everyday persona.

Even he knew time was running out when the girls started packing their textbooks away, as if to leave. "I'd love it if you came with me, Suki," Guy said. That's when he remembered that he'd brought two of the condoms with him.

Suki seemed embarrassed and speechless.

Guy waited. He helped Suki with her jacket.

"I have boyfriend. I am so sorry," she said, and left, without looking at Guy.

He grabbed his large cup of root beer and hurried outside. "Forget the peace museum," he whispered to himself.

Mr. Black,

Post me for Nippon P.I. Detective #1. Thank you, thank you. Exist, we try, she coming. He coming. Boat late, me no. You happiness, mine, it is double. Case example and following as off ship into limousine. No hand in them, no kiss. Virgin Road maybe. Ring MIA. Example of love no. Example of friend yes. For them you say gratefulness. Smile and photo. SEE PHOTO #1 FOR PROOF #1. Example of Aki Mary not happen in limousine tinted. Follow. Shiodome arrive comes in Conrad Hotel Area. 2 bags. Old. SEE PHOTO #2 FOR PROOF #2. No ring. Romance absent. Smile. Receiving they up bye bye. Waiting. Lobby good. Waiting. Still lobby good. Maybe sleeping. Maybe love. Maybe no. Lobby. Man say why. Car, me. Car no good. Maybe Aki coming but no. Morning Aki come no Mary. Aki rain, Aki cold. Aki up. Shift complete. You say one okay. Home. Writing. I charge 12 not 24. Special. $2400. Tomorrow big understanding. Auto. I drive the weekend. Now time night clothes pajamas.

Have a good tomorrow,
Kenji Kumoto
Nippon Private Investigators
Tokyo, Japan

CHAPTER TWENTY-EIGHT

There is no Longer Beauty or Consolation Except in the Gaze Falling on Horror

FORGIVING AKI: IT WASN'T until the long break between the fatty tuna and mackerel courses at the sushi bar on the ninth floor of an office tower in Tokyo's Ginza district that it became possible. We'd stuck through the rest of the cruise together, saying much less than before. It was the same at the hotel once we'd arrived in Tokyo. Something happened inside me that was irrevocable. This would be a new Mary Black, less possessive, conventions thrown aside. Poonah came as a shock, but maybe I was off the mark on some level. It wasn't that he lied to me, or meant to upset. With the forgiveness came a catharsis so strong I started tasting the food on a whole new level.

Nothing would be taken for granted anymore.

We were the only customers left that night at the counter. The other four, all businessmen, left several courses earlier. Not everyone has Aki's appetite. At some point I had to stop, but not Aki. He was on his third sea urchin hand roll. Now and then Aki would translate something from his conversation with the sushi chef. It was about where the fish came from and why it all tasted so perfect today.

I thought about how cute Aki looked after I forgave him, his eyes filled with tears. Tell me that isn't moving, seeing a blind man you love in some deep part of you in such a state.

He had made me love man again. Imagine that.

Aki ordered a third small bottle of cold junmai sake.

This would be our last night at the hotel, and I wasn't sure what was next for us. We hadn't said a word about the future yet. Perhaps it was some kind of unspoken pact. Something had to change. My money would run out in no time at the Conrad, our hotel. Frequenting the best sushi spots in Tokyo wasn't helping either. I figured out a way to introduce the subject to Aki. "When am I going to meet your family?" After I said it, the nuclear effect of the sentence hit me. Besides, we had been in a cocoon together, away from everyone.

Aki twitched. He kept talking to the sushi chef. I didn't think that I had interrupted them when I said it, but maybe I was wrong. It happens to me when deep in thought.

"Aki?" I asked five minutes later. "You stopped listening to me now that you've been forgiven."

"What family are you talking about?"

"I don't know, maybe your mother," I said. A sore subject, it seemed, given his pinched face. I'd feel weird, too, if Aki asked about meeting my family, even if I didn't have one anymore. There was Mark, but that was a different story. "Or your uncle with the cabin."

"We can't meet them," Aki said, lifting his sake glass my way. "One day I will tell you why."

Not good enough, Mister Aki, Osama of the Wondrous Appetite, the only man I love. I stewed over it while he kept eating hand rolls and talking Japanese to the master chef. Aki placed his left palm on my right thigh. I'm guessing he could tell I was upset. I told him I was going outside to smoke a cigarette.

I stood in the busy alley and watched people smoke.

By the time I came back, I had made my decision: I had to know who Aki was.

"I've to hear what happened to your family," I said. "You can share it with me. I promise you that I'll understand."

Aki fidgeted in the seat. He breathed in as if to speak, but no words came out. His hand was on my thigh again. He moved his head like a Noh actor wearing an oversized mask. "I am alone in the world. There is no one."

"You mean alone alone. They're dead?"

"Yes."

"But what about the uncle who was selling the cabin?" There was a lot that I didn't know.

"There is no cabin. I had no uncle in America," Aki said, lowering his head. "I invented them."

It was a test of feeling, to see if it was possible to get beyond feeling. I tried standing up to leave, but he pushed down on my leg, urging me to stay.

"What were you doing in the woods that night?" I asked.

"You want to know?" Aki was the one that was getting angry. He said something to the sushi chef that sounded like he might have been asking for the check, then turned to me. "It doesn't matter. If you want to know me, the past will be an obstacle. The same goes for me discovering you. Why else do you think I don't ask you? Did you think I was naïve and childish? That's what you wanted. You never even thought to ask why my English was so good. No, I didn't want to know who you were. I have that right. You can't live with that. Perhaps it is true that all beautiful women are doomed to unhappiness." He gestured to the sushi chef as if to apologize for his outburst.

"That's fine with me. It isn't as if I'm simplistic," I said. "I don't want what other people want. And I don't appreciate being lied to."

"I told you I am full of shame for it. If you want, I will leave."

"I'm not saying that. I don't enjoy being lied to."

"But at least it was a story, and it was a beautiful story," Aki said. "I gave you that as a gift, instead of who I was. Now you have to decide which you want, that story, or the stupid person that is me." He gestured to the chef that he wanted more sake. "Do you need to know what I was doing in the forest? Think about it. Think double hard, for both of us."

CHAPTER TWENTY-NINE

From the Standpoint of Redemption

Dear Wendy Douglas,

I am looking forward to hearing from you about the quote for a custom quilt with the following aphorism printed on both sides of it. Sorry, it took me a while to dig it up again. Then I had to edit it to make it readable. I'm so glad you can make it! It will be one of a kind.

My husband's birthday is coming up, and I think he'll love this.

Sincerely yours,
Mary Black

The only philosophy which would still be accountable in the face of despair, would be the attempt to consider all things, as they would be portrayed from the standpoint of redemption. Cognition has no other light than that which shines from redemption out upon the world. Perspectives must be produced which set the world beside itself, alienated from itself, revealing its cracks and fissures, as needy and distorted as it will one day lay there in the messianic light. To win such perspectives without caprice or violence, wholly by the feel for objects, this alone is what thinking is all about. It is the simplest of all things, because the condition irrefutably calls for such cognitions, indeed because completed negativity, once it comes fully into view, shoots into the mirror-writing of its opposite. But it is also that which is totally impossible, because it presupposes a standpoint at a remove, were it even the tiniest bit, from the bane of the existent. The more passionately thought seals itself off from its conditional being for the sake of what is unconditional, the more unconsciously, and thereby catastrophically, it falls into the world. It must comprehend even its own impossibility for the sake of possibility. In relation to the demand thereby imposed on it, the question concerning the reality or non-reality of redemption is however almost inconsequential.

Theodor Adorno, <u>Minima Moralia</u>, Aphorism 153.

NEW YORK POLICE DEPARTMENT

ARREST REPORT

ID/Event # 2388254

Arrestee's Name: Black, Mary K.

Date: September 9, 2007

Time: 5:00 AM

Charges: Grand Larceny

Circumstances of Arrest:

That on September 9, 2007 at 0500, at the location of XXXXXX, Bronx, NY 10471, Mark Black became the victim of a grand larceny over 250.00 Dollars and Battery Domestic Violence at the hands of his wife who he identifies as

Mary Black. Mary Black physically assaulted and battered Mark Black and took his cellular phone valued at 322.17 Dollars. The following details are given in support of the charges.

That Mary Black was out with friends at Basta Pasta Restaurant when she returned home at 0230. She entered his residence and found Mark Black talking on the telephone. Mark and Mary Black began having an argument during the telephone conversation. Mary Black was upset because Mark Black was talking to another woman on the phone. Mark was upset because he wasn't invited to the restaurant. Mary Black was getting more upset and loud and Mark Black made a phone call to the Police. Under Evt. # 400904-0889 NYPD Patrol Officers were dispatched to the residence due to a domestic disturbance. Mary Black advised officers that no battery had occurred. But she wanted Mark Black to leave the house where they both lived. Mary Black wanted to evict him but officers explained to Mark Black that there was an eviction process. During the event Mary Black understood the eviction process and left the house.

That under Evt. # 400904-0978, Mary Black returned to the address of XXXXXX, Bronx, NY 10471 at approximately 0500 Mary Black was accompanied by a male friend by the name of Carl Friedrich. Mark Black was sleeping on the couch in the living room. Mark Black stated that while he was sleeping on the couch Mary Black was yelling at him and holding his cell phone and reading text messages on his phone. "Are you having sex with someone?" she asked. "No, I'm not." Mary Black grabbed Mark Black by his hair and began striking him several times with a closed fist. Mary Black pulled him off the couch by his hair and twisted his right arm. Mark Black stated that Mary Black began yelling, "I am going to kill you and the woman you are messing around with." She also stated "I'm going to have you both disappear." Mark Black tried to fight her off of him. He said he thought of trying to break her arm by twisting it behind his back. Mark Black screamed for Carl Friedrich to call the police. Mary Black turned to Carl Friedrich and said that he should call the police. Carl Friedrich advised that he had seen Mary Black hitting and kicking Mark Black.

NYPD officers arrived at the scene and Mark Black was taken to Montefiore Hospital and treated for facial injuries. A crime report was completed. Detective L. Strongin conducted a verbal interview with Mark Black at Montefiore Hospital. Strongin also took digital photographs of Black's injuries and downloaded them onto the NYPD On-Base System. Mary Black called Mark Black at 0626 on his cell phone and told him not to come back to the house. Mark Black hung up on Mary Black.

Mary Black was listed as the primary aggressor in the domestic battery and also the person who without permission took the cell of Mark Black.

That on 9-10-2007 at approximately 0930 Mary Black and her attorney, Barry King, came to XXXXXX, Bronx, NY at the Detective Office to turn herself in. Then Detective V. Tontti placed Mary Black under arrest for grand larceny and a charge to be considered for 1 count battery domestic violence. She was taken to the Metropolitan Detention Center and booked accordingly.

CHAPTER THIRTY

You Shall Not Eat of it, Neither Shall You Touch it, Lest You Die

AKI SAID HE HAD a taste for goat Vindaloo. I, Mary Black, didn't. Going somewhere else was my priority, but Aki had something he needed to do. He sat beside me while I slurped a bowl of lobster ramen near the Tokyo Ginza subway, so I promised to do the same for him and join him at Rai Palace. I could smell the noxious spices from a block away, but we still had to take the elevator up to the restaurant on the fourth floor.

Once the doors to the elevator closed, and there was no going back, Aki revealed the actual purpose of coming to Rai Palace. "This is Poonah's son's restaurant. She's meeting us here."

You have to take what life gives you, even if I didn't want to in this instance. I thought we were long done with her. Meeting the woman who gave Aki an enema and who knows what else was low on my wish list of things to do. It wasn't too late to let him go without me, but I had no intention of seeming weak. Machiavelli would tell me that Aki was doing me a favor by introducing us. "Perfect. I was hoping you could see her again." Knowledge is power, and there was no reason to hide from reality, if I wanted to succeed.

A petite Indian man with a unibrow and dark eyes twice the size of most eyes was standing there when the elevator door opened.

I figured he'd been watching us with the security camera in the elevator. Palms together, he executed a half-Indian, half-Japanese bow. Then he grabbed two very long menus and led us to our banquette by the window, with a view of a crêpe shop across the street. Young Japanese students dotted the tables. It was a generation that had grown up with bowls of curry rice and hamburgers instead of their ancestral diet. The whole place was lit up as if it were still Christmas. There was no older Indian woman anywhere. After Aki finished ordering, I decided to ask the man with oversized eyes where Poonah was. This sent a clear signal to Aki about the kind of person I am.

"She's headed here," the man said, Indo-British accent on display. "She called ten minutes ago and inquired whether you'd arrived as yet."

Aki's oily samosas were brought to the table, followed by a bowl of creamy black beans. Still no Poonah anywhere to be seen. Then the extra spicy curry plate was served in a copper pan.

I passed on eating and sipped a mango lassi, decided to reopen the topic of Aki's past. I'd waited long enough, and was starting to imagine the worst. "Being here in Japan makes me want to know who you are. I told you I want to know about your past." Aki stayed silent after I said this. His eyes were difficult to read. Sometimes it seemed as though they communicated something, reflecting his inner state, at other times a blankness. I decided to keep talking. "My father used to tell me that until I met someone's parents, I didn't know who they were. At the time I was so young and it didn't make any sense to me. Now it seems wise."

"I agree with your father. We are nothing but our past," Aki interrupted. "I'm like you. But I told you that you can't meet my parents because they are both dead."

I've been there. "And your uncle, is it true that he didn't have a cabin?"

"Yeah, and he's dead, too." Aki put his chopsticks down. "Now I guess that means that you want to know about what I was doing when I first found you."

I told him that I decided it made sense. We couldn't go on like this forever, pretending the past has no relevance.

"I warned you that the story was better, but you weren't satisfied with that. So I will tell you." He put the samosa he held in his chopsticks back on the plate. "Life got so difficult for me. I lost my job at a restaurant and I couldn't find any work," Aki said. He pinched his lips together. "I didn't want to talk about this."

Was there some big dark secret that he needed to hide? He kept insisting there wasn't. "That still doesn't explain how you ended up in the forest in the middle of the night."

"Once I share it, everything will be different. But I have to tell you, now that you need to know," Aki said. "I wanted to make you my Calypso. Now I don't know if I can keep thinking of you this way. Because without the illusion, love disappears."

"Whatever," I said. That was the least of my worries.

He patted his face with the traditional small hot towel the chef's spouse gave us when we arrived. "My wife kicked me out of the house. She screamed until I couldn't take any more. She wanted to humiliate me. I decided that our marriage was over and I started wandering around. We lived in that stupid town called Sundown."

I never suspected that he was married. So was I though, and it didn't take anything away from my feelings for him. If it wasn't for the incident with Guy, I wouldn't have told him about Mark just yet. The fact that I suspected that Mark was eager to protect me was also kept from Aki.

Back to my big Japanese lover. I squeezed his hand. "As shocking as that is, it isn't as bad as what I started imagining."

"Oh really," Aki said, laughing. "Is that right?"

"Conceal a flaw and everyone will imagine the worst," I said, quoting Marcus Aurelius. "So you lied to me."

"I have regretted it every day since. Everyone has something they are ashamed of."

I had to grant him that. All are flawed.

Our bickering had to stop.

In the distance I could see Poonah walking out of the elevator in a blue sari, holding hands with a puny, wiry child. I didn't remember her from the boat. She looked even older in person than in the photograph. She came straight over to our table, wearing a pair of worn flip-flops. "Mary dear, with the beautiful gray eyes, I'm so pleased to meet you," she said, as she sat down with us.

It didn't ring true.

The child turned out to be the owner's son, making him Poonah's grandson. She bragged about how her son had moved to Tokyo two decades earlier, started working in the sewers, became a waiter, and opened this restaurant over time.

Poonah scratched the right side of her jaw, where there was a most obvious cyst.

This is going to be a long, tortuous night, I said, to myself.

CHAPTER THIRTY-ONE

Indian and Update

From: Guy Persons <persons411@usa.net>
Subject: Indian and Update
Date: January 28, 2011 1:04:35 P.M. PST
To: Mark Black <mblack5742@me.com>

Mark,

I'm having a great experience here in Tokyo, even though I spend most of my time standing in one place waiting for Mary and Aki to go somewhere. I am working hard, but you must realize that there is nothing for me to do but figure out something to make note of. They are in the hotel all the time. Rooms start at over six hundred dollars a night and they have a suite, so I imagine she's spending a lot of dough. Drinks are prohibitively expensive at the bar, which is so beautiful you wouldn't believe it. They seem to leave the hotel for one reason: meals. It has been several days like this, following them in the middle of the night to the main fish market and then a couple patisseries in the afternoon. A few times they've gone to an 11-seat tempura place with Michelin stars. They feast and then they go back to the room, and I am the dope who waits outside all these places, wishing I could be inside. Mary comes out of the hotel with a different set of clothes every time, and Aki wears either a beige velour jumpsuit or an Asian looking black getup that's somehow traditional. I stand outside the lobby on a concrete bench most of the time. I wish I had more to report, but unless I were to somehow hide in their room, I can't say much more. They are not all kissy kissy or anything, but I can't imagine they stay in the hotel as celibates. You've told me many times how sexual Mary is. I tried bribing a couple taxi drivers for information, but they didn't take kindly to my request. People have too much pride here, and it gets annoying.

Tonight was weird because they were at an Indian restaurant for three hours. I walked up and down the same street a thousand times. When they came out Aki was holding Mary on one side and this old lady in traditional Indian clothes on the other. She is less than five feet tall and weighs ninety pounds tops. I figured she was some old friend of his, but then they got into a taxi and all went to the Conrad hotel again. I followed them in a taxi and I checked the bar after they went up (the hotel starts on the 28th floor) and they weren't there. So I decided to call up to their room from the in-house phone. Mary answered and I said, "Apologies, I made wrong number," with my version of an Indian accent, and hung up. So they're in the room together. I stayed outside most of the night in the freezing cold and the Indian lady came out by 11:00 A.M. and took a taxi as soon as she was outside. I had to go back to my room and rest. I've been following them for three days without anything more than an occasional cat nap, and that's grueling.

This Indian lady is at least 65 years old. I don't know what Mary is doing, but maybe she's involved with some kind of business. But why would she sleep there? The Indian lady came out with wet hair, as if she'd showered. She had on the same bright blue clothes she went in with, and shuffled along in what looked like slippers.

I'm not sure what you want me to do next. I tried finding a copy of that book you wanted me to get (by Rex Feral) but it is getting harder and harder to, since the triple murder and the lawsuit. I asked your old neighbor to check again with the movers. Mary's copy wasn't at the house. We did find a first edition of *Fanny Hill*, but it was unmarked. Even so, you were right to have me read it before I left. Besides all the smut, I found the section on masturbation with Phoebe and Fanny as amazing as you had described it. Fanny did remind me of Mary, but you would know better. Also, I recalled an incident of participating in frottage with a girl on the field hockey team my senior year. We then moved on to axillary intercourse, in fact. My understanding is that the axillary is something that fascinates you personally, as well as in your studies. Anyway, I had Eileen forward the book to your address in Saudi Arabia, with a different book jacket, like we did before with your hardcover of *The Better Sex Guide to Extraordinary Lovemaking.*

Back to business, I don't think the Indian lady is the type to be armed. I suppose she could have something in her sari, but I wouldn't count on it. I wish I had better news. This is one messed-up situation.

Cheers,
Guy

FROM THE DESK OF MARK BLACK

Dear Kazu Komatsuto,

I believe you are already aware that I would be contacting you, as I am the old friend of Shlomo Bernstein's, of London. He says that we met there at his gentleman's club, and I do remember it. It is most kind of you to offer your people, and I can promise you fair reimbursement. It is my feeling that you fulfill an important need in society, because justice must be served, and modern governments will not do so. I am located in Saudi Arabia but am going to Jerusalem by the end of the week on business.

You know THE REASON I am contacting you and I don't need to tell you that we must proceed with THIS MATTER immediately. I was notified of an additional member to the concerned party, with an unclear connection to the two you are already aware of. Our local sources were able to investigate her. She is Poonah Barot of Agra, India. She is on a tourist visa, visiting her relations who are the owners of Indian restaurants in Tokyo. I don't believe that she is dangerous, but I would appreciate it if your staff also looked into the business affairs of Rai Palace. If you would confirm that you received the photographs provided by my investigators in Canada, it would be helpful. Please phone me on my satphone so that we can discuss the details of how we will do what we must.

Regards,
MB

CHAPTER THIRTY-TWO

Flees to the Moon

February 1, 2011
Dear Professor McConnell,

A lot has happened in a short time. This is one of those accelerated periods in my life, the opposite of stasis. I did in fact embark on Beckett, my horse, and left the Bronx for the mountains to the north, ending up in a cave where I spent most of the night weeping, believing I'd erred. To soothe my mind I started interviewing myself when, in the middle of the night, this special person came into the cave. I had assumed that I could live there undiscovered for months, if I chose to. The stranger was a very large man from Japan who speaks somewhat like a sage.

Fast forward to a few weeks later and everything changed again, due to this person. I returned the horse to his owner and Aki and I went to Vancouver for fresh crabs and then took a boat to Tokyo, where I am now. I still have the sack of coin and the armor, but I don't know what to do with them. I had once trained in judo and kendo and always thought of myself as a samurai. I'm not sure how long we will stay in Japan because meeting Aki complicated everything.

I am a married woman who never wants to see her husband again. Aki, as it turns out, is a married man with a complex past as well. He confessed that he was booted out of his house the night he found me in the cave. My husband is looking for me and I will make sure he doesn't succeed. You know how complex the emotion of love is, given your medieval systematic analysis of all aspects of the mind.

As of yesterday we have a third member in our party, an older woman from Gujarat that Aki begged me to accept into our journey. In the past I have been a possessive lover, but relinquishing that understanding may be what I need to do next in life. It led to total failure with my husband, for example. I can't go into the details but this woman serves some function to Aki that I am told that I must respect. He is a blind man and blind people have different needs than us. He needs to feel more than the rest of us.

It took a lot to get him to open up about his past. For a while we existed as people without a past, reduced to an identity fixated on the present. We couldn't sustain it, and that makes me sad.

Aki and Poonah are discussing what we are going to do next. I have asked them to remember that I am on a special journey and have placed my life in their hands. They will protect me from my husband. It is due to the kindness of strangers that I'm here at all.

Warm regards,
Mary Black

༄

GENERAL PROCEDURE OF THE GOVERNMENT OF JAPAN

Agency: Office of the City Attorney General

Division: Judicial Police

Department: Homicides

Offense: Homicide

Official Letter: PJE 230-957-2776

MATTER: INVESTIGATION REPORT

TOSHI SAKAMAKI

PUBLIC PROSECUTOR FOR

LOCAL MATTERS

BY HAND

In response to your official letter number CHI 7083-31-2040/957-277-6 dated March 18, 2011, in which you request that the corresponding investigations of OUD 3102-60-1434/669-1702/5159-2-2011 be made; such investigation was initiated for the offense of HOMICIDE committed to the detriment of GUY PERSONS against WHOEVER RESULTS LIABLE, I herby inform you of the following:

At about 0900 hours there was information by
Mika Ono, Personnel of the Security of Hotel
Paramount Akasaka, that inside the sewerage
pit of Akasaka, Ken Namba, maintenance
supervisor, found on opening the pit a corpse.
Personnel of the Red Cross under the charge of
paramedics told me they would take the corpse
out of the sewerage pit. Let me also inform that
in the same place Dr. Shinji Kyushu, expert
in criminalistics, was on board the forensics
ambulance. Then, after some complicated
maneuvers, the body of the murdered person was
taken out of the said pit, wounds on the body
were not visible at first sight, the body was naked
and in a state of saponification. The prosecutor
attested to the facts.

In like manner, I inform you that that the
undersigned had knowledge by Tateru Yoshino,
Commander of the State Judicial Police for the
Hotels area, who was present in this place of
occurrence, that due to the characteristics of the
corpse it could be the missing man, reason for
which the fact-finding report PGBK/RRAR/
NSWS/002/2011 had been initiated. Therefore,
following up the investigation with a person said
to be named Sachi Yasuda, 27, working in this
city, who mentioned that on February 2, this
year that he was informed by the supervisor of
housekeepers named Candy, of a guest who was
missing in the facilities of Hotel Paramount. She
found out about the search for the missing guest
and realized that the lid of the sewerage water
treatment pit was not properly closed, and when
she took a look inside the sewage she saw a body
floating and therefore interred that it could be
the missing person.

Continuing with the investigation we went to
the home of Ichirou Rakutei since there was
information provided by the Chief of Police in
his previous report and there was a complaint
filed by this guest of room 709 where he said
in said report that he heard very loud noises,
like people fighting and he heard the voice of a
man screaming for help. There was screaming,
crying and arguing since 0600 hours and these
terrible noises woke up his children. There
he proceeded to inquire who the guests of
this room were and corroborated that it was a
single American man. His children told him it
sounded to them like a middle-aged woman's
screaming and it sounded like stuff was being
dragged in the aforementioned room. This
was corroborated by the son of said family.
They reported the incident to the SECURITY
SUPERVISOR after the parent, Ichirou Rakutei,
woke up. The Security Supervisor carried out the
corresponding surveillance but the perpetrators
of the crime had left the Paramount.

In like manner, I inform you that we also
interviewed a guest at the hotel, a person who is
said to be named Kevin Mattson, 34, native to
Australia, married, having a college degree and
he said he was outside the Paramount at 0630
hours by the side of the building preparing to
go for a run when he realized that two persons
were leaving the lobby and he remembers that
there was an oversized Japanese man walking
with a small elderly Indian woman who was
arguing and crying with the Japanese individual.
He picked her up and, in an unusual display of
public affection, kissed her face several times.
They left the area in a taxi.

At this time we have no suspects in detention.

Respectfully,

Justice For All
The Officer of the State Judicial Police

(SIGNED)

TOSHI SAKAMAKI

(Sealed)

CHAPTER THIRTY-THREE

The Only Choice For Those Who Choose Only the Best

February 3, 2011
Dear Ms. Black,

This is regarding confirming your reservation for a Business Boeing jet, given the 4989 mile distance between Tokyo Narita and Jammu (Kashmir), India, as per your request to book an aircraft that is capable of traveling without refueling. You can save on the costs of booking a private plane should you choose to allow for one stop along the way, as I sense based on your communications that budget is an issue. I am sorry, but the price I am quoting you for this aircraft is the lowest our company can offer. We understand that you have an emergency and need this plane right away.

We would need to confirm the destination of the aircraft and would prefer not to change the country destination mid-flight, as you inquired about. Exceptions can be made, but there are penalties for that and so I suggest you figure out where you are going ahead of time.

Regarding your third passenger, yes, we will need to have that person's passport. We are unable to carry people across national borders without documentation, for obvious reasons.

We have arranged for a South Asian vegetarian meal for your business partner and will guarantee that there are plenty of rose petals (approximately five dozen red roses) on the bed so that she can sleep.

A charcuterie course with goose breast and a foie gras terrine has been arranged and our master sommelier has chosen vintage Bordeaux pairings with high ratings. We have arranged for a shiatsu masseuse from Tokyo to be on board who can offer treatments at any point during the duration of the journey.

We will arrange to have all the shades down once you board the airplane. Your privacy is important to us. It is possible to book the reservation under the name of someone in your party, as you preferred, and still have you pay for the booking under your debit card. We would prefer a credit card, however.

A bulletproof all-terrain vehicle with two armed guards will be waiting for you by the tarmac and will take you to your undisclosed location in Kashmir. We understand and respect your privacy regarding the matter and have made sure that once you enter the country of India you will be able to travel anonymously.

Please sign the attached contract so that I can hurry the jet to your location. I understand the urgency of your request and will do whatever I can to get it there. We need three hours from when you sign the contract. The jet is in Seoul, South Korea as we await your answer. I hope that I have addressed everything.

Sincerely,
Lucas U. Spalding
White Star Jets, London Branch

CHAPTER THIRTY-FOUR

They Only See What is Near at Hand and Should Not Exist at All

Dear Mark Black,

Thank you for contacting me again about your familial situation. I understand your concern about finding your wife. My services and advice as a skip tracer shall remain confidential.

As far as finding your wife, I will require a copy of her passport and a retainer of $4,000.00 to find her location. That said, if anyone can find her, I believe that person is me. I have over two decades of experience with international cases such as this one. This information will be available to you within two business days of receiving your go-ahead. To determine the specifics beyond her next port of entry, we will need to hire a local professional. That will be more expensive than the above amount, as you can imagine.

Based on my experience with finding people on the run, it is difficult to say where she's disappeared to after Japan. The Philippines and Myanmar are obvious choices, but any number of dubious nation states could be her destination. Considering what you've told me about the murder of your friend, I'd say that they are rather disorganized and desperate. The amount of money in their possession is an issue. The fact that she closed her bank accounts before leaving is a sign that she knows what she is doing. I am guessing that she has another arrangement, but tracking that is difficult, unless she is wiring money, which is possible. You've told me that she is detail-oriented, so I assume she is going to be hard to track down. Once we know where she is, we can open up the topic of extradition laws, and discuss other options.

The fact that your wife figured out that you'd sent someone to follow her means that I wouldn't be surprised if she has a vengeful plan, targeted at taking your life. It would behoove you to hire security and arm yourself in the coming weeks, until we find her. Riyadh's expatriate community is rather small, so finding you is easier than you might otherwise realize. She seems to know the right people to hire.

I shall consider her and her crew armed and dangerous.

Sincerely,
Erik Soderbergh, Skip Tracer

❧

Mary,

Thank you for reaching out to me! As your therapist, I must confess that I am concerned about your well-being, on so many fronts. When you get a chance, I think we ought to do a session on the phone. I will try to address your main points in this note.

What your husband does is beyond your control. You can only control how you live. It is all about you. That you've taken a new lover and that your lover has taken a new lover is rather dangerous to the psyche. In my experience this never works out. Devotion to another person and monogamy seem to me to be the natural state of humanity as we know it, but exceptions exist.

Regarding your concerns about not being able to experience sexual pleasure with your lover's lover, I would say that you shouldn't punish yourself or believe that you are homophobic. Your lover has an open eroticism with the feminine, but you've always been more discriminating. It is essential to be true to yourself. You don't have to wear a sari if it doesn't turn you on. You also don't have to take the sari off Aki if you don't find it to be something you want. The point is that you shouldn't have to do things that go against your will. The same goes for all those enemas they keep giving one another. BTW, are they in therapy???

You may need to make the choice not to share the bed with the two of them. What troubles you is not that she can pleasure him, but that their way of making love is not something that appeals to you. If you are leaving the bed to eat a bowl of lentils, as you describe, then something is off. You've tried being open to their role-playing and let the new woman try to please you. There is nothing else to be done. The resentment you are feeling will become hatred.

Another point: I spoke to my Indian friend and said I had a client in India. My understanding is that there are travel advisories in Kashmir and that you shouldn't plan on staying there for the indefinite future. It might be as beautiful as you say on that houseboat, but if all you're doing is having failed sexual experiences and cooking for them, I think you'll tire of that. That you care so much about Aki's pleasure is a positive sign to me, as long as he is not abusive. This means that you can trust that you are recovering from how you and Mark treated one another. It sounds like your lover no longer wants to be with his wife, but these things are complicated. Both of you may be haunted by the past for a long time. We are vulnerable creatures, most of all with lovers.

Do keep in touch if there's anything else.

Warmest Regards,
Dr. Cheri Adrienne

February 8th, 2011

Winfrey: So, I'm glad we've this chance to meet again.

Mary: Me too. I feel so far from everything now.

Winfrey: I'd say. The last time we spoke we were in a cave, this time it is in the middle of a lake on a colorful boat.

Mary: Exotic, I know. But I have my own theories about what is happening.

Winfrey: That's why you've asked me here. I'm curious to know your thoughts on what you're doing.

Mary: I believe we are all the same person and that we are in one of multiple universes with infinite space. I don't feel I exist in a way that's different from you.

Winfrey: So this place is the same as the cave and whether it is you or me talking it is the same thing.

Mary: Something like that. This collection of particles that I am could be your consciousness and each of our thoughts and actions occurs somewhere else at some point an infinite number of times. We are each born with the same imaginary penis that wasn't there.

Winfrey: Now, sister, how did you come up with that?

Mary: There are so many reasons, but let me give you an example. My lover is named Aki, and his lover, who is also here on the boat in another room, is Poonah. The three of us sat on the dining room table last night wearing saris. Aki and I don't care for saris, but Poonah's primary fetish is blue saris. So we oblige. We unwrapped our saris at the same time and masturbated on the cold marble. We each found the marble cold and we each wanted to have our butts warmed so we each put a right hand under another person's butt while that person masturbated. We climaxed at the same time. Each of our masturbating hands tasted similar afterward, as did the ones under each other's butts.

Winfrey: That might be more than I needed to know.

Mary: Exactly. And that's because you can imagine your butt getting cold on that marble table, too. You know the odors I am talking about. What we each imagine as the ultimate pleasure at any moment overlaps. I was thinking about riding Aki from behind and he told me he imagined Poonah as a young woman taking off her green underwear. Poonah said she wanted to please Aki and me while wearing her sari. All of this was going on while we each touched ourselves. I'm guessing that at that moment in the world there were at least one hundred million people masturbating and we were all thinking more or less the same thing. Add to that the number of people who are inside one another and the numbers are staggering. The latter group is still masturbating, but they are led to believe that their pleasure is somehow linked to the other's, but I don't accept that it is that way anymore.

Winfrey: I can't say I see things this way.

Mary: Each of us carries around our versions of our imaginary vaginas and imaginary penises. How we each own our organs and how others have handled ours has a definite effect. We pretend to be innocent and unique, but we are all the same, wherever we happen to be. That's why my husband hated the sight of condoms and dildos.

Winfrey: What is your relationship to your husband? It doesn't sound like you're close any more.

Mary: We are still close. Because once you open your secret world to someone else, they will haunt you forever. That continues even after they can no longer please you. Mark no longer pleases me. It has been this way for five years. That's on a practical level. There is another realm. I know how to enter him from over here. He can't handle my power, if I learn to access it. When we spread our legs it is too much for any man. You remember the story of Medusa. I can send a thought to him in his dreams, though it may take a year or more for him to get it. But that pattern exists, and it will get picked up in this infinite expanse of repetition. When he looked at my vagina he was stunned that my penis was missing. I know that he doesn't want me to feel pleasure, and he knows that I would love to emasculate him. This will go on after he and I are both dead, because even what comes will be nothing but a variation of who I am here and now.

Winfrey: So thanks to all those repetitions somehow I ended up on this boat.

Mary: And we will have this conversation again, with ourselves, an infinite number of times.

CHAPTER THIRTY FIVE

And What Followed Was the Apparition of Somebody in Me

Fajita Avenue
Dabab St., Suleimania
Riyadh, Saudi Arabia

Mark Black made the restaurant reservation from his satellite phone in order to request the corner booth. All the tables were hidden behind beige curtains (this was Saudi Arabia and women must be sequestered from non-husband men), but he wanted the corner. He was armed with a small Beretta pistol, in case there was any foul play. Risks weren't acceptable, but any plan involved risk. He arrived twenty minutes early so that he could take the bench facing out towards the restaurant and waited for Omar Amir. Mark had partnered with him several times before. Omar was not the kind of man that was commonplace for most people to cross paths with. He is, more or less, what is called a wanted man. In other words, a crucial link to international terrorists. Finding money was his specialty, and that's how Mark was able to assist him in the past. When a prominent Arab came to Mecca on pilgrimage with fantasies of discovering illicit sexual pleasure, people like Omar knew that Mark was the person to contact. Mark didn't ask clients about anything personal, except what kinds of girls or boys they desired.

Al-Qaeda is an organization sustained by money, like any other, and Omar was one of those with a Vertu phone full of important contacts that could be nudged into contributing to their cause. Rewarding men with sex in the desert was at least as old as the stories in the Bible.

Mark ordered a virgin strawberry juice with extra ice and read the technology section of the local Asharq Alawsat newspaper from the day before. The curtain was pulled back and the Mexican waiter led Omar to the open bench. "I'll take a juice as well," Omar told him, as he sat.

Omar had let himself get round, was now in his mid-fifties. Originally of Kuwaiti descent, he spoke impeccable English, having been educated at a London prep school. Today he wore a white linen suit and straw hat. The contrast of all that light fabric with his black as charcoal mustache was dramatic, if not tacky.

The two of them spoke about how business had been since they last met. They'd both been hit hard by the world recession. Everyone was traveling everywhere less, including to Dubai, which the Saudi economy depended upon more than the locals would admit.

"You've been the one to help me in the past," Omar said, while smoking a cigarette with his hand kept still just above his head. "Our tradition is to return the favor. You said it involves something about Kashmir."

"Yes, I have a situation there. I didn't know how to handle it. I was starting to panic," Mark said. "I panic when I feel like I am starting to fail, and I know it."

"I'm the same way," Omar said.

"I did a Google search for *How to Kill Someone in Kashmir* and that led me to some articles on the local political scene. My understanding is that the Kashmiri resistance is now more connected to international networks. That's when I thought of you."

"That's right, we have people there," Omar said. "Kashmir doesn't belong to India. It is no more Hindu than Alaska."

"I get your point," Mark said. He knew their agenda. He didn't care about their agenda.

The waiter startled both of them when he came to the curtain and asked if they were ready to order.

"Two plates of chicken fajitas with extra guacamole." Mark was getting tired of eating lamb and rice, the regular item on menus. "Otherwise, leave us alone."

"Si, Señor."

Mark turned back to Omar. "I need someone captured," he said once the waiter was out of earshot. "She is somewhere in Kashmir, with two others, and they are armed." Mark took a sip from his virgin drink. "This person killed my friend and she has no idea that I paid a specialist to find her. The problem is I don't have any more than that. Your people will need to take over."

Omar asked for physical descriptions of the three. "My people track everything. We are very organized."

"What about the police?"

"Forget about the Indian police. Useless. I think it is easier to kill someone than to apprehend. If you want them captured, that will be trickier. The Kashmiris know how to kidnap, but they've been known to fail. Killing is much easier. I will be contacting a special group who can do this for us."

"Fine, let's do that. But I want the Indian price, not the American."

Omar smiled for the first time since he arrived. "I understand. Let me make a few phone calls this afternoon. I'm sure we can take care of them by the end of the week, at the latest."

(**Aki, February 9, 2011**)
Dear Maria Jose,

It isn't as if I can stop thinking about what happened before I left. I hope you are feeling better where you are. I have been through a lot myself, but worries about you won't go away. I fear what you've done and how it won't help you. It is miserable, for you and for me. One day we will unite again. The love can't disappear because of time and how it punishes us. Try as I may to get away from you, I can't help but feel we are still together. Or think that we should be together again one day. It was miserable in that house, with you on the edge of destruction. I did everything to try to please you, but every day you would wake up in that same pool of misery. Sometimes, from afar, it feels as though I made you up so that I could heal you. It would be like fixing the world, which has always been my deepest desire. We know that it is all wrong and all broken. You sit in my imagination and I want a version of you back, the one that understands pleasure as a form of deliverance. But we could never sustain it. Neither of us is enough of a sexual invert.

Maybe I am mistaken to think that the striving for unity between man and woman has anything to do with the joy of life. I don't wish to concern myself with men, however. I've two women with me now, and it is as dangerous and perilous as every triangle is. I fear for the future and what it will bring us. My days may be numbered, too, and this is why I needed to write you, as if you didn't end your life.

These are things thought out during the night of February 2 and February 3, 2011, but I hesitated for several days to pretend to send them to you.

Love,
Aki T.

CHAPTER THIRTY-SIX

The Advent of the Inevitable, and Other Struggles With Her Osama

"The Veil: Towards a Sexual Politics of Kashmir's Daughters of Allah," by Janelle A. Carrier, McGill University, 2011.

The following is based on research at Princeton University for my doctorate on the women of radicalized Islam. While in most Muslim societies the women are sequestered to an extreme, it was in Kashmir where I found women organized on a political level, under the banner of the Daughters of Allah. For six months I was given access to these women, for they were eager to get their voice out to the world. I watched them practice military maneuvers, martial arts, target practice, etc. They consider it their duty to martyr both themselves and their children as servants of the divine.

A little about myself: I'm an anthropologist by training, with a background in psychology. Had I been a political scientist or historian I would have focused on the political agenda of this armed group. My area of interest is in the personal understanding of sexuality and gender politics and how it relates to the phenomenon of female Islamic rebellion. For works about men I can recommend the following articles:

"Patterns of Homoerotism in the Mujahideen," Silver, Paul. *Middle East Bulletin*, Winter, 2002.

"Male Fantasies of the Death Wish in Egypt's Islamic Brotherhood," Loevy, John. *World Psychology Journal*, September, 1996.

"Patna Purdah and Castration: An Examination of Indian Writings," Singh, Smirta. Indian Institute of Technology.

Fundamental to understanding these women I lived with was the notion that all people are the same on the outside. Coming from a society that emphasizes personal expression through the external signs of the fashion industry, I could recognize some truth to their contention. Their bodies are sacrificed for religious purposes. It wasn't as if the veil communicates nothing about the women. This is another way of saying that no matter what we do, the sexual is expressed, even as an absence. This is utilizing a neo-Freudian approach.

It may come as a surprise that these women were forthright when it came to discussing their sexuality, although I often wondered whether I was hearing the whole truth. That's something that we as researchers have to wrestle with, as we try to present an accurate version of what is. When it came to physical descriptions of sexuality they would speak at length, most often in reference to expressing dissatisfaction with their husbands. The personal aspects, perversions, inner desires, etc., I would say, were difficult to access. All of this had been purged from their minds, on the grounds that it was unholy. What they perceived to be negative they considered part of the djinns, the devilish aspect of the supernatural. The veil became a private acceptance of sexuality with the one other who is invited to remove it, in the sanctity of the marital arrangement. The erotic is not for other men to access. Repeatedly, women told me that without the veil it is impossible to control the sexual appetites of other men. They see it as the only option for people who wish to live a simple, monogamous life. Every woman I sat with complained about the groping of women in places like buses. These Kashmiri women were able to defend themselves from the gaze and touch of the masculine, through the boundary of the veil and their ability to fight. Kashmiri sex ring operators have been challenged by this organized militia of women. The police were corrupt participants in the prostitution networks. The issue of how sexuality is handled there is a complicated one.

I heard from the women that Western society was hypocritical. It was their feeling that liberation could be achieved only through the veil. Any expression of public sexuality was one step away from rape, in their eyes, and was an explanation for why rape was so common in the West. It is because men cannot handle the sexual power of women. Unlike their grandmothers, these women chose the veil not because men demanded it, but to protect them from other men. Whereas in other Islamic societies I found that women in veils bought the finest of lingerie, in Kashmir the armed women wore simple village clothes, no négligées.

I confess that it was difficult to accept the prohibitionist tendencies of these people. While I was there they would organize attacks on beauty salons as well as shops selling alcohol. The outrage they felt against non-Islamic culture told a different story than the puritanical tendencies of modesty and family values, as they were willing to be violent to advance their cause.

It may be that they are right when they say that all of our erotic lives will be forever veiled. It may be that the actual veil intensifies the erotic charge of these nations, leading them to the extremes of personal self-expression, including martyrdom. Annihilation and death become fused with a celebration of femininity. They do not want to be the puppets of men. The extent to which they succeed, or any of us do, is debatable.

CHAPTER THIRTY-SEVEN

We Never Forget Who We're Working For

THE TIMES OF INDIA, "Tourists and Police Die in Kashmir Explosions," February 11, 2011.

As three additional wounded tourists struggle for life in critical care facilities, the death toll has risen to ten in Friday's deadly bombings in Srinagar. These numbers include previously unreported explosions that occurred in this week's violence.

Indian tourists and local police have been killed, and more than twenty persons, mostly holiday-makers, were wounded in a series of grenade explosions on the scenic Dal Lake of Srinagar.

Indian officials said that all six police officers killed had responded to a series of blasts on houseboats on the lake. The four tourists killed were on the first boat that exploded, and officials say that all four came from the city of Hyderabad.

Responsibility for the incident has been taken by the Daughters Of Allah, a Muslim separatist group fighting New Delhi's rule over the disputed Himalayan State divided between Indian and Pakistani controlled parts.

Officials are researching the veracity of the claim by the Daughters of Allah. Extremists are targeting tourist locations, especially after the police increased surveillance and pressure on members of armed groups in the recent months. General Lieutenant Rahman Baluchi said, "Our message to these groups has been clear from the beginning. Killing innocent people will not be tolerated. We will find the perpetrators and bring them to justice one by one."

According to witnesses, an unidentified assailant tossed several hand grenades at two houseboats where the tourist victims had been sitting. The first houseboat had six people on it, but the second had no occupants. Two survivors from that blast are in critical condition at a local hospital. At a press conference last night in Jammu, Kashmir, Police Chief Mohammed Salah said, "When officers came to the site of the grenade explosions, they found four persons already dead, including three sisters." He added that the assailant then proceeded to disappear on a boat, according to local sources.

Less than thirty minutes after the attack, an SUV in the heart of the city caught fire. A group of American tourists inside the vehicle were injured. "They were brought out of the burning car with great difficulty," said a nearby shopkeeper. Bela Nuss was one of the Americans. "It all happened so fast. We were on our way to the airport, when I saw this woman coming towards our car. By the time I saw the grenade, it was too late." Police and a local resident engaged in a shootout with the two assailants of the car bombing. Additional police were hurried to the area. Six officers were killed before catching the two women who were responsible for this blast. It is believed but not confirmed that the explosions were linked.

Minutes later, three more grenades were exploded by a private taxi, near the Tourist Reception Center, injuring at least a dozen more tourists, witnesses said.

The grenade explosions have caused panic in parts of Srinagar, and people have begun to withdraw from the streets.

Friday's attacks were the latest in a series of acts of violence against tourists in the area. Soon, many tourists who were to spend another few days in this unforgettable land nestling in the lap of the dazzling, snowcapped Himalayas cut short their visit and returned home. The predominantly Muslim valley has yet to come to grips with the attacks perpetrated by women. Noted tourism pioneer, Ahmed Ahmed, sees a systematic pattern in the select targeting. He points out that first it was tourists from Gujarat and now it is from Hyderabad and the United States.

Authorities are not ruling out that some agency is behind the attacks. There may be a personal rivalry at play.

Former Chief Minister and leader of Peoples Democratic Party Muhammed Velayat said, "If we've learned anything from this latest series of attacks, it is that we need to do much more to protect our police officers so that they can go about their jobs of protecting citizens and tourists in the area. There is no other choice."

❧

"Wake up."

"What is it?"

Aki was with me tonight. Poonah decided to stay with relatives at an apartment by the main train station.

We were staying at a hotel near a temple. It wasn't much of a room, but it was better than staying with Poonah's family. They start early here. The bells forced me up, not him. I went down, got chai, the paper, and brought them back up to the room. "Listen to this article." I read it aloud to Aki.

Aki couldn't see the cover photo, but it was all clear to me. "Those three sisters they mention are the ones we talked to when we were going to dinner a couple days ago."

"Yes, they are."

I owed my life to Aki.

Two nights before, returning to the houseboat from dinner, he couldn't sleep. He packed up our stuff by the time Poonah and I woke up.

We thought he'd gone mad.

"What the hell are you doing?" I asked him when I saw the suitcases.

"I was in bed going in and out of sleep and I had this bad feeling, like there were people around," Aki said. He looked funny when he spoke, his head poking out from under the blanket. "I went outside and there were a few women talking. I didn't recognize their voices. They were far away, but something about their voices scared me. I felt vulnerable from then on."

I reread the article four times. *We were supposed to die in there.* Aki finished the rest of my tea.

"How did your father pass on?" Aki asked me, ending the silence.

"Cancer."

"So your husband didn't kill him," Aki said.

"No way," I answered. "And he won't kill me, unless he has no choice."

"I hope I never understand why your husband has it in for us."

CHAPTER THIRTY-EIGHT

One Exception is Found, the Floating Bridge of Dreams: That Craving He Feels is Evidence

Fajita Avenue
Dabab St., Suleimania
Riyadh, Saudi Arabia

"We're fucking doomed."

They were there again in the back of the Mexican restaurant, deciding what to do about Mary. Omar Amir had to stop chewing before answering Mark. Omar wore the same white linen suit he did the first time, this time with a pink Italian shirt. "I don't know what to say. Nobody saw them leaving."

Mark hadn't slept since he received the call about the botched attempt in Kashmir. Time and again Omar reminded him that no one would be able to link him to the explosion. "I'm not worried about the Indians," Mark said. He hadn't taken a bite from his plate. "But I'm sure the American investigators will go through everything."

"Not in a country like India," Omar said. "The important part is finding your wife. The clue, I mean the big clue, is the Japanese man. There's no way he can hide for long. I promise you, he'll turn up on our radar."

"Hope you're right," Mark said. "Anyway, you want a girl?"

"I won't say no," Omar answered, as he filled a soft tortilla with charred chicken. He didn't seem to notice that Mark had yet to touch his food. "What do you have?"

"You name it."

It was the price of business for Mark.

"I was thinking of one blonde and one Asian this time," Omar said. "Not too skinny, if possible, and no tattoos this time. I prefer overweight."

"Virgin?"

"Doesn't matter. I'm not like you."

Mark ignored the jab. He had seen everything when it came to desire, setting up as many as a dozen at a time for men like Omar. When you order a shipment of buttons from Taiwan, deliveries are handled by specific carriers. Millions of buttons cross the ocean on ships, and somehow that portion of the economy organizes itself so that all those buttons get used. Every business has its protocol. The arms trade requires governmental approval. You make a rifle and you'll figure out who wants it.

The same applies when it comes to exporting sex workers. There will always be customers. All Mark needed was a corporate account at a hotel and access to people who knew how to smuggle them in. He was the man in the middle, connecting people to the fantasies they had no idea how to create alone. "I assume the same hotel is fine with you," Mark said. "I'll text you tonight with the details."

ॐ

MARY REALIZED HOW LUCKY they were to have a break in the weather only after they'd arrived by jet to the one narrow runway in the state of Ladakh, the mountainous tip of India. Flights had been canceled all week and would be for days afterward, making for a full plane. The roads had been closed most of the year, due to the high passes. Poonah considered it the safest place to rest until they determined what to do next.

All the Kashmiris had gone away for the winter and wouldn't be returning to their tourist shops until the summer. Even the mosque was closed.

None of the three had acclimated to the high Himalayan air so they stayed inside in their suite at a guesthouse in the center of town. Two hours after landing, the snow continued all day and night. The only times they left the room were to eat breakfasts and dinners in the main dining hall. Lunch was little more than dried apricots, hard bread, and a yak jerky served in the room.

There was one other Western tourist who had kept to himself the first two nights. He didn't even say hello to them; they didn't know where he came from. He was tall, so tall that he had to be careful where he walked; the houses were designed for short Ladakhis, with low ceilings that meant less to heat during the interminable winter. But this time, as Aki and Mary went to their table (Poonah stayed behind, in the room, with an upset stomach), the man gestured for them to join him.

"I'm Cyril Helbling," he said, taking off his long, colorful scarf.

Aki and Mary introduced themselves. "You're German," she said.

"Pure Swiss."

For a small country, their citizens seem to know how to pop up everywhere.

Cyril took a bottle of whiskey from his small Patagonia backpack. Foreign alcohol wasn't easy to find in the backwaters of India. "I got this in Kazakhstan. You'll share some with me?"

Aki filled his glass to the top and started talking. "In my tradition, when you meet a stranger in the snow, it has a special meaning. It reminds us that life is a dream. That is how Mary and I met. Now I have that feeling about you."

Cyril turned to Aki and smiled. "I'm going to be honest with you," he said. There was a slight wildness in his eyes, like a man who had spent a lot of time alone. "I have been almost everywhere. I have crossed Mongolia on foot, and most of Central Asia. I'll tell you something. This is the best place in the world to hide."

Mary wasn't the type to divulge anything, simply because someone else was.

When you yourself are on the run, it may not be wise to be honest to someone who also is.

The owner of the guesthouse, Stanzin, brought plates of steamed root vegetables and rice.

Cyril took a bag of key limes from his backpack. "These keep you from getting sick. When I'm in remote places, I squeeze it on everything, even cereal. Have some."

Mary took one for herself and one for Aki.

"The reason I love the snow is that it covers everything," Aki said. "The past disappears in it. I don't know why we're here. Maybe we're hiding, maybe we're moving. Things happen to us and we react. The lesson is that it doesn't matter what happened before we arrived."

"So you live in the present," Cyril said.

"They call it the present. But that assumes something else, a past and future," Aki answered. He finished the last of his whisky. "I don't give it a name."

"You're being too quiet," Cyril said to Mary. "We men need to hear women speak, even though I find your friend to be amazing."

"I am aware that I have a past and I know I have a certain future. My character is my fate," she said. "I wish I was more like Aki though. But I can't lie about it."

"I'm more like you," Cyril said. "Let me ask you something, are you married?"

"No, we're not married," Mary said. She took her left hand from her pocket and squeezed Aki's leg.

"I meant you," Cyril said.

"Me, personally? I am, but the marriage is over." Mary's voice was drained of feeling.

"I had a feeling you were married. But it wouldn't be fair to ask you what you're doing here," Cyril said. "I respect that. I wish I had your luxury, but I am in a different circumstance. I need to tell you about my life."

"You have no option," Aki said, "because you have been destructive."

"I don't know, yes and no." Cyril lit a cigarette. Only after he had answered Aki did he show his confusion. "What exactly do you mean by that?"

"You are not good to yourself," Aki said. "If you are bad to yourself, you are destructive. Right?"

"Yes, I suppose you're right. I'll be honest. I've been destructive, and that's why I need you both. I don't mean I need you in the sense that without you I'm kaput. But I need you. I need you like a hungry man needs some bread. Notice I didn't say a dying man, I used the word hungry."

"And your point is," Mary said.

"After dinner I would like to show you something."

"Very mysterious," Mary said. "Swiss man in the snow needs to show us something."

"For you it is mysterious. For me it is the biggest burden of my life."

୧

THE MOON WAS NEARLY full again. It made it possible to sludge our way through the mounds of snow, following Cyril. Time seemed to be moving slower than ever. It has a way of doing that when you don't know what's happening.

Cyril was someone who seemed to have spent too much time on his own. Surely he must recognize how odd it was for us, two strangers, one blind, to be traipsing into a meadow in the dark. We'd gone far enough from the house that it was out of sight. We were on a narrow trail lined by high stone walls and bare poplar trees.

This was so much his life that he didn't seem able to see it for what it was. As Aki paused to catch his breath, Cyril turned around and showed that his sclera were bloodshot. He looked crazy. "Come on! A bit further and we're there."

"I'll never get used to the lack of oxygen up here," Aki said. "This must be what death feels like."

I held Aki's hand from here on out. He seemed so delicate in the darkness, even though his world was always dark. That's when I realized we were both vulnerable. For all I knew, Cyril was planning on killing us. It wasn't likely, but it was possible. I didn't know him, and as he walked further ahead, I tried remembering details about his face. Cyril was handsome in an anguished way. His hair, a bit too long and wild, was probably cut by himself.

It was colder than I expected it to be. My nipples poked into my bra, despite the coat and blanket I wrapped myself with. I told Aki about it. He said something about how his privates were having the opposite experience.

We continued on another several minutes, Cyril always at least twenty feet ahead of us. It felt like an eternity. We were already on the outskirts of town, climbing the road towards a monastery high above us. I wondered if that had something to do with it. Again, we were far from everything, in what seemed like another century. When I realized this, I felt like I had another thing to congratulate myself for, going this far from home. But it was too cold.

Cyril stopped by the beginning of another stone wall, not far from a brook, one of many carrying the high mountain water down to the Indus, where it would travel through India and Pakistan then on down into the Arabian Sea. He fell to his knees and started digging through the snow with his bare hands. The top layer was powder, but whatever he had was buried deeper and harder to get to. We stood over him and he said little, except to himself in Swiss German. I assumed he was cussing.

There was nothing around, no houses.

About four feet into the snow we heard Cyril hit something. "Fantastic," he said. But it wasn't coming out, whatever it was. Cyril tried getting his hands around it, but I assumed it was buried in ice. "It is completely stuck. Either of you have to pee?"

"As a matter of fact I do."

Cyril stood up and turned his back to me. "Great, go ahead."

"Really?"

"Don't worry, it is sealed."

When I had the four cups of mint tea with dinner, little did I know I'd be discharging it this way. I unbuttoned my jeans and squatted over the hole Cyril had dug, aiming for the edges around what looked like a box. "Don't turn back around until I tell you to."

As soon as the sound of my pissing finished, Cyril ignored my request and ran over, before I could pull up my pants. He reached into the area where I had just peed and didn't seem to care, putting his fingers right into it. He struggled for a few minutes before knocking the object free. He lifted a metal case the size of a book and rolled it in the snow, getting the urine off of it. He smelled the case to make sure it was clean.

"Brilliant," he said. "Let's go back to your room, I'm frozen."

Ich don't think so. "What's in the case?"

"I'll show you as soon as we get back to your room," Cyril answered. "I would've had you wait at the house if I knew it was this cold."

"You won't open the case here?" Aki asked.

"I can't," he answered. "It's a long story. Better if we go back to your room. I'll lose my fingers if we stay out here."

"Is that right?" Aki asked.

Cyril kept emphasizing needing to go to our room.

"I don't see why we can't come to your place," I said. Perhaps I'd have a better sense of who he was if we went there. Plus, Poonah was probably asleep by now.

"I don't have a room," he said. "I've run out of money. I'm in a tent. The family was thoughtful enough to give me food, in exchange for English lessons for their daughter. They gave me a room, but I prefer the tent."

"You have money," Aki said.

"What?" Cyril asked.

"The voice of someone who doesn't have money is different," Aki said.

I don't know what came over me but I reached forward and surprised Cyril by grabbing the case from his mittens. It was difficult to hold on to with bare hands. That's when I saw that it had a numerical lock on it. "What's the code?"

"Not here."

"Open the damned thing!" I yelled in frustration.

"Trust me. It's better if we waited. We have to."

CHAPTER THIRTY-NINE

Both Are From the Same Penis, and the Same Anus

STATE OF NEW YORK

VS.   Case No. 08-CF-5094

MARK BLACK

TRANSCRIPTION OF TAPED CONTROLLED

PHONE CALL

TRANSCRIBED BY:

Will Shaheen

LAURA SIMON REPORTING GROUP

APPEARANCES:

NAJIB KHAN

MARK BLACK

CONTENTS:

NAJIB: I'm glad you finally called.

MARK: Too much going on. Hard times.

NAJIB: Where?

MARK: Israel. The Saudi scene is better. We've got issues in Israel.

NAJIB: Police.

MARK: No, never.

NAJIB: Then what?

MARK: We're losing money to Lebanon and Syria. For a while, I couldn't figure out what was going on, but one of my Russian girls told me.

NAJIB: They're cheap girls from Iraq, true. That's true.

MARK: I'm getting desperate.

NAJIB: I would, too. How much have you lost?

MARK: Ten percent each year over the last three years.

NAJIB: Fuck. But you know I can help you. How many more do you want?

MARK: Start with a dozen. I hear they're good.

NAJIB: They'll do anything.

MARK: But I don't want any younger than fifteen.

NAJIB: You're mistaken. People want younger. The average starting age for them in Israel is eleven.

MARK: I don't give a shit. Even if I'm going to drop my prices for tightwad customers, I need girls that know how to manipulate men, keep them coming back. That's where the real money is. This has nothing to do with morality. And it isn't about satisfying the men sexually, like the young ones think. You have to know how to manipulate their sex drive, because that's something that will never get satisfied. The sexual need does. Young girls don't get that.

NAJIB: I don't know, it doesn't really matter. That's too theoretical. You know, it is like bullshit.

MARK: That theoretical BS is why I'm a success and a whole bunch of other guys aren't. Listen, before we bring them here, we have to know how these girls think. When a girl is too young, she doesn't know who to be. You have to see that. It isn't about spreading the legs.

NAJIB: What do you want me to do?

MARK: Let's start with a few and see how it goes. I can always take them to Saudi Arabia. Do they have an issue with screwing Jews?

NAJIB: Good point. I'll find out.

MARK: Yeah, do.

NAJIB: Anything else?

MARK: Has Mary called you?

NAJIB: No, not lately.

MARK: What do you think about contacting her?

NAJIB: It would be awkward.

MARK: Tell me, I wonder if you ever call her on your own. Or would she know I was behind it?

NAJIB: No, I've emailed her. We have an independent relationship, you could say.

MARK: She's pretending to be out of this racket. But I know she's still in it.

NAJIB: I don't know, the last time we spoke she told me she was out. That was a while ago.

MARK: Contact her, would you, tell her you're getting out of it, too. Act like you were wondering how she's doing.

NAJIB: What for?

MARK: I'm worried about her. I want to know where she is, so I can see her.

NAJIB: You aren't going to hurt her?

MARK: No.

NAJIB: You're saying you've got yourself under control now.

MARK: I always loved her. She's a bitch, but still.

NAJIB: Harsh. I don't know, let me see what I can do. I'll call you on this line.

MARK: Right. Bye, *habibi*. Don't let me down.

NAJIB: You're crazy.

(THE CALL ENDED.)

I, Will Shaheen, certify that I was authorized to and did transcribe the foregoing proceedings, and that the transcript is a true and complete record of the tape recording thereof.

CHAPTER FORTY

A Corner of the Mournful Kingdom of Sand

Mary Black

Poonah complained about being stirred awake when the three of us came back from the cold, metal box in hand. We bunched the chairs together by the wood stove to warm up. Poonah got out of bed to go to the tiny bathroom wearing a mauve bra that held her comically sagging breasts and a matching pair of nearly see-through floral underwear. She didn't look her best and I could tell Cyril seemed confused by us, though he was still polite when introducing himself.

Cyril held the metal box on his lap with a menacing smile on his face. He seemed too happy in our presence, given how confused and hassled we were. I resented his childish exuberance. Aki climbed into the bed closest to the stove and sat up with a stack of pillows behind him and kept his heavy sweater on.

I asked Cyril to start, but he pointed at the bathroom. "I want your friend Poonah to hear everything."

"Fine." He was definitely annoying.

We stayed quiet for a couple minutes, but then we could hear Poonah on the toilet.

"Where are you thinking of going next?" he asked, as we waited for her. "Thailand is fantastic this time of year."

I knew the budget travelers circuit, how they bussed between Bali, Laos, and Goa, staying as long as their few thousands lasted in third world currencies. "Who knows? It's been snowing so much, we've barely seen Ladakh."

"It is a magical place."

Finally, Poonah came out of the bathroom and we could get past the chitchat.

"You see that box, Poonah," I said. "That's why Cyril is here. He dragged us out into the snow so I could pee on that thing."

"Wait, that's part of it. It isn't everything," Cyril said. "You complete the picture. The reason is that I am entrusting you with it. I already decided that."

I could hear giant Aki breathing.

Alas, Cyril started explaining. He took out a piece of paper and began reading from it. "Let me continue without being interrupted. I know, I've been a bit oddly behaved. Listen, for I can write better than I can speak. If you wait a bit longer, it will all come together. Dear Strangers, From the moment I saw you in the dining room I knew that our meeting was destined. You would play an important role in my life. Strangers meeting in places as remote as the high Himalayas have this effect on each other. I am someone without a home, by choice. I believe I am only living when I am wandering, totally rootless."

Oh give me a break. Who do you think you are? Cicero? I had no choice, and interrupted him. "Just tell us what you need. One of the things I abhor most is being read to." The three of us were on the verge of extinction when we met Cyril. We had been trying to live truly, and yet we faced tragedies at every turn. We found out that our dreams weren't what they seemed to be. It comes down to care. I want to care, but the struggle and the pain had become too much. We suffer too much to be regular travelers, and that's a beautiful thing.

"Fine, you don't want the story, I understand," Cyril said. He lifted the aluminum box and unlocked it. The heavy-duty item looked like it was made for NASA, by the best of Nordic designers. "1450 is the password. You'll need that." He looked at us, hesitating before lifting the top. "I have to warn you. This is a bit shocking."

The case was padded with yet another package in it, sealed in what looked like a dark glass canister. It was frozen shut and frosted. "You can see it from the bottom." He turned the canister on the side and I figured out what it was.

My eyes doubled in size and Poonah came closer so she could look inside. "My God, that is a penis you have in there!" Poonah seemed indignant. "I was expecting diamonds or rubies. What the fuck in hell is this?"

It was an erect penis, complete, floating in some kind of liquid that had discolored it. Something about it made me feel sick.

"Is it true?" Aki asked.

"This is my penis," Cyril said. "You can see why I wanted to tell you the story first."

"I don't know what you're thinking, but don't get us involved in your crazy life," Poonah said. She seemed to be looking for confirmation from me.

I was more curious than her. I would've been disappointed if it was some bounty he stole. Besides, if there's something I've learned in life, it is that everything is possible. Watch the news at night and tell me any of the gore seems realistic. Friends run into each other on opposite sides of the globe, someone somewhere finds a valuable painting in an attic, you open a book and find the one and only line that relates to what you were obsessing about: all the odds make our days a miracle of sorts. Pretend you know what will happen in so much as an hour from now, but be ready to be wrong. My feeling was that we'd ended up here for a reason, and I was going to see where it would take us. "Give him a chance, Poonah." I held the canister in my hands and looked at the penis through the rest of the bottle. Normal in every way, I thought, and yet so gruesome. There was nothing else in there, as far as I could tell.

"That's where you come in," Cyril said. "I need you to take this to someone for me. I can't do it myself."

"I see. You cut off your penis. Then you save it for a crazy stranger to deliver it somewhere?" Poonah asked.

"It is more common than you might think," Cyril said.

I felt sorry for him. And no, it wasn't so common. But you never know.

He continued. "There are people in India that specialize in this. That's part of the reason I came here. I had been hurt by a man several years ago. You could say I was damaged. I want him to know what he led me to."

"What does any of this have to do with us?"

"Nothing, except that I'm asking you to bring this to him."

"When did you do this to yourself?" Poonah asked. She was sitting in a chair with her back to Cyril.

"A month ago."

"Pull down your pants." Aki had been silent in bed until then.

"What?" Cyril asked.

"I need you to pull down your pants," he repeated. "I can't see and I don't want to touch. Show these ladies what you did."

"I'd rather not," Cyril said. "It isn't pretty."

"Neither is what's in that bottle, and you showed that," Aki said. "That's not your penis."

Cyril's jaw twitched, and he lifted his chin to the side.

"Is it true?" I asked.

Aki might have done it again.

"Fine. He's right. It isn't mine."

"Are you dealing in body parts?" Aki asked. "You may as well leave right now if that's what you're doing."

"No, that isn't it. I swear," Cyril said. "My intention wasn't to lie to you. I didn't want to go into everything."

I told him to sit down. "We aren't conventional people, if you haven't noticed by now. Tell us the truth about the penis and we might even help you. Besides, you might be able to do something for me."

Cyril paused, almost smiled. "We all do something we regret. For me it has to do with money. I was home, living with my parents in a small apartment outside of Lucerne. Maybe you've been there. It is the most beautiful hell mankind has ever created."

I understood what he meant, but for me the Alps were always heavenly. I could think of worse places to be.

"My family doesn't understand what I need, why I travel so much," Cyril said. "I can never get anywhere with them. They're cruel. Whenever I run out of money, I have to go back and live in their house. I find a job and start saving again."

"I knew you were a hired man the minute I met you," Aki said. "You're desperate."

"You're right, I used to be desperate," Cyril said. "I was working as a carpenter at this stone castle on a small island near my hometown. It is owned by a Swiss guy, an industrialist. He was busy doing trading in China and so he had a couple of us making him an outbuilding for his art. After two months he showed up and invited me into his office for a drink. That's when he proposed the plan that led to me having this glass bottle. He handed it to me and told me what I had to do. Much money was promised if I did this for him."

"He was gay," Poonah said.

"Exactly. His name is Oscar Stein, and he's a brilliant man. He had this younger lover who lived with him, a pianist from the Italian part of Switzerland. But they were often apart because of work. Oscar always suspected this lover of being unfaithful, so he had me follow him. He gave me the case and the bottle and sent me here to India to castrate him, if he came to bed with me. And that's what happened. We met at a hotel and we went up to his room and I proceeded to treat him like a lover. He had no interest in anything other than a casual fling. I laid him down in the bed and reached into my pants for my knife and with the man's eyes covered with a towel I pretended like I was going to please him. I'd never done anything like this before. I tried keeping my composure so he would stay relaxed as I took my left hand that clutched the blade and cut across him in less than a second."

"That's disgusting," Poonah said.

"Worse than disgusting. I put his bloody thing in a bag and ran out of there. I called Oscar and we figured out what to do next. To get paid the rest, he wants the penis delivered to him. I can't do it because I know they'll search me if I go back. He had me swear that I would have someone else bring it back. He was worried that they'd trace my disappearance to India and see the overlap with his lover if I returned. He won't let me ship it either. He isn't allowed to leave the country, since all this happened. The Swiss have an investigation going on so it will be tricky for you."

"A photograph of it isn't good enough?" I asked.

"No, he wants the penis," Cyril said. "Believe me, I've tried everything, but he's being stubborn as fucking hell about it."

"We'll figure out how to do this," I told him. "I know how to handle these things." I saw Poonah looking at me with contempt, but I didn't care, to tell you the truth. "Aki?"

"Of course we will," he said.

Cyril fell to his knees and prostrated in front of me. He had tears in his eyes. Aki was right, he was desperate.

"But I have something I need you to do for me, and you're the only person who can do it," I told him. "Fair is fair."

"Anything," Cyril said. "I mean it."

"I will need you to get one more penis," I said. Cyril listened to what I told him about my background, how this married woman ended up in a Himalayan village in the snow with these two companions. I told him everything I could about Mark and his life, and explained how he could find him in Riyadh.

"Do you have his picture?" Cyril asked.

I still had one in my purse that I couldn't bring myself to throw away, taken outside a movie theater in Paris. It was from our honeymoon, and we had seen a melancholic Resnais film.

Cyril studied the picture. "Forgive me for saying so, but you both seem so happy here."

"It changed."

"Love does that," he said. "You look so similar. I can't believe it. Even the eyes have the same expression. I guess he came from another vagina."

"Yeah."

"It reminds me of how dogs resemble their owners. Anyway, well, I'll help you, but I do things my own way," he said. "I am going to walk to Riyadh. That's normal for me."

"You're serious?"

"I crossed Mongolia in the snow. Trust me, I can handle this. I can cut one more, if that's what I have to do."

It was all coming together, somehow.

"Like I said, I've crossed entire countries before," Cyril added. "Give me forty days and I will be in Saudi Arabia."

In the morning, on our walk over to the main house for breakfast, I saw that Cyril and his tent were gone. He had already earned my trust. I knew he would do his best to deliver on his promise. Meanwhile, I had to figure out how to fulfill mine.

CHAPTER FORTY-ONE

Without Noticing Their Absence in Myself, Without a Trace of Any Gruesome Feeling

Bronx News, February 13, 2011

"New Findings in Alleged Bronx Teen Sex Trafficking Network"

INWOOD—It started in the ugliest way imaginable. The 13-year-old girl begged Muhammed Faraj to let her return to her home in Iraq so she could be at her brother's wedding. The girl met Faraj at a restaurant in Mosul, across the river from Baghdad, he told investigators. She was smuggled into the United States from the Canadian border, with promises of work in the garment district.

Worn out and tired of working as a prostitute, the girl insisted to Faraj that she had a right to leave.

"This is why you're here. This is what you were brought to do. So be quiet and do it," Faraj told her, according to the police affidavits.

U.S. Magistrate Judge Nina Roberts ordered Faraj to remain in custody as his human smuggling case proceeded through the federal courts. Faraj, 31, was one of three men arrested by New York City police last week during a routine traffic stop.

Entering the Holland Tunnel, police became suspicious of the white van and asked them to pull over. Faraj, Nosaka Mochizuki, and the 13-year-old girl were found inside. Faraj finally presented his concealed weapon permit to the investigators and admitted a 9 mm pistol was in the glove compartment.

It was at this point that they knew this was more than a routine traffic stop. "They noticed the young girl was trying desperately to get the officer's attention," U.S. Immigration and Customs Enforcement Special Agent Roger Huzam testified.

Federal agents questioned the girl, who told them she'd been smuggled into the United States to work as a seamstress. But after she arrived in New York, Faraj, Japanese national Mochizuki, and another unknown man, believed to be the leader, held the girls at gunpoint and wouldn't leave the apartment where they stayed.

The girl was one of three teenagers held against their will to sell their bodies for sex, authorities allege.

Faraj and Mochizuki both face federal and state charges in the purported sex trafficking case. Another suspect, Dick Breslav Jr., 17, is wanted on state charges.

NEW YORK LEGISLATION

New York put a human trafficking law on the books in 2007. Bills making their way through the New York Legislature this year would make the offense a first-degree felony, punishable by up to life in prison. According to a press release from the governor's office, the laws would make sex trafficking and labor trafficking separate felonies.

Faraj and Mochizuki face three counts of aggravated sexual assault—for each of their alleged victims, ages 13, 15, and 18—in state court.

The three men are being charged with the smuggling of Aliens and are being tried in U.S. District Court. Authorities are hoping to be able to charge them also with human trafficking, where they'd face much longer federal prison sentences and fines per each count of conviction.

Human trafficking convictions are more difficult to make because the burden of proof is on the victims. They must demonstrate in the court of law that they were held against their volition.

Faraj's defense lawyer, Alphonso "Big Al" King, said he doubts the alleged prostitution ring will escalate to a human trafficking case.

"These women knew exactly what they were getting into. I don't know who they're kidding," he said in an interview.

Faraj is the only U.S. citizen among the three charged in the purported prostitution ring. But because of his family and property ties to Alex Paul Hoffman, the judge refused to set a bond in his case.

King alluded to the possibility that the case could become more severe in the coming days.

David Burr covers courts and general assignments for Bronx News.

CHAPTER FORTY-TWO

Would I Lie to You?

Dear Mary Black,

Greetings from Ramayana Tours. Many thanks for your mail, helicopter is not possible. You have to book a flight from Leh to Delhi. The most economical option for this sector and capacity with private air:

Pilatus PC12, single engine turbo prop with 05 passenger seats + 01, air hostess, or 06 passenger seats.

Flying time: 02:15hrs, Cost: Indian Rupees 347,445, all-inclusive.

The nearest international gateway is New Delhi. Attached is a contract to fax to my name so I can inform pilots of your necessities. I do not need to know the nature of your emergency, but if you need this plane by sundown call me right away. Travel over high Himalayas is dangerous and not always possible.

Regards,
Captain H. Parvizeh

SOME TIME AFTER BREAKFAST, the proprietor of the house, Stanzin, came back from town with a bag full of chunks of fresh meat. Too bad, after a few days of eating nothing but rice and root vegetables, I was feeling like a carnivore. He thought we were staying for dinner, but I apologized, informed him that something urgent had come up. With perfect Ladakhi grace he told us that he understood, and hoped we would one day return.

Checking out, Aki and I followed him to his office, set around the corner from the dining room. Poonah stayed back. She wasn't one to pay for anything. The walls to the office were lined with religious books and enormous accounting ledgers, like something out of Casablanca. He lit the hand-rolled incense and I was too embarrassed to beg him not to. He took a chipped abacus out from under his desk and shuffled the beads around. There was no computer or calculator, but he didn't seem to need them.

He handed the invoice to Aki, who already had a stack of rupees out. We were happy to get rid of the soiled bills. Aki handed him the pile of cash for our stay. We could have remained in Ladakh for a year and it wouldn't have made a dent in our savings. In winter, they charged about a dollar a day. Amazing, but we needed to be careful once we left. We were going through my account much faster than I had intended. It was true that I was prepared to spend everything I had, but just not at this pace.

"By the way, there's something I need to know. What time did Cyril check out this morning?" I asked.

"Who's that?" Stanzin asked. He spoke English with a Londoner accent.

"The man in the tent."

"Oh, him, yes. We were sleeping when we heard a car door shut in the middle of the night. I looked outside and saw this Swiss leaving in a taxi. He wasn't staying here at our inn," he said.

"What do you mean?"

"This fellow showed up after you arrived, and asked if he could camp out in our yard. I deemed it weird, but I've seen my share of such travelers. They're on budgets. We get plenty of them, from all over."

A different story from Cyril's, a problematic story. What about all the walking he talked about, I thought. I trusted Stanzin.

"Are you sure he arrived after we did?"

"Absolutely. I thought it was peculiar because we haven't had a guest in months."

If only he knew how peculiar.

"Wasn't he teaching your daughter English?"

"No, I handle her lessons," Stanzin said. "Is this what he told you?"

It all made sense; Stanzin's English was better than most people's. I shared with him some of what I knew, leaving out the issue of our glass container.

"All he did was camp out in the field, and then, you saw, he would eat his meals in the corner there," Stanzin clarified. "I didn't ask more than that. I don't know who he was and what he was doing here."

CHAPTER FORTY-THREE

Life Closed Twice Before it Closed, or Where the Heart Must Either Break or Turn to Lead

**WIKILEAKS: Viewing cable 09JEDDAH443,
UNDERGROUND PARTY SCENE IN JEDDAH:
SAUDI YOUTH:**

Classified By: Consul General Martin R. Quinn for reasons 1.4 (b) and (d).

¶1. (C) Summary: Behind the facade of Wahhabi conservatism in the streets, the underground nightlife for Jeddah's elite youth is thriving and throbbing. The full range of worldly temptations and vices are available—alcohol, drugs, sex—but strictly behind closed, often lavish, doors. This freedom to indulge carnal pursuits is possible because the religious police keep their distance when parties include the presence or patronage of a Saudi royal and his circle of loyal attendants, such as a Halloween event attended by ConGenOffs on [DETAIL REMOVED]. Over the past few years, the increased conservatism of Saudi Arabia's external society has pushed the decadent nightlife and party scene in Jeddah even further underground. End summary.

¶2. (C) Along with over 150 young Saudis (men and women in their 20s and early 30s), ConGenOffs accepted invitations to an underground Halloween party at Prince XXXXXXXXXXXX residence in Jeddah on XXXXXXXXXXXX. Inside the gates, past the XXXXXXXXXXXX security guards and after the abaya coat-check, the scene resembled a nightclub anywhere outside the Kingdom: plentiful hard alcohol, young couples dancing, a DJ at the turntables, and everyone in costume. Funding for the party came from a corporate sponsor, XXXXXX, a U.S.-based energy-drink company, as well as from the princely host himself. Royalty, attended by "khawi," keep religious police at bay.

¶3. (C) Religious Police/CPVPV (Commission for the Promotion of Virtue and Prevention of Vice) were nowhere to be seen and while admission was controlled through a strictly enforced guest list, the partygoers were otherwise not shy about publicizing the affair. According to a young Saudi from a prominent Jeddah merchant family, the Saudis try to throw parties at princes' houses or with princes in attendance, which serves as sufficient deterrent to interference by the CPVPV. There are over 10,000 princes in the Kingdom, albeit at various levels and gradations—"Royal Highnesses" ("Saheb Al Sumou Al Maliki") signified by direct descent from King Abdelaziz, and mere "Highnesses" ("Saheb Al Sumou") from less direct branches of the Al Saud ruling family. Our host that evening, xxxxxx (protect), traces his roots to Thunayan, a brother of Mohammad, Amir of Diriyyah and Nejd (1725-65), King Abdullah's direct ancestor, six generations back. Although Prince XXXXXXXXXXXX is XXXXXXXXXXXX not in line for the throne, he still enjoys the perks of a mansion, luxury car fleet, lifetime stipend, and security entourage. (Note: Most of the Prince XXXXXXXXXXXXs security forces were young XXXXXXXXXXXX men. It is common practice for Saudi nobles to grow up with hired bodyguards from Nigeria or other African nations who are of similar age and who remain with the prince well into adulthood. They are called "khawi," derived from the Arabic word "akh," meaning "brother." The lifetime spent together creates an intense bond of loyalty. End note.)

¶4. (C) Alcohol, though prohibited by Saudi law and custom, was plentiful at the party's well-stocked bar, patronized by Halloween revelers. The hired Filipino bartenders served a cocktail punch using "sadiqi," a locally-made "moonshine." While top-shelf liquor bottles were on display throughout the bar area, the original contents were reportedly already consumed and replaced by sadiqi. On the black market, a bottle of Smirnoff can cost 1,500 riyals ($400 USD) when available, compared to 100 riyals for the locally-made vodka. It was also learned through word-of-mouth that a number of the guests were in fact "working girls," not uncommon for such parties.

JEDDAH 00000443 002.2 OF 002

Additionally, though not witnessed directly at this event, cocaine and hashish use is common in these social circles, as has been seen on other occasions.

¶5. (C) Comment: Saudi youth get to enjoy relative social freedom and indulge fleshly pursuits, but behind closed doors—and only the rich. Parties of this nature and scale are believed to be a recent phenomenon in Jeddah. One contact, a young Saudi male, explained that up to a few years ago the only weekend activity was "dating" inside the homes of the affluent, in small groups. It is not uncommon in Jeddah for the more lavish private residences to include elaborate basement bars, discos, entertainment centers, and clubs. As one high society Saudi remarked, "The increased conservatism of our society over these past years has only moved social interaction to the inside of people's homes." End comment. QUINN

STATE OF NEW YORK

VS.   Case No. 08-CF-5094

MARK BLACK

TRANSCRIPTION OF TAPED CONTROLLED

PHONE CALL

TRANSCRIBED BY:

Will Shaheen

LAURA SIMON REPORTING GROUP

APPEARANCES:

MOHAMMED FARAJ

MARK BLACK

CONTENTS:

MARK: You're right, I'm getting nervous. I've got a lot on the line right now.

MOHAMMED: You start complaining whenever you think you might lose money.

MARK: That's not it this time. Did you see the Wikileak thing I faxed?

MOHAMMED: So what?

MARK: Those are my parties. My women.

MOHAMMED: But you're covered. You've paid off half of Riyadh.

MARK: Maybe. It is a lot easier for me when I can work in quiet. I don't like when the things I'm doing get fucking attention. At any moment they could decide to kill me.

MOHAMMED: They love your coke and whores too much.

MARK: They can get them from someone else.

MOHAMMED: True. At least things are quiet here in New York. I'm on top of it all, so you don't have to worry.

MARK: God I hope so.

MOHAMMED: Where are you?

MARK: Jerusalem. For some reason this year I've got a bunch of Canadian Christians to supply. It must be cold there or something.

MOHAMMED: Women?

MARK: Boys, too.

MOHAMMED: And where's Mary?

MARK: On a plane to Switzerland.

MOHAMMED: You said India last time.

MARK: She's on the run.

MOHAMMED: But you know where she is all the time.

MARK: I've got my people. This time it was a Bulgarian guy posing as a Swiss. He owed me a big favor.

MOHAMMED: To kill her?

MARK: No, not yet.

MOHAMMED: I can help you with Switzerland, if you need it.

MARK: I'm handling it. She's going to be followed.

MOHAMMED: You know as much as anyone how crazy it gets over there.

MARK: She doesn't know who she is anymore. If she was the old Mary, yeah, I'd be worried. But now that she thinks she's on the high road to goodness, she's a lost cause.

MOHAMMED: You know what she's doing there?

MARK: No. That's the part that confuses me. My man was supposed to keep her in India for a while. I've no idea why she's going to Switzerland.

MOHAMMED: Where is he now?

MARK: Missing.

MOHAMMED: So that's why you're worried.

MARK: I'm not worried, I'm scared. Terrified, actually. She can be psychotic, as you know. And when that happens, anything is possible.

MOHAMMED: I always liked her, but I can't understand why you don't just kill her.

MARK: I know, but she's the one woman I've ever loved.

MOHAMMED: Crazy.

MARK: Yup. Anyway, let me go, I'll call you soon.

MOHAMMED: OK, sir. Do that.

(THE CALL ENDED.)

I, Will Shaheen, certify that I was authorized to and did transcribe the foregoing proceedings, and that the transcript is a true and complete record of the tape recording thereof.

CHAPTER FORTY-FIVE

I've Been to the Mountaintop

"WHAT DID HE SAY?" Poonah asked. From Lucerne, the three of them had taken the gondola to the top of Pilatus and were seated at a long wooden bench at the cafeteria restaurant when Mary got the call back from Oscar Stein. They'd been waiting three almost frantic days for it.

"It wasn't him that called," Mary answered. "Thalia is his assistant. That's also my sister's name, and I can't get along with my sister."

"Why is that? I wish I had a sister."

"We were always at odds. She had issues with my brother and me," I said. "Anyway, this new Thalia said she's working out of an office in Geneva."

"Are you sure about this whole thing?" Poonah had curry ketchup above her lips from the basket of fries she was in the middle of eating. "I have a sick feeling again."

"He's sending a van to pick us up at the hotel," Mary said in a low voice. They were sharing the bench with a Chinese couple who didn't seem to understand English. "At first he was going to meet us in public, but she said it would be safer if we went to Oscar's house."

"Did she say anything about our penis case?" Poonah asked.

"She did. They're looking forward to relieving us of it."

"They better be," Poonah said, with a tinge of anger. "And did she say anything about paying us something for all this?"

Poonah had been agitating Mary for several days. She'd started asking a million questions ever since they'd left India. At first Mary assumed it was because Poonah was excited about going to Switzerland. She'd taken photos continuously from the moment they'd seen the Alps in the airplane. Even worse, Poonah had been pointing out everything she remembered from her beloved Indian movies, locations where Raj Kapoor and other Bollywood legends had honeymooned.

"No, she didn't. And if you ask me one more question about what people might be saying, I just might push you off this mountain, Poonah."

"Aren't we bitchy?" Poonah said. "I don't know what's wrong with you, but I'm asking only for your sake. He owes you for this."

Aki stopped chewing his pork sausage. "You need to tell Mary what's bothering you, Poonah. Hiding it isn't working."

"It is none of her business."

Aki cupped his hands and blew into them. Fog was coming in, the temperature dropped with each minute. "I will. Basically, Poonah always wanted to die in Switzerland."

"You mongrel," Poonah said. "I told you not to tell her."

"What does that mean, Aki?" Mary asked.

"We all have a feeling about where we should die, and Poonah thought it should be here in Switzerland," he answered. "I think that's why she's behaving so crazy."

"I thought we could all die here. Not just me," Poonah said. "This is done by visitors, you know. I'm not the only one with this idea."

"You guys lost me," Mary said. "I didn't come here to die. We could have stayed in India if this was your intention."

"Ever since Kashmir, Poonah has been talking to me about suicide tourism," Aki said. "Certain places have become destinations, like Zürich. That's if someone wants the easy way. Otherwise they go to San Francisco, to the bridge."

"You want to die?" Mary asked Aki.

"I'll do whatever you decide."

It was strange how he spoke about it without a hint of anxiety.

He continued. "You have to stop thinking of me as water. I'm more like fire. To me life and death are the same."

"You don't mean that, Aki. When it comes down to it, you want to live," Mary said. "You like sex with me too much."

"You have a point," he said. "But you are my friends and we have been on an adventure together. If it is time for us to end it, I'll do so. I am devoted to you and Poonah, and whatever you want."

CHAPTER FORTY-SIX

A Balance of Fluids in the Human Body, the
Loudest Expression of the Little Civilization of Me

CASE DETAIL REPORT
Hans Hansen, HPI Private Investigation For Mark Black
Case Number: Black297.3
Hire Date: February 16, 2011
Date Filed: February 17, 2011

ACTIVITY REPORT:

Followed the subject one day during the week of February, 2011.
The subjects have been in their hotel in Lucerne around the clock
since the 16th. There has been nothing to report, I'm sorry to say.
It happens. The only hours I have not been stationed outside have
been to sleep, from midnight to 0700. In the interest of efficiency,
all meals are from street vendors. I do recommend having a
second agent so we can work in shifts, but understand the client
is concerned about the expense. All times are for a 24-hour period
starting the date of February 16th, 2011, at 0900 and ending the
date of February 17th, 2011, at 0900.

0900—Palace Luzern Hotel, where the subjects are staying. I stand outside, strolling along the lake all day, trying to make it look like I belong here. Zinggentorstrasse and Gesagnettmattstrasse are rather beautiful, although touristic, as evidenced by all the Asian people everywhere.

0945—Bathroom break.

1015—Stationed once again in front of the hotel, but no activity. Ate the best bratwurst in my life, however.

1130—Aki appears and strolls up the street alone, westward. He is wearing headphones that disappear into his jacket. I decide it best to follow him. He walks for a couple blocks and enters the Casino Luzern.

1145—I decide to enter the casino and find Aki playing one of the more expensive slot machines and drinking scotch. He plays slowly and methodically. This place is pretty awesome, I must add.

1300—An Indian woman arrives wearing a blue sari and sits down next to Aki. She begins playing the slots also. She carries a Ziploc bag of shelled peanuts and shares them with Aki.

1310—I sit near them and listen to their conversation. Whatever they say concerns lunch. The Indian woman is tired of eating in the hotel. She wants fondue at a place she walked by.

1330—The Indian woman goes to the bathroom carrying a purse, comes back ten minutes later, stands over Aki and kisses Aki on the lips for a good solid fifteen seconds, and leaves. I must emphasize that she seems at least twenty, or closer to thirty years older than him. I'd say he weighs 400 pounds, while she seems to be about 80.

1350—Aki has a platter of bread and cheese brought to him in the casino.

1430—Aki leaves the casino without going to the cashier. He walks back to the hotel without stopping.

1445—Bathroom break.

1520—Still no sign of anyone, especially Mary. The room is under her name, but they are not accepting incoming calls.

1700—A white pest control van pulls up to the hotel and Aki and the Indian lady are met by a tall woman in her thirties, with hair as long as Crystal Gayle's (down to her butt). Something is up. I get into a taxi and watch as they introduce themselves. The two go into the back of the van and I tell my driver to follow them.

1710—Continuous. The woman drives at quite a pace, it is hard to keep up. She drives south and up into the hills of an area the driver tells me is called Eggen. Then she makes a turn and heads further up into the hills and back north, above the hotel. She loops around the hills and my driver starts to get angry. I ask him what he thinks she is doing and he said he had no clue. She goes in circles, across the city, but always from above it. Finally, we go over the lake and stop in front of a place called Olga's Hair Salon.

1740—Continuous. This is turning into one expensive taxi ride. At this point the driver and the Indian lady go inside the hair salon. I can't see into the back of the van, but I assume Aki is there.

1755— Mary is now with them, coming out of the salon. Her reddish hair is short and choppy, like the singer in Eurythmics. She gets into the back of the van and they begin driving again, very fast. We go back upcountry, start crisscrossing the hills all over again. It is agonizing, mostly because my driver won't stop complaining. I had to promise him extra money because he threatens to take me back to the hotel. I'm not sure why he was so grumpy. I tried talking to him, but he wasn't interested in anything I had to say. Anyhow, we weave all the way back past our hotel and towards Eggen again.

1820—The van stops, parks at the Sunset Bar, and four of the Subjects walk down to the Churchill Quay where a stunning speedboat waits for them. Stamped on the boat in Helvetica font is the boat's name, *Die Pracht*, which translates as The Splendor. They jump aboard and hurry away. I am not prepared to travel by water and must apologize. There is no way to follow them. I try seeing where they are headed, with my binoculars, but after a mile or so they vanish.

1830—I decide to go into the Sunset Bar and have dinner, keeping my eye on the van outside. The manager tells me he doesn't know the owner of the vehicle. I have raclette, by the way, and it is an amazing sunset.

2030—The four of them returned to the bar by boat and went straight to the van. I'm able to take a taxi and follow them once again. This time they take the direct route back to their hotel, thank God.

2045—Back at Palace Luzern Hotel where it is now cold as hell outside. Winds come off the lake that go straight through a person. The tall lady drops them off and drives away, heads south, towards Eggen. I stay on watch by the hotel.

2359—I wait until midnight and only then return to my motel to sleep, with nothing more to report.

0700—I am back in front of their hotel where I stay for two hours, with one longer than expected bathroom break in the middle, but there is nothing to report. The client asked that I stop at this point, because of the budget. I waited an extra hour, because I was curious, but still not one of them came out.

INVESTIGATION FINDINGS:

It isn't possible to determine the nature of the activities of Mary, Aki and the Indian lady. The pest control van was suspicious, and when I looked up the name Franck's, I was unable to find a listing match. Enclosed are photos of everything I have described, including the very tall lady with very long hair. As mentioned, the Indian lady and Aki seem to be involved on a romantic level, though it is almost inconceivable. I recommend hiring me for a longer period if you wish to get to the bottom of this. Oftentimes, as was communicated to the client upon commencement with the investigation, four days aren't enough. Now that they seem to be leaving the hotel again, it would be a shame to depart from Lucerne, as you've requested. Also, though the Palace is a more expensive hotel, being able to investigate inside would be recommendable; I suggest that I relocate here, if you'd like me to continue. This is my suggestion, and my flight back to New York is not until tomorrow evening, so whatever the client decides is fine with me.

Hans Hansen, HPI Private Investigation

CHAPTER FORTY-SEVEN

And the Trim-Coiffed Goddess

I WISHED THE BOAT RIDE would never end. Each of us sat, glass of dry prosecco in hand, weighed down by the heaviest of wool blankets as Thalia captained us in breathtaking speed across Lake Lucerne. *What a way to live. It doesn't get better than this.* The boat was Oscar's, not mine, and I'm sure after a month of pleasure with his purchase, he'd begun taking it for granted. Something told me this man we were on our way to was an aesthete, and most of those that I've known are unhappy being in this world. It can't ever be beautiful enough for them.

By the time we approached the private dock it was almost dark. There was no house in sight. Following Thalia, we climbed fifty steps to a clearing where only then could I see our destination, a small glass box of a home. My guess was that it was fifteen hundred square feet in size. Nothing much, but perfectly beautiful. It wasn't the manor house I'd been expecting ever since Cyril described this world to me. Behind the glass box was another small building, the one that Cyril might have made, a mysterious round wood structure with a tapered roof. It had no windows pointed this way and wasn't very large. A fence made of the same wood lined a walkway between the two buildings. Three black Irish wolfhounds lounged outside on the lawn, ignoring our arrival.

Thalia slid the blocky front door along the track and requested we go inside. "I'll ask Oscar if he's ready for you. Please, make yourself at home over there." She pointed at the white leather sofas that faced a view of the lake and mountains. A plate of Linzer cookies were laid out on the coffee table, as well as narrow bottles of French mineral water. Thalia brought over a bowl with four golden apples and placed them in front of me. Gothic electronica played on an elaborate Bang & Olufsen system in the corner. He even had their television.

Poonah kept eating biscuits.

Aki had been quiet the whole ride. He had a puzzled, or disgusted even, look on his face.

"What's on your mind right now?" I asked.

"Honestly, nothing," he said. "But I can't put my finger on the smell in here. You notice it?"

I didn't. I tried to, but all I could smell was a bit of the leather off the couch. I asked if that's what he was referring to.

"It reminds me of when I was a child," he said. "A classroom."

"I don't smell a thing," Poonah interjected.

We waited twenty minutes, chatting about nothing, until the door slid open again.

"He'll be coming in a moment," he said. "Oscar is stuck on a call to Shanghai." Thalia's long hair was now in a ponytail. She went over to the dining room table and lit the incense. Ugh, it was getting to be a bit much, all this incense everywhere. "I warn you, he's in a horrible mood today." Thalia paused in front of the incense and took three deep breaths, entering a state of what seemed like her version of a meditation. I wanted to tell her she looked ridiculous. Then she lit a cigarette and walked over to the open door, looking out for Oscar, I figured.

"This is a wonderful place," Poonah said, breaking the tension in the air.

"*Ja, ja,* I suppose it is, at first," Thalia said without even looking over. She put out her cigarette in a Veuve Clicquot bottle by the door. "Did you see the peacocks yet?"

We hadn't.

"Oscar loves them because he says they have one hundred eyes," Thalia added.

From a distance I could see an old man approaching, an ugly, stocky creature. Was this really Oscar? This minuscule hunchback of a person in shabby clothing, looking like he could croak at any moment, cigar dangling out of his mouth. Set against the pristine nature, it gave him a hateful aura.

Thalia came close behind me and sat beside Aki.

Poonah gave me a look of bewilderment.

"So I guess that's Oscar," I said to Thalia.

"That's him, *ja, ja*," she said.

I already wasn't crazy about the way she kept adding those two words when she spoke.

Thalia turned down the music and grabbed a biscuit.

Wealth makes for strange situations. At that moment I would have paid to have seen a picture of the lover whose penis we were carrying. What did this old man expect? A saint wouldn't be faithful to him.

Oscar entered the room and grunted a command to Thalia. "Close the door, it's freezing in here." I couldn't peg the accent, but it wasn't entirely Swiss.

Thalia, in no particular hurry, walked over, shutting the door while he hobbled on over to us. He acted as though we weren't there. I said hello, but he didn't answer. Poonah then tried. Perhaps he couldn't hear well anymore. It went the way of his bathing, which he could do more often, were you to ask me.

Stiff and decrepit, he dropped himself into the Herman Miller chair with a mangy blanket on it. So far he hadn't looked in our eyes, though he was across from us. "The fucking Chinese," he repeated to himself twice, reaching for something in his pocket before giving up. "I need a napkin."

Thalia said nothing in response and went over to the kitchen area.

Oscar looked up, only he was staring at Aki. Some good that did those of us who weren't blind. "The best thing I ever did was buy this land. Franz Burri sold it to me. What a man. Thalia, why don't you tell them about Franz."

"I think you should," she answered, from a distance.

"A lot of good are you," he said. "Franz was my uncle's friend. None of us liked him too much. He was from the old, nationalist school, you see. This passionate man thought he could convert the Swiss to Nazism. As you know, he failed. When I bought this property, he had his house on it, full of his life's memorabilia. The first thing I did was burn it down. That's the kind of man I am."

"You wanted no trace of him," Aki said. "Sometimes we need to destroy."

"Precisely," Oscar said. "When Mr. Burri died, I was the physician in charge. That's how I came to know him again, later in his life. As a corpse. And the one thing I saved from everything that I had to do with him was his penis."

Too bad Cyril wasn't with us to do some explaining.

"I hated him so much he became my first one," Oscar said. "Open that door there, Thalia, show them."

"Which one?" she answered. "All of them?"

"Why not?"

She pushed the heavy cart with the Bang & Olufsen television to the side and pressed a button that moved the wall over six feet, revealing a gallery of canisters matching the one we'd brought him. A trio of halogens came on, to showcase the objects. We were far enough away that it wasn't clear what we were looking at, but I had my guess: body parts?

"Then whose penis is this that we brought?" Poonah asked. She was livid.

"We'll get to that," Oscar said. "What you are looking at is remarkable. Take it in, because there is nothing else like it in the world. This is the collection I've spent a fortune on."

"Is he really a doctor?" Aki asked Thalia, a voice low enough that he wouldn't be heard by the old man.

"Supposedly," she answered, "but no one knows for sure."

"I told you to show all of them," Oscar said to Thalia, pointing at the bottles with his cane. "Open it for them. All the way. Let them behold it."

Thalia pressed another button and revealed four more shelves of these special objects, again identical to the one in our case. There must have been two hundred of them. "Those on the right are all al-Qaeda."

"What do you mean?" Poonah asked.

"Bring over Usama al-Kini." To my ear he said it like an Arab, not like a Swiss.

Thalia opened a drawer under the gallery and took out a laminated piece of paper. She read it to herself, then reached for yet another bottle and brought it over to Oscar.

"This Kenyan prick cost me 40,000 Swiss Franks. Why? I'll tell you. He was a commander at one point, helping to expand al-Qaeda out of Pakistan. He was killed in an explosion in the tribal areas, but my people were there to bring this to me."

"You have people in Pakistan?" Poonah asked. "I thought you were a doctor."

"I'll get to that, but not just yet," the old man said. "This isn't a personal meeting where we get to know each other. What you need to realize is that I have connections that other people need."

"So those are all penises?" I had to ask. Maybe it was a dumb question, but this was getting too weird.

"Yes, of evil men. All of them are of evil men."

"In my country we worship those," Poonah said. "But still, why would you possess so many penises?"

"That's such a pedestrian question. No, it is a fucking stupid question," he said, chewing on his unlit cigar. "If there's something I hate, it is explanations."

I can relate to that. At least there was something to relate to.

He continued. "If I serve you a cup of tea and it is delicious, you should not expect me to tell you where I bought it. Just fucking drink it. Nobody knows how to just drink anymore. This is an appearance of destiny, you see."

"Fine, I understand that. This is your home, and those are your rules," Aki said. "It is getting late and we planned on having dinner at our hotel tonight. So, if you don't mind, we'll give you the penis and get back to town."

"You can leave the penis, then get out of here," Oscar said. "But you should know that there is more, and I'll discuss it tomorrow at your hotel, at ten thirty. I need to go into town for an appointment with my doctor, and I'll come to you after."

"We'll see you then," I said, leaving the case on the coffee table. "One-four-five-zero is the password Cyril gave us."

"His name isn't Cyril. We call him The Bulgarian."

Figures, I thought. There's no shortage of lying going on. "Tell us about him, Oscar."

"At this point all you need to know is that he could have brought the penis himself, if that was what I wanted. That wasn't my plan. We're not done with each other, you see. In fact, we might just be beginning."

"Take a look at these hands," Aki said. He stood up and walked towards Oscar, turning on the reading lamp next to the man's chair and began moving them underneath it. "I know what you're talking about."

It was odd behavior.

Oscar ran his index finger across both of Aki's hands. He squeezed Aki's left thumb at the base and then pushed Aki's hands away. "I don't know what you are implying, but they're beautiful."

"You must have felt it," Aki said. "These hands have an appearance of destiny, too. Unlike you, they will sacrifice everything for something approaching love. I am the opposite of people like you."

CHAPTER FORTY-EIGHT

Doesn't Like to Talk to Reporters

Excerpted from: YALE QUARTERLY, Fall 2006

Reclusive Poet Agrees to Interview **by Gary Owens**

Mark Black, author of *Further Problems*, the 1989 award recipient for the Yale Younger Poets Series, and a National Book Award nominee, discusses his career.

The Journal for Contemporary Literature, Gary Owens, Contributing Editor.

Editor's Note: Our Journal has made a great effort to secure this interview with the iconic author, Mark Black. The publisher of Further Problems, *Yale University Press, cannot give out specific information about the author and seemed very nervous when we even brought up the subject. They hadn't been in contact with the author for over two decades.*

There'd been rumors that he corresponded from offices on an island off the coast of Yemen, as well as a cabin in Grinda, Sweden.

Having found Black on my own, with the help of an international lawyer, after three years of negotiating he still wouldn't cooperate. All that changed one afternoon as I sat grading papers at a coffee shop in Brooklyn, well after I'd given up on the interview. Out of the blue he phoned me to say he would honor my request, that he wanted to put certain rumors to rest. I got on an airplane that week and met him at the Connaught Hotel in Athens, for afternoon tea:

GO: Your book created a sensation in poetry circles, with critics hailing you as the voice the country had been looking for. Yours is the top-selling Yale Series book ever printed. People called you the next Frost or Eliot. Yet you haven't published another book in all the years since. Your readers have never understood why. What do you have to tell them?

MB: I had one book in me. Or I had one book too many in me. My feeling was that the most poetic expressions of life are never written. So I was tired of being a hypocrite, of staring at myself in the mirror, at this person who was involved in artifice. That's what art is, and I decided to take on life.

GO: That dialectic informs much of the contemporary discussion about art. It still doesn't explain why you couldn't have both. Many of us can't fathom how you walked away from something you were so good at.

MB: You'd have to go to the graves of people such as Socrates and Rimbaud for the answer. Socrates wrote nothing down, despite having the greatest mind of his millennium. Rimbaud gave up the word by the end of his teenage years. As for me, I don't have any idea why I wrote. Nor do I care. And I don't consider my book to be anything special. Nothing about the contemporary discussions holds interest in my life. My mind is elsewhere, and in my work I deal with the poetic imagination of my clients. That means more to me than writing another poetry book.

GO: Could you say more about your life? As you know, many of us have hunted for information about what you've been doing and came up empty.

MB: This single interview is all I have to offer my readers after all these years. What they have is the book. I do not wish to speak about my private life, and that includes my employment.

GO: I understand, and I must say to readers here that we agreed to honor your wish not to explore your current profession. We also don't know where you live. But can you tell us a bit about your personal life? The nature of how you dealt with the autobiographical in your poetry still informs the narrative about your work.

MB: Is that so?

GO: Yes, of course. I suppose that means you don't follow the scholarship on your work.

MB: That's the scholarly community's business. It has nothing to do with me. What I know is that there's quite a bit of controversy, and I can live with that. If I touch a raw nerve in this heartless world, reality will be the better for it. As far as my personal life, what I can say is that I live what's called a normal life. That means to me it is normal, just like every other oddball on this planet who believes that what they're doing is more or less mundane. I know that's hard for the readers of my poetry to believe. They prefer to think of me as impossible, or despicable.

GO: So you're married with children, two cars in the garage, take the occasional trip to Florida? Somehow I don't see that.

MB: I am married, I've never been to Florida, and we've no children. My wife and I are in business together. She's my partner in crime, and the reason my life is what it is. The best part is, she has never read my poetry.

GO: Is that because you're ashamed about the lack of morality in your poems? You've upset a lot of people with your brutal look at life, your defense of certain forms of incest. What does your wife have to say on these matters?

MB: She is a lot like me, only a whole lot worse. It is partially a joke to say that. Neither of us is moral, in a conventional sense. If there's one thing I stand for, and my reason for agreeing to meet you, it is that I've held that human beings have no rights unless granted by children. We are the rotting ones, not them. They get it. They're the ones who are supposed to rule. As for my wife, our relationship is grounded in life. That's why she doesn't need my poetry. It isn't who I am. There's nothing evil about the truth, and if people and their mores are simplistic, those of us that aren't don't have to bow down and submit.

GO: But there are all the thoughts of one flesh in your poetry, how two people unite in order to recreate a bit of Eden in this hellish world. It amazes me that she would marry you and somehow doesn't know about that.

MB: It isn't as though we sit around naked pretending we're Adam and Eve. William Blake might have done that, but my name is Mark Black. Like I said, poetry is something private to me, divorced from what is said about it. The way to keep it alive is by encouraging people to read. The talk about it kills it.

GO: I think one of the things I've always related to in your writing was how you handled the emotional. You had a way of bringing up the most horrific and painful of realities while giving it a human face, the opposite of what you'd call a melodramatic treatment. But then there'd be a line that would be an uppercut, if you know what I mean. A huge punch.

MB: I see.

GO: You have no comment?

MB: All I did was write the poem. Talk about poetry isn't poetry. That's fine for them, but I've no interest in their dialogue. Nor anything to do with poets. You know what a poet is?

GO: I have an idea. But I'd like your answer.

MB: Somebody who doesn't know how to live.

GO: So you've abandoned it, your poetry.

MB: Talking about anything doesn't cut it for me. That's because at the heart of everything we are dealing with lies and liars. There's no point in pretending we're approaching a truth when we communicate. A version of life is all we get, and it is always flawed. That's what reality is. And how we fool ourselves.

CHAPTER FORTY-NINE

This Thing is Truly Heroic

O SCAR WORE THE SAME clothes and arrived thirty minutes late on the terrace where Poonah, Aki, and Mary waited for him at a cherry table, halfway through a bottle of champagne. This time he shook hands with each of them, as if to make a positive impression, looking them in the eyes even. The cigar was a bit shorter today.

"I don't drive the boat as quickly as Thalia," he said. "Sorry I'm late."

"Not very Swiss of you," Mary said. She still couldn't figure out what his roots were.

Oscar didn't volunteer anything about himself. He grabbed a bread stick and called over a waiter.

"Where is Thalia today?" Poonah asked.

"Oh, she's home. Thalia was feeling nauseous."

"Is she pregnant?" Aki asked.

Oscar took a breath. "Yes, she is. And since you're probably curious, you should know that I'm the father."

"Congratulations," said Poonah, raising her flute by the foot, using the wrong fingers. She said it the way people do when they don't mean it.

"Don't bother. It isn't for me, this child," the old man grumbled. "I'll be dead before he can walk. I better be."

The waiter, a Frenchman with the thickest of accents, came over and they each ordered what most people would call a lunch (sandwiches, soups, etc.), except for Mary, who asked for a huge bowl of lettuce.

"You mean salad, Mademoiselle?" the waiter asked.

"No, just lettuce. Bring me a big bowl of uncut lettuce," Mary said. "The more, the happier I'll be."

He took the menus from each of them and walked away, as though he had been offended by her request.

"I needed to see you again because there's more to do," Oscar said. "It would be too much to ask you to come all this way to deliver a penis."

"Not really," Poonah said. "Granted, the penis thing was stupid. But we always wanted to come to Switzerland."

"Yet Mary has been here before, have you not?" Oscar said.

Mary said nothing for ten seconds. "Yes, a few times." Mary brought both her feet up on her chair, almost curling up. "And you're from Montenegro, aren't you?"

"Indeed." Oscar seemed charmed at the moment—he was still the cold man with cold eyes.

"I'm glad we finally meet," Mary said. She reached across the table pretending to shake Oscar's hand. "So you must have heard that Mark and I are no longer together."

"Cyril, you know, the Bulgarian, was your husband's spy," Oscar said. "When you survived the blasts in Kashmir, Mark called on certain people. He was desperate. He didn't know that I was already giving them much more money than he ever would."

"Good," Mary answered.

"Is it?" Oscar asked.

"Poonah, Aki, let me make an introduction. This is the man who stole about 150 million cigarettes from Mark and me, all going into Albania. That's sixteen trucks full of cigarettes," Mary said, then turned to the old man. "Sure, I'm glad to see you now."

"I want you to come and live with me. You can even have my house all to yourself," Oscar said, as the waiter brought their food. "Let's work together, we can destroy him."

It seemed questionable to Mary, this kindness. "Cigarettes again?" Mary asked.

"No, now it is alcohol. These Moslems love it more than nicotine. Or even sex," Oscar said. The waiter placed a square plate of breaded veal chops and buttered asparagus tips in front of him. "We'll use Mark's routes. But instead of delivering women, it'll be alcohol."

"Maybe, but they'll see the alcohol," Mary said.

"Not so fast. We get it out of New Jersey, dyed and labeled as mouthwash or cleaning solvent," Oscar said. "There is huge money in this."

"Tens of millions of dollars," Mary said.

"Possibly. So the house will be yours to use, but I ask that you not leave," Oscar said. "I won't allow that."

"What does that mean?" Poonah asked. "We aren't zoo creatures you can leave in a cage."

"I'll need to trust you. That means all of you. Three times a week, food will be delivered. All my phones and computers are tapped. It isn't that I wish to do this to you, but I think you understand that I haven't a choice."

"I understand, it's like the peacock, with all the eyes," Mary said. "But I have my conditions, too. Everything is fifty-fifty, between you and me. That's the net profit split. No negotiating, nothing. Plus I'll need a small advance, in case we fail. Fifty thousand will do."

"Deal," Oscar said. "I'll call Thalia and tell her that you'll be moving in today."

Though it seemed like a perfect day, they could hear thunder in the distance.

CHAPTER FIFTY

In Which We Learn About Happiness

"LET ME TELL YOU what I know about happiness," Aki said, "because I've felt it more than most people."

They were alone on a gondola traveling high into the Alps again. Aki resembled one of those majestic mountains, even more so because he was blind. It wasn't only the view that drew them. Poonah had developed an attachment to the hot dogs served on top of Pilatus; she hadn't stopped talking about them since the first time they'd gone up.

Rain pounded into the gondola—Mary had objected several times to going but gave in to Poonah in the end. It was to be their last journey before moving into Oscar's dominion, where they'd be too busy for leisure.

Aki took off his shiny silver jacket. "If you love life, you rise above everything. You stop caring. Being part of it is a killer."

Clouds were so thick it was almost dark outside.

"So you're not worried about staying at Oscar's for a while?" Mary asked. She had Aki hold her as she went to sleep the night before. She expressed that need because Oscar was putting her on a direct collision course with Mark. "Because I fear something terrible is going to happen."

"There's no issue. We can always leave," he said. "And the worst he can do is kill us."

"That doesn't sound like happiness," Poonah said. She had oiled her hair and tied it in back. It looked like she hadn't washed it in days. "If you want to know about joy, ask me. A real woman knows pleasure more than any man."

"In sex?" Mary asked.

"Of course. It is calculated that a woman's pleasure is nine times a man's," Poonah answered. "We have three times the taste buds and a hundred times more points of sensitivity than the penis."

Aki wasn't talking about sex. Aki wasn't even talking about the world. Seeing the world was a distraction. The point was that it was easy for him to make it go away, and for that he was grateful.

CHAPTER FIFTY-ONE

This is an Excellent Time For You to Become a Statistic

The Salvation Army Missing Persons Inquiry Form

Return this form with a $25.00 nonrefundable registration fee (check payable to The Salvation Army).

The Registration fee is only a token charge. It does not cover the cost of setting up a case or searching for your missing person. Your further contributions to help offset the cost of this service are welcomed.

All inquiries are confidential. Please answer all questions. Give more details by letter if possible.

SOCIAL SECURITY NUMBER 563-52-0764

CITIZEN OF USA

NATIONALITY <u>American</u>

EDUCATIONAL BACKGROUND <u>Self</u>

PERSONAL DESCRIPTION:

sex <u>Female</u>

height <u>5'10"</u>

weight <u>130 lb.</u>

eyes <u>Greenish</u>

hair <u>Sandy Brown or Red</u>

race <u>Mixed Caucasian</u>

complexion <u>Olive</u>

scars <u>One long set of stitches under right underarm and inner leg. Birthmark on right side of face above lip. Lips are large.</u>

tattoo marks <u>Never</u>

Physical handicaps or mannerisms by which the person might be recognized: <u>Mary is extremely fit.</u>

DATE LAST HEARD FROM: <u>January 9, 2011 (BY MAIL)</u>

LAST KNOWN ADDRESS <u>675 West 252nd Street, Bronx, NY 10471</u>

REASON FOR SEPARATION   <u>Marital issues, strife.</u>

EMPLOYMENT: trade or occupation Self-Employed, Importer

EVER DRIVE CAR/TRUCK No

LICENSED IN WHAT STATE New York

DRIVER'S LICENSE NUMBER Unknown

EVER INCARCERATED Yes

WHEN 2006 WHERE Piscataquis Jail, Maine

EVER FINGERPRINTED Yes

WHEN 2006, when convicted, I assume

WHERE see above

Missing Persons Services

PO Box 635

West Nyack, NY 10994-0635

Case No. 7987851

SECTION I

INFORMATION ABOUT THE MISSING PERSON

FULL NAME(last, first, middle) Black, Mary K.

NICKNAME or ALIAS Sugar, Mmmmm Mary, Aphrodite, Lover

MAIDEN NAME Black

DATE OF BIRTH (month/day/year) <u>June 1, 1976</u>

PLACE OF BIRTH <u>Yokosuka, Japan</u>

FATHER (even if deceased) <u>Martin Mortensen</u>

MOTHER (even if deceased) <u>Helen Black</u>

MOTHER MAIDEN NAME <u>Norcross</u>

SECTION II ADDITIONAL INFORMATION ABOUT THE MISSING PERSON

Missing Person's Marital Status: <u>Married</u>

(list names and dates of birth)

Husband or Wife: <u>Mark Black</u>

Wife's maiden name: <u>Black</u>

Children: <u>None</u>

List Previous Marriages: <u>None</u>

Brothers or sisters: <u>Two sisters who are no longer in touch with Mary, for over a decade.</u>

Which of the above individuals have you contacted:

I have not contacted anyone. The entire family, aside from her sisters, is no longer living. She's a loner. Add to that description that we are a private couple who doesn't socialize much. Also our business takes us to other parts of the world, so we don't know too many people in the USA.

Clothing Worn When Last Seen (Note: color, brand, pattern, size):

<u>Photo attached of Mary at her last location, wearing a white linen dress. Notice the use of a ponytail. That's new to me.</u>

Note: She is skilled in disguising herself, so it is incumbent upon researchers to contact international authorities rather than rely on recognizing her. She may be considered armed, but I wouldn't call her dangerous.

Church membership: <u>No religious affiliation</u>

Name of pastor: _____

FULL NAME

Mary K. Black is my wife and she has been missing for a couple weeks. She was last seen getting on a speedboat on Lake Lucerne, in Switzerland. She checked out of the Palace Hotel (Lucerne), and there's no clue beyond that about her plans and movements. My private eye lost her. Before that she was in Ladakh, India, a high mountain town that I have no idea why she was visiting.

REASON FOR INQUIRY

I am concerned about her wellbeing. I would like to know her location. As stated, we have had our share of marital bickering, but she's disappeared at this point. She is still my wife. All problems aside, we need to fix them.

WHAT HAVE YOU DONE TO LOCATE PERSON

Pretty much everything. I have hired private investigators, but they failed to trail Mary once she began using marine transportation. We weren't prepared for that.

PLEASE LIST ALL DOCUMENTS ENCLOSED

Three photographs of Mary Black.

Two photographs of her mysterious traveling companions, a rotund Japanese fellow and an elderly woman of Indian descent.

A copy of Mary's passport, although I suspect she may be using a fake.

A letter from Mary, the last she wrote me.

Our marriage certificate.

Deed of ownership of our home, in both of our names.

I understand that the whereabouts of the person located will not be divulged without his/her express consent. By signing this form I am giving permission to release my address and phone number to the missing person if located.

MARK BLACK, February 18, 2011

CHAPTER FIFTY-TWO

Among a People Intensely Susceptible, With a Mind Befogged

"EXACTLY," MARY SAID, FROM the low couch in the living room, while talking on the satellite phone to Najib Khan. "This will be the biggest single bounty of smuggled alcohol into Saudi Arabia ever." She'd decided it would be far better to execute the shipment in one chunk, under the watch of several bribed customs officers, rather than spread it out over time.

Oscar remained in his chair, listening on speakerphone. Ten days and Mary had figured it all out. He wouldn't have been able to accomplish the same in six months without her contacts. The Italian team he'd gone to in the past was under strict watch by Swiss prosecutors. A third financier running out of Ticino was now serving a five-year sentence. Oscar expressed deep concern that they'd come after him next.

"How much is Mark paying the guards?" Mary assumed Najib Khan would share his information. Many times he'd revealed to her how much he mistrusted Mark, earning her allegiance. Sure, he was in the middle of helping Mark transport hundreds of women from Iraq to Saudi Arabia, but that was more complicated. You couldn't just put them in a warehouse. Much forging of documents was involved. The promise of bigger money was enough for Najib to delay in assisting Mark, which Mary was eager to exploit. She knew that's all it would take. "We need to give them at least thirty percent more than he is."

"That isn't difficult," Najib said. "But we'll need a paper trail for all this window cleaner. There has to be some record of someone exporting it."

"Fine, I'll take care of that," Mary said.

She watched Poonah shuffle in and out of the kitchen, from the hallway leading to the master bedroom, wearing nothing. The custom began when they moved into the house, and the more Mary complained about it, the more Poonah would indulge. She had a pot of chai on the stove and used the dainty glasses they had picked up in the hotel shop. Mary begged her to use larger cups (fewer trips to the kitchen naked), but Poonah wouldn't. She said that she felt freer and happier than ever in life, and that no one had the right to take that away from her.

Oscar sipped his whiskey, never looking up at Poonah's body.

This was a serious day, one that could erupt.

"The trucks will start delivery on Saturday. That's when the bribed officials will take over the length of the journey towards Najran," she told Najib. The plan was to empty the trucks at an agricultural warehouse west of Riyadh, then distribute the goods throughout the country over time. The entire operation was operated by a tribe that used to run frankincense around the region. Nothing had changed over the centuries except for the introduction of pavement. This meant the alcohol was a six hours drive, on highways built by the Bin Ladens, from Mecca, instead of several nights on camel.

"And Mark? Does he know we're talking?" There'd always been tension between Mary and her husband when it came to figuring out how to handle their networks. It could get violent. People along the chain of command need to know who's masterminding the operation, but be paid off enough to keep quiet about it. The balancing act wasn't for everyone, and many lives would be destroyed along the way. It took diligence not to raise the red flags of Mark and his people.

"That's the beauty of doing this in one day," Najib answered. "He doesn't have to know anything. Mark isn't even in Mecca."

This was the first Mary had heard of it. "Now you tell me."

"I assumed you knew he was in Tel Aviv."

As much hatred as she felt for Mark, jealousy seized her. "There's someone there for him, right?"

She wasn't putting Najib in an easy position. "You know Mark. It is all business."

"But is there a woman in Israel?" Mary needed to know. *A woman has a right to certain things at certain times.* "Jerusalem is where he does business with all the religious people. Tel Aviv isn't his territory."

"Do you mind?" Oscar interrupted her. "We have millions at stake and you're yapping away about your stupid relationship. Ask him about the chemicals."

Oscar was referring to the smuggling of chlorine gas that he had purchased on his own. It was now being stored in Yemen, in use already by the government there. Mary had told him she wouldn't get involved with the shipment of chemical weapons.

"What's he talking about?" Najib asked.

Mary watched one of the peacocks pass in the field next to the house. "Nothing, he's being an asshole."

CHAPTER FIFTY-THREE

Peace is not the Absence of War

NEAR DEAD CENTER IN the middle of Iran, Cyril had taken the overnight bus into cosmopolitan Shiraz, having walked enough days since he left the Himalayas. He was relieved to be in the city and out of the wild. The mountains had been teeming with foreign soldiers and everyone, especially the local tribesmen, was on high alert. One wouldn't call Cyril a peace pilgrim, but his mission had nothing to do with their war.

He checked into the Eram Hotel, showered and went out into the streets. It was a perfect spring day, fuzzy unripe almonds already on the trees. The plan was to skip the tourist routine of heading out to Persepolis. Instead, it was to wander, take a taxi back to the room later in the day, and sleep.

He took the crowded road past the city hall and the famous Vakil Mosque, stopped at an awe-inspiring structure called The Narenjestan Garden. Built in the nineteenth century by wealthy merchants, Cyril could imagine living out his life in the luxurious surroundings, even if the reality was that he was planning on leaving Iran within a day or two. Children, on what he assumed were field trips, hurried from room to room of the house. Cyril went around back to the expansive, geometric traditional Persian garden, with its series of fountains. Compared to all the arid and rocky places he'd been, he found it stunning to be in a place so lush.

Cyril wouldn't be alone for long. In fact, he'd been followed ever since he left the hotel. He was standing in the shade of a mulberry tree when the stranger approached him.

"You are from Europe?" he said, revealing his yellowed teeth. He wore a brown suit with no tie, and looked like he hadn't shaved in a week.

Like many solitary travelers, Cyril didn't mind the company. "Switzerland, yes," he answered. "You're from here?"

"Not Shiraz proper. I was born in a village nearby, and I never left," he said. He stood close to Cyril and still had the smell of cigarettes on his breath. "There is too much gravity here."

There was some elusive quality drawing Cyril to the man. Maybe he was simpler, more grounded than the people Cyril often dealt with. His was a different kind of intelligence. Cyril invited the man for tea, the national pastime. He could use the company.

The man introduced himself as Kamal.

They walked together to a café a short distance down the road, sat outside on the noisy sidewalk.

"You haven't told me what you're doing here," he said, staring Cyril up and down. "Or maybe you didn't notice that the world has forgotten about my country."

Cyril had spent enough time in this part of the world to know that men staring at men wasn't meant to be rude, or evocative. In this part of the world, men did this to each other. "Yeah, ever since Khomeini arrived, tourists have skipped Iran. But I'm not staying either. I am on my way to Saudi Arabia."

"Why would you go there?" Kamal asked. "Unless you like criminals."

Perceptive, Cyril thought. But he had an alibi ready, what with all those hours alone in the desert. "I'm writing a book about the Middle East."

"Oh really," Kamal said. "I'm a writer, too. Well, a poet. That's why I love my city so much." He extended his hand towards Cyril, even though they already shook hands.

Now, Cyril wasn't stupid and he knew that to a writer he wouldn't pass as a writer. He wasn't educated enough, for one. "I'm thinking about writing a book that describes the people I've met in the Middle East. I'd like to give the world a real idea of what this culture is all about."

"That's a cliché, you know," Kamal said. He lit a cigarette. "There is one culture, and you either have it, or you don't." For the first time since they met Kamal seemed to stop putting all his attention on Cyril. He said something in Persian to the man seated at the next table, and now these two were carrying a conversation.

Cyril wondered what they were talking about. He was trying not to take it personally.

After a solid two minutes of chat, Kamal gestured to the stranger by putting his hand on his heart and looked again at Cyril. His mood was now different. "You have the eyes of a wild animal. Do you know that, my dear?"

Cyril was taken aback. "I didn't know."

"Well, you do. And a wild animal who goes to Saudi Arabia, that's a curious thing," Kamal said. He spoke as if he didn't care who he was speaking to. "Why are you really going there?"

Here he was, far from all that was his life. Cyril could tell him whatever fib he wanted, but sometimes a stranger brings out the truth in us. "I'm supposed to find someone, a husband."

"And kill him?" Kamal still didn't seem phased.

"No, I won't kill him." Cyril said. "I'm not a killer."

Kamal laughed. He had a menacing look on his face, as if he knew how to do this to people. Kamal could disappear into the alleyway behind, never to be seen again. "If I were thinking about eliminating someone, I would have you do it instead. You're a perfect killer."

"No, that's not true. I'm a peaceful man." The words brought tears to his eyes.

"Trust me, one day you're going to kill someone." Kamal gave Cyril a kind slap on his shoulders. "But don't worry, I'm just a poet. I sell fruits and vegetables in a small store. What do I know?"

STATE OF NEW YORK

VS.   Case No. 08-CF-5094

MARK BLACK

TRANSCRIPTION OF TAPED CONTROLLED

PHONE CALL

TRANSCRIBED BY:

Will Shaheen

LAURA SIMON REPORTING GROUP

APPEARANCES:

NAJIB KHAN

MARK BLACK

CONTENTS:

MARK: Things well over there?

NAJIB: Absolutely.

MARK: Not for me. Hell no. I've got a lot of shredding to do, thanks to those idiots that had to go get themselves caught.

NAJIB: So what are you doing about it? The Feds are all over everything.

MARK: Muhammad may spill the beans. Not about himself, of course. He'll try and pass everything off on us. We have to be prepared for that. More me than you anyway.

NAJIB: We had nothing to do with it.

MARK: You and I know that. That's why I don't live in America. But I don't feel like I want to explain myself in the court of law. And it doesn't help that Muhammad is a liar.

NAJIB: So true. Where are you at this point?

MARK: Pirate Alley. A den itself this time. I'm staring at the minarets as we speak, roasting away in this heat. It's awful, like hell. I've to wait on some boats coming in.

NAJIB: You're in Yemen? You never told me what happened in Israel.

MARK: It was taking too long. The shipment has become impossible to arrange. It's all mixed up. That's why I'm calling you. I don't understand what's happening, but all of a sudden everyone is giving me the cold shoulder.

NAJIB: Maybe it is the trial in New York. People are talking.

MARK: Possibly. Yet I don't think so. The Israelis are craftier than that.

NAJIB: No one is answering my calls either.

MARK: You see.

NAJIB: Yeah.

MARK: But Mizrahi told me he spoke to you.

NAJIB: Not really. It was quick.

MARK: Don't hide things from me.

NAJIB: I never do. And what's coming into the port this time?

MARK: Eighty by way of Somalia.

NAJIB: Young cuties?

MARK: Not too young. The issue is I needed to get them here yesterday. Ramadan is coming up.

NAJIB: When is it?

MARK: End of July, but I need to break them in, not all at once. You know how crazy it gets that month.

NAJIB: Crazy is an understatement. You still have time.

MARK: They've been laying low in Djibouti for a week already. I have to feed them and all that. At least they're eager to get working.

NAJIB: It shouldn't be so hard to get them into Yemen.

MARK: No, but once they're here, I don't have time. I need to deliver into Saudi Arabia. And that's what's killing me. The Yemenis are trying to destroy me. I don't know what I had to do with them. So you have no idea?

NAJIB: No.

MARK: That's surprising. Well, you better not be lying to me right now.

NAJIB: So you're threatening me.

MARK: Only if you're lying. I love you, but if you've got something that I need to know, things are different. I'll fuck you so bad.

NAJIB: That won't be necessary, *Habibi*. I'll poke around, make a few calls.

MARK: Do more than poke. But don't even try to outwit me.

(THE CALL ENDED.)

I, Will Shaheen, certify that I was authorized to and did transcribe the foregoing proceedings, and that the transcript is a true and complete record of the tape recording thereof.

CHAPTER FIFTY-FIVE

Men are the Protectors and Maintainers of Women

February 20, 2011
Mary K. Black
Postlagernde
Lucerne General Post and Telegraph Office
Switzerland-CH 6000

Dear Ms. Black:

We have completed the initial property records search, following your request for our services last week. You can have faith that we did an investigation in multiple facilities where records are kept here in Saudi Arabia. We executed online legal searches, researched city sales files going back seven years, as well as banking public records pertaining both to foreigner sales and securing insurance. Given your warning that your husband is a secretive man I think you'll understand that we have been unable to locate his holdings at this time. Additionally, the businesses whose names you provided have all been closed, as well as the commercial offices and phone numbers associated with them (two years ago, to be exact). Your husband's name doesn't appear on any of the contracts for those properties. Are you certain that he is in this country? If so, do you happen to know if he has been traveling under a different name and/or using an illegal passport? This is the reason his name would not have turned up yet. We have even gone to local officers (without revealing the purpose of our inquiry) and the closest and most dubious we were able to find was a certain Will Black Ray of Portland, Oregon, whose business is medical technology. We assumed that there was no link to your husband and that if he's using a different name it is rather unlike his own.

Thank you for your wire dated February 19th, 2011. Please let us know if you have any additional information that might allow our firm to reopen this matter. Most important would be the names of either his company or of a local woman whom you believe he has married. Barring such information, at this moment we will consider the case closed until we hear from you.

I wish I had better news, and offer my best wishes.

Mahmoud Arshad, Attorney at Law
Al-Omri Law firm (Riyadh Main Office)
Al-Umam Commercial Center, North Tower, 18th floor
Sitteen Street, Malaz
P.O. Box 6691702, Riyadh 11361, KSA

Deadly Shooting Outside Babylon's Strip Club

Updated: Thursday, 21 Feb 2011, 8:14 P.M. EDT

By Claudia Bester, Associated Press

LONDON, ENGLAND—It happened outside Babylon's strip club on Tuesday night. Shots were fired. Three people were wounded, one fatally. Najib Khan, an international businessman and citizen of Canada, died from blood hemorrhaging in the ambulance on the way to the hospital. He was shot several times in the head. Khan had been staying at the £525-a-night Landmark Hotel in Marylebone, central London.

"I heard the gunshots, and the first thing I did was fall on my floor," said Soho neighbor Michele Ports. "When I looked out, I didn't see anything, but I knew something had happened."

Though neither he nor his unnamed female companion who was with him as he walked towards his vehicle were armed, they were hit with no less than thirty bullets, killing Khan and wounding the woman and the club's valet.

"This is a tragedy. I've lost a close friend who was in town visiting me. I knew him for many years, and Najib was a total gentleman," said Babylon's manager Maroun Tahyoun. "As far as what happened, we are cooperating with authorities one hundred percent. We're doing what we can, but as far as anything else, we have no comment."

There have been a few acts of violence around Babylon's in recent years. In one case, a customer drove over a valet driver. In another, a valet driver shot and killed a would-be carjacker. According to local sources, police authorities had already been investigating the club.

"That's what's going to happen when you have the clientele that's hanging out at that bar," Ports said. "I, as a member of this community, am really sick of it."

Neighbors complain about liquor bottles and prostitutes littering the area. They also say the music from the club is especially disruptive.

"From midnight on, the music is loud in there, and then once the club is closed, they come out to their cars. They're drunk, they're high, they hire women, just loud noise all night," said neighbor Beth M. Ramsey. "You find condoms, whiskey bottles, they don't care about you and your life. Children walk to school in the morning on these streets."

People in this neighborhood are calling for more police patrols and are demanding the city to keep an eye on the club.

"It's a nuisance, but it has not always been like that," said Ramsey. "Recently, it has gotten out of hand."

London police have arrested two men in connection with the murder. Police have charged Edward Rashidian, a thirty-two year old

Nottingham resident, and Moshe Simontov, a forty-six year old also from Nottingham. Police sources aren't releasing information about the motive. The death is being treated as suspicious and is being investigated by officers from the Met Police's Homicide and Serious Crime Command.

Mr. Rashidian and Mr. Simontov were taken into a central London police station where they remain in custody.

۶&

MARY: IT HELPS TO talk to you, as a woman. Sometimes I think you're the only one who understands.

Winfrey: You can call on me any time. I am here for you when you need me, like I am for so many people.

Mary: There's been a ton of bad weather and hours and hours of thunder. It makes me fear again. A lot can go wrong, not only to me, but to my companions. I feel responsible for them, their safety. They've been so good to me.

Winfrey: I don't know about that. They're lucky to be with you. The biggest adventure you can ever take is to live the life of your dreams.

Mary: And if it destroys you? I mean, I wonder if what you're espousing applies in that case.

Winfrey: Breathe. Let go. And remind yourself that this very moment is the only one you know you have for sure.

Mary: Now, don't take this the wrong way, but I can't digest that way of looking at things. It might get you high ratings, and I respect that. But this situation requires a bit more than taking a breath and smelling the flowers.

Winfrey: This is a call to arms. A call to be gentle, to be forgiving, to be generous with yourself. The next time you look into the mirror, try to let go of the story line that says you're too fat or too shallow, too ashy or too old, your eyes are too small or your nose too big. Just look into the mirror and see your face.

Mary: That isn't it. I can't bear to lose to Mark. That's what it comes down to. And I don't want him to own me.

Winfrey: Your calling isn't something that somebody can tell you about. It's what you feel. It is the thing that gives you juice. The thing that you are supposed to do. And nobody can tell you what that is. You know it inside yourself.

Mary: That's just it. I have a plan. But it is the most painful and disruptive imaginable. That's how it feels to me, and I don't know if I have the courage to go through with it. You're a woman, maybe you understand.

Winfrey: Do the one thing you think you cannot do. Fail at it. Try again. Do better the second time. The only people who never tumble are those who never mount the high wire.

Mary: Exactly, and I won't have a second chance. I see my destiny as a woman in front of me, but I can't accept it.

Winfrey: Think like a queen. A queen is not afraid to fail. Failure is another stepping stone to greatness.

Mary: To greatness?

Winfrey: I trust that everything happens for a reason, even when we're not wise enough to see it. Understand that the right to choose your own path is a sacred privilege. Use it. Dwell in possibility.

CHAPTER FIFTY-SIX

So Long as Men Can Breathe

I T WAS A CRISP spring day with clear skies, the kind that makes the Swiss a tad more jovial, and a pair of golden eagles flew overhead. Mary gazed out the front windows holding her third glass of a twelve-year-old Glen Ord the moment she decided she'd had enough. Oscar behaved as though he had the power, since he was the one fronting the cash. Mary understood that her contacts were even more important than money. She'd been careful to safeguard certain bits of information as she set up delivery of the alcohol to Saudi Arabia. So long as Oscar kept his word there would be no issues. She'd decided that from the beginning. He wasn't one to do so, however, and she ascertained that the instant she met him.

Mary had arranged the meeting for after lunch and they were all present, except for Poonah, who napped in back.

Mary was about to lay hard into Oscar when she noticed a man walking up the field. It took a long moment to realize that it was Cyril, the Bulgarian, with that same bright orange hiker's backpack, as if he'd walked all the way from the Himalayas. Mary assumed he'd be in Saudi Arabia at this point. Something had gone wrong, she surmised.

Cyril looked down the whole time, went straight to the front door and knocked it several times. Thalia rushed up and opened the door for him, invited him inside.

Mary could tell Thalia didn't care for him. She was more concerned with keeping his dirty backpack out of the house than asking how he'd been and what he was doing here.

Mary walked over to him and extended her hand. Cyril gave her a quick smile, muttering a customary whisper of a *Grüezi*, and went over to Oscar who was in his chair, in his usual foul mood.

"I was at the other house and one of the workers said that I could find you here," Cyril said. "I hope I'm not interrupting anything."

"Perhaps you are, but it doesn't matter," Oscar said. "Mary called us up here because they've got something to tell me. Prepare yourself a drink and take a seat. That's if you're thirsty. Otherwise, just sit." Oscar lifted his wooden cane and pointed it at Mary. "What is all this about anyway?"

"You know, I've been asking you for my advance since we started," Mary said. She showed no fear of him whatsoever. "I trusted you to handle that. Now, I don't feel like hearing another one of your excuses. We called the bank today and it still wasn't in the account. The money to everyone else in our network shows up, however. That tells me you care only about them."

"I told you that there was a problem with that wire," Oscar said. "Two million dollars has gone here and there in the past week, so you should know I'm good for it."

"Not good enough, Oscar," she said. "What do you think, Aki?"

"You've been too nice to him," Aki said.

"What the fuck do you know?" Oscar punched his chair as he said it. "I've given you my house and this insensitive bitch has the gaul to ask me for money. All I've done is give and give. Who's feeding you? Who pays for all this French wine you drink? I showed you the letter from my bank proving that I made the wire, and they admitted to being responsible for the mistake."

"So have them send another wire," Aki said. "Let them find the missing money on their own time."

"I can do that, but don't come in here accusing me of foul play. I don't appreciate it."

"I'm giving you until tomorrow," Mary said. *Something is making me hate you.* "If it isn't in my account, we're leaving."

"Then leave."

"And when I do, I won't tell you where we're going." She had to make it hurt. "Now listen, you will be out everything. The alcohol is not where you think it is."

"Is that so?" Oscar asked. "Is that fucking so? I have the address of the warehouse already."

"Those are my contacts, those are my people," Mary said. "The alcohol is in a warehouse, like I promised. But not the one you know about."

"I don't believe a word you're saying," Oscar said. "Besides, I don't let anyone talk to me like this. Thalia dear, do what I said."

And just like that with those few words everything in the room changed forever. Thalia reached into her purse and revealed a Sphinx pistol, pointed it at Mary, as she stood in the front of the room.

Twenty feet separated the women. Mary could tell that Thalia wasn't an experienced shooter, holding the gun more like it was a cell phone. But a gun is a gun and who knew what would happen.

Thalia shot the first bullet into the ceiling, sending a pile of plaster to the floor.

"No, I meant shoot straight at this bitch," Oscar shouted.

Aki started to stand, but Mary screamed at him to stay put. A blind man wasn't any good against a gun.

Thalia pointed the gun at Mary and pulled the trigger. Mary stayed still and the first segment of thirty square feet of window behind her shattered. She ran closer to the door and Thalia fired again, this time hitting the gallery of penises. The glass bottles fell over each other and at least ten landed on the dark wood floors, broke into countless pieces.

Shot three brought even more bottles crashing down.

Oscar looked at Cyril. "Do something!"

"I can't any more," he said. "I'm a changed man. I no longer believe in violence."

"You no longer believe in violence?" Oscar screamed. "You know how hard I worked to get the penises!"

Distracted at that moment by Oscar and Cyril, Poonah, who had been listening from the other room, was able to sneak behind Thalia.

Oscar shouted at Thalia, telling her to watch out.

But the warning came too late. Poonah struck her shoulders with the bottle of scotch, missing her head. Thalia fell to the floor. It was enough of a blow to cause her to lose the grip on the gun. Poonah was able to take hold of it, moving faster than she ever had.

In an instant she stood over Oscar with the handgun. "Here you go." She turned and fired several more shots at his collection of penises. The scent in the room had gone from one of an African spiced cinnamon candle to formaldehyde. "My Baba trained me to shoot at our ranch in the Punjab." Next she pointed at Oscar who was helpless in his chair and fired two bullets into his stomach. She tucked the gun into her sari.

Thalia rushed over to Oscar's side. He was already unconscious.

"Stop this! He didn't want me to shoot you," Thalia said, as she slapped Oscar in the face, trying to bring him back to consciousness. "You people are crazy."

"Maybe," Mary said. "So you don't want him to die?"

"No, I do not." Thalia said it with conviction.

Mary took the gun from Poonah, put the bullets in her pocket and threw the weapon on top of the penises on the floor.

"I forgive him," Mary said. "You shot at me for no reason. But I forgive him, right, Aki?"

"We have no place for hate in us," he said.

"Cyril, carry him. Then you'll stay back, take care of the animals. They'll be hungry soon."

"I can do that," Cyril said.

"We might be a while," Mary said as she grabbed her patent-sleeve trenchcoat. "We'll drive the boat to the hospital. But we need to hurry. Oscar needs to be taken care of."

CHAPTER FIFTY-SEVEN

And Now Women Found

Capital Eritrea News, **February 26, 2011. Asmara.**

Thirty-five people drowned and another five were feared dead while crossing the Gulf of Aden this week, including an incident in which a naval boat ignored the migrants' cries for help, a U.N. refugee agency said Friday.

A first boat carrying mostly Iraqi refugees and at least one Israeli man ran into strong winds and rough waters after it set sail from Puntland. It approached the Yemeni coast the next day, but fearing interception by coastguards, smugglers kept the boat out at sea.

"The passengers, who by then were dehydrated and hungry, began crying and shouting," said Peter Navasky, spokesman for the Commissioner for Refugees, an independent human rights agency.

The Somali captains in charge of the boat tried to catch the attention of a cargo vessel and a foreign naval ship. However, "The naval ship approached their boat but ignored their cries for help," said Navasky.

Also, a boat carrying mostly Ethiopians which set sail on January 11 arrived close to Yemen's coast on January 13. However, smugglers forced the passengers into the sea even though the boat was still in deep waters.

The refugees frequently fall victim to vicious smugglers who brutalize them after taking extortionate fees for the passage.

As of late yesterday, forty bodies had been recovered by the Yemeni navy. One person is known to have survived, a sixteen-year-old woman who swam for almost a day before reaching the Yemeni coast near the port of Bir Ali, some 400 kilometers east of Aden.

In 2005, thirty-nine people who had been stranded for days in the Gulf of Aden between Somalia and Yemen were rescued by a Danish vessel. They are the lucky ones among the rising wave of illegal migrants from the Horn of Africa who make the perilous journey to Yemen and other Middle Eastern countries to seek a better life elsewhere. Some eighty-nine people have drowned in January and February of this year while making the perilous voyage across the Gulf of Aden, compared to fifteen for the whole of 2010, the commissioner said.

Angela Braybrooks
Capital Eritrea News

Excerpted from: INVESTIGATION INTO HUMAN TRAFFICKING TO SAUDI ARABIA

===

HEARINGS

ONE HUNDRED NINTH CONGRESS, MEETING 728, ASSOCIATION 43

JUNE 19; OCTOBER 2 AND 3; AND DECEMBER 4 AND 11, 2009

Serial No. 349-83

SHOULD THE UNITED STATES DO MORE TO EXTRADITE FUGITIVES IN SAUDI ARABIA?

ASSOCIATION ON GOVERNMENT ACTIVITIES, Washington, DC. The Assoc. met, pursuant to notice, at 12:06 p.m., Dulles House Office, Hon. Paul Drew (Chairman of Assoc.) presiding.

Mr. Davis. Good afternoon, please be seated. Because we have a quorum we can proceed. We have exhibits provided us so it will be made part of the record. For those that haven't already, we request that you and your staff have an opportunity to review them.

Mr. Johnson. OK. That is fine. I ask unanimous consent that all articles, exhibits, and extraneous or tabular material referred to be included in the record, and without objection, so ordered.

Mr. Walker. What is happening in the Middle East right now is critically important. We have strategic interests. We have economic interests, and we have military interests. So it is imperative that we win the war on terrorism, and to do that, we have to have strong allies in that region. We need access to airfields and military bases there. It is also imperative that we preserve the flow of oil from the Middle East. We get about 55, 56 percent of our oil from that area.

Mr. Caston. We've seen cases where men have violated court orders, taken women away against their will, and kept them for years. Despite the fact that arrest warrants have been issued for some, the Saudi Government has refused to lift a finger to help us solve these cases. In fact, the Saudi Government has created a safe haven for them in a country where women and children are treated like property.

Mr. Davis. We can't let this go on. Our relationship with Saudi Arabia is important, but this just can't be allowed to continue. The only way we're going to resolve this problem is by elevating this issue, letting the American people and people throughout the world know about it. This has to be raised with the Saudis at the highest levels. I am preparing a letter to the President, and I'm going to ask all of my colleagues on the committee to sign it. We're going to ask the President to raise this issue with Crown Prince Abdullah to try to get it resolved. We have examples of our own citizens who are now fugitives from justice traveling freely and doing illicit commerce without abiding by international laws.

Mr. Caston. Just last week I was at a human rights convention and everyone was talking about the Saudi young women who were burned to death.

Mr. Johnson. Prince Saud states that the law regulates and guarantees all humanitarian rights without any prejudices. Do you think that law protects women's rights without any prejudice? It doesn't sound like it. I don't want to continue to put you on the spot with this. But the fact is they recognize men.

Mr. Caston. The Saudi Government refuses to cooperate in the investigation of human trafficking. Religious freedom is forbidden by law, and women have few rights in Saudi Arabia. The U.S. Commission on International

Religious Freedom has recommended that
Saudi Arabia be named a country of particular
concern, placing it in a category with North
Korea, Iran, Iraq, and Sudan.

Mr. Walker. One way or the other we must stay
after this. I want you to know that I know you
guys do a good job up here. And I didn't bring
you up here just to beat the heck out of you.
But what I wanted to do is make the case that
with the Saudi government, you have got to be
careful. I know, because they are paying you
and if you say the wrong thing they are going
to cut you off. But the fact is they have lied and
lied and lied to us. They have lied and lied and
lied to everyone. They have been roadblocks to
getting American fugitives back in this country,
and it is something that will not be tolerated.
We must keep the heat on them until something
happens.

CHAPTER FIFTY-EIGHT

This is Another Paradox:
What is Soft is Strong

FROM REST THE IMPRESSIVE speedboat tore out onto the lake with Poonah at the helm, Mary hollering directions over the engine. She was anything but distracted.

The wind was nearly calm, the water so clear as to seem tropical. It was the first time the lake appeared this way in weeks.

"You're going the wrong way!" Thalia shouted, pointing the opposite direction, into the horizon. She had the frustrated look of someone who was used to being in control. "Lucerne is behind us!"

"Trust me," Mary said to Poonah, keeping her hair from blowing over her face. "Don't worry about her."

"Why aren't you going to the hospital?" Thalia clutched her cell phone. She had just finished shouting to someone in German. "This is bullshit. Total fucking bullshit." There was even more cursing than that.

Aki was left to deal with the wounded Oscar, who went from delirium to an unconscious state and back. Poonah had gotten the bleeding to stop, at least. What few words he did say were about how they wouldn't get away with ruining his collection of penises. It wasn't looking too promising at the moment for Oscar.

Something tragic seemed ahead of them.

Think of how you would not want to be on that boat of sorrow. Mary behaved as though she feared nothing any longer.

She'd studied Thalia, registered how unhelpful she'd been with attending to Oscar. Earlier, Aki had asked Thalia to hurry with some bed sheets to wrap Oscar with, but Thalia at first complained that they were all *Charlotte Thomas Bespoke,* and wondered if anything else would work.

"I don't care who made them," Mary shouted. She decided that would be the last thing on her mind if her love had just been shot several times. Her suspicions regarding Thalia from the beginning were being confirmed. "Maybe that's not Oscar's child in there, is it?" A test, the kind of thing Aki would say. Mary had been learning from him.

Thalia pushed her lips forward as far as they would go, contorting her face. "Excuse me?"

"You don't love that old man," she said. "I always knew this. But now I'm starting to think you didn't screw him either." Mary had gone back to the house for the gun, just before they left on the boat, in case Thalia tried anything.

"Get us to the hospital," Thalia said. "There's no point in talking to you."

"You're too good for me, I guess," Mary said. She then told Poonah to stop the boat. "But don't turn it off."

"Here? In the middle of the lake." Poonah seemed confused. "Is everything okay?"

Mary hurried to the stern and kneeled in front of Oscar, reaching her arm under his crotch.

All was quiet for a few seconds.

It must have been a great shock to the others, sitting still in those waters. One could hear the piercing screams of an eagle flying overhead.

In one quick movement Mary hoisted Oscar on her shoulders and with all her strength stood up, held this bloody creature on her as if he were her prey.

"You care about him, Aki?"

"You know he's no good," Aki answered.

"And what temperature is the water?"

Aki reached over, dipping the round tip of his thumb into the lake and no more. "Almost freezing. It is so cold, but it is also so soft."

"I've always wondered why people like this exist," Mary said. She leaned her body overboard and dropped Oscar into the water. Adrenaline was on her side.

As soon as Oscar's body hit the lake he woke, thrashing for something to hold onto. You can't grab water. It doesn't care about anyone, no matter how old, or pitiful.

"Hurry up, before he manages to hang on," Mary told Poonah.

"But he's going to die if you leave him there."

"Exactly."

Thalia remained speechless as The Splendor raced away, with Mary now pointing the gun her direction, glancing behind them, watching Oscar, now a dot in the distance, struggle with all his might to stay afloat.

She gave him no more than ten minutes before he'd die of hypothermia.

They were now headed towards the widest portion of the lake, about four miles. Mary had studied the map the day they moved in. From Mark she'd learned to plan for these sorts of occurrences more than other people.

"If I were you I'd be crying right now," Mary said. "Look out there at that tired pathetic hunk of flesh."

Thalia didn't flinch. She didn't turn back at Oscar, and said not one word to Mary.

"The father of that little creature inside you is dying, and you have no tears for him," she continued. "Because you're not who you say you are." With the gun still pointed in the direction of Thalia's navel, Mary walked over and wrenched the black Hermes purse from her.

"You have no right," Thalia said. "You lost your mind."

Mary took out objects one by one, including a pocketbook full of cash, various combs, a designer mirror, prescription sunglasses and dark lipstick. "No passport in here?"

"No."

"Hand me your phone."

Thalia gave Mary a defiant look, putting it under her thigh.

Mary shot one bullet into the air. "I said I want your phone."

Aki grabbed it from under Thalia and threw it in the direction of Mary.

Mary started playing around with it, going straight to the contacts to see if she recognized anyone. Nothing. Then the text messages.

Two minutes later she stood up. "Poonah, I need you to stop again."

Poonah obliged. She took a moment to readjust her sari. There were cliffs of rocks towering above them, at least sixty million years old.

"Country code 966." Mary walked over to Thalia. "Who's in 966?"

"Look, I have no idea what you're talking about," Thalia said. "Oscar used my phone all the time."

"That's a phone out of Saudi Arabia," Mary said. "You even called there last night."

"It was Oscar."

"Bullshit. That's your story? I know the father of that child, and that makes us enemies. I've succeeded in discovering your destiny," Mary said. "You had Oscar fooled. No wonder you hated him so much. And that poor child in you, with no idea of the evil in this world. What can be worse than coming out of a womb like yours?"

"All wombs are perfect, Mary," Aki said. "We are all born innocent."

"We remain innocent," Mary said. "Protectors."

Mary walked, almost skipped, over to Thalia, lifting her hand-stitched dress shirt halfway up, despite the resistance and objections, and pointed the gun once again with the barrel inches away from Thalia's shiny belly. It was the first time she'd seen it, and it was a holy thing. Mary caressed the belly and looked up at Thalia's face, making sure they both knew what was happening. Mary had entered a trance, with some overwhelming feeling taking over her body.

With their eyes locked on each other Mary let go of not one but two quick shots straight at the belly.

Blood everywhere. The noxious smell of urine. Fountains of blood and miscellaneous tissue landing on Mary's face. Now Thalia cried, more like a squeal. She fell back, hyperventilating. Mary pulled down Thalia's pants and found there a silky pink Victoria's Secret thong. She grabbed the soft cloth and moved it aside, leaving dots of blood on the top, placed the barrel above Thalia's shaved labia. They were swollen. Still there was no pity for the woman. She shot the third bullet into her vagina. More screams. They were an animal's screams, the ones you can't bear to hear. Those you can't ever forget, no matter how long you are alive. It was a slaughtering. A deer or German shepherd hit by a speeding truck kinds of sounds.

What contrast with this glorious boat, the perfect Swiss day.

Mary reached into Thalia with her bare hands and grabbed the mangled fetus from the womb, but it had already stopped breathing. A bullet had ripped through its heart. She handed the tiny girl to Aki.

"Mark is the father?" Aki said, holding it in his left hand. "This is all about jealousy. You are possessed by it."

She wasn't listening to him. "Move out of the way, let me lift her up," Mary said, as she grabbed onto Thalia. "I have to be the one who kills her."

And moments afterward, from the freezing center of the lake, Poonah had turned the boat around, captaining it towards Lucerne in a frantic scramble, Thalia's mutilated, ivory body coming ashore not until three weeks and two hours later.

CHAPTER FIFTY-NINE

The Representation of Femininity is the Profoundest Art

Facsimile Page One of One

Mrs. Mary Black
Widder Hotel
Rennweg 7
CH-8001 Zürich
Telephone: 4144 224 25 26, Telefax: 4144 224 24 24

Dear Mrs. Black:

As a follow-up to your initial consultation on the telephone we have confirmed the possibility of an early appointment for your surgery in ten days. We are unable to do so sooner, and please understand that this is a confidential matter. This is not how medical matters are handled, but given your urgency concerning time I am doing all I can to accommodate you. Therefore, there will be additional charges for this elective procedure, as one would normally have to wait at least a month.

Additionally, it is my professional opinion that having a hymen reconstruction after you're pregnant poses risks to the embryo, and would strongly suggest that you consider other options, such as the Chinese products that have become popular in places like Egypt. This is an over-the-counter, inexpensive solution that you would insert inside yourself. When it would come into contact with your partner's, this thin plastic Chinese hymen would be punctured. Your blood would be in the object so it would appear that it was your hymen that had burst.

Should you, however, choose to proceed with surgery I will have to sign off on all risks both to you and your unborn child, if you are indeed pregnant. Waiting until after the surgery to conceive a child is my first recommendation. You are at additional risk because this would be your third hymenorrhaphy.

Following the procedure you will find sexual contact to be uncomfortable for at least a month. Most women aren't able to engage in sexual acts until six weeks after the surgery, some complain of pain for even longer. The reconstruction method where we take a flap from your vaginal lining to create the new hymen takes three months to heal. Two days after the surgery you will be in no position for penetration, so I strongly suggest you reconsider. This is a serious matter and I advise you to consider the risks associated with your plan.

If you are committed to having this surgery, please be in touch with my office and I will arrange for something as described above.

Sincerely,
Dr. Kenneth Anthus
Forchstrasse 224, 8008 Zürich

CHAPTER SIXTY

The Selection of a Course of Action, but They Weep Here

Fajita Avenue
Dabab St., Suleimania
Riyadh, Saudi Arabia

Reservations to the Mexican cantina were made this time via the satellite phone Omar Amir had been using for the past two years, eluding international terrorist hunters. He asked for the same corner table Mark had gotten them the previous two meetings. You never know how people will follow and how people will listen, so you can never be too careful. Omar had changed the satellite number several times during this period, between carriers out of Ankara and Abu Dhabi. Home was whatever hotel room he happened to rent—under various pseudonyms. They were common Islamic names that were too difficult to trace. He owned no cars and traveled by small aircraft or his friends' planes. Money was buried in various vaults in Turks and Caicos, Geneva, and Australia, and there were also significant real estate holdings in both Las Vegas and Toronto, under partnerships. The number of Semites like him roaming the planet using the same services, with both Arabic and Israeli nationalities, was anybody's guess, but it was more than people realized. Some of these gophers and salesmen did very well for themselves, when they didn't get caught.

It took Omar three attempts to convince Mark to meet. Mark had been depressed ever since the women drowned along the Yemeni coast. Nothing else had been working out either. Omar had promised Mark an offer that was meant to end his unlucky streak and provide him with the women he needed to run his affairs during the religious pilgrimages.

Mark was waiting for Omar when he arrived, dressed in a white T-shirt and blue jeans. A scruffy look for this part of the world, Omar probably thought. And totally unlike Mark. He wasn't even wearing socks. It was a good thing no one but the waiter could see them in their curtained booth.

By the time Omar sat down, two plates of garlic cheese bread had come to the table. It is a violation of Gulf etiquette to order before your guest arrives. Mark knew that.

"You have to taste these, Omar," he said, breaking some of the hot bread off the plate. "I already had one plate. And waiter, how about some of those chicken wings with the blue cheese?"

If not for the promise of moolah, Mark knew Omar would probably have excused himself.

Mark reached into his pockets for a flask, took a long sip. He offered it to Omar, who turned it down.

"Are you okay?" Omar asked.

"Fine," Mark said. "Just fine. But I'm sick of this part of the world."

"You were in Israel and Yemen. You told me you've been traveling a lot."

"Sure, true, but I lost big bucks in Yemen. It wasn't easy. They had hundreds of policemen combing Aden, rounding up everyone they thought might have been bringing these women in," Mark said, with three tortilla chips crunching away in his mouth. "They're not stupid. And they know the U.N. and everyone else are going to be on them if they don't do some proper inspecting. So I had to bribe more."

Mark's report checked out with what Omar reported hearing from his sources. There was cause to worry that Mark would try to conceal his recent failures, in hopes of capitalizing through Omar's network. It was never advisable to admit weakness in such circles.

"Aren't you going to eat anything?" Mark asked.

"Sure, I'll get to that."

Mark took a peak out the curtains, shut them, and downed another couple ounces of hooch from the flask.

"Look, I don't have all day," Mark said. "I've got this Kuwaiti coming in on his Lear Jet and he wants at least six women, handpicked from twenty. I sent him photos, but he didn't trust those. He may end up with all twenty, the pervert."

"More money for you," Omar said. "I don't understand why you're complaining."

"Because deep down I hate fucking hypocrites." Mark reached into his other pocket and took out his phone. "Look at them, these people I know. Mahmoud Karawi, three wives, eight kids, built four mosques and last time he was here he spent a long weekend in a hotel with a little Thai boy, told everyone he was in Abu Dhabi. Ramin Al-Hosseini, biggest insurer in the Gulf, and he's on the board of an Islamic foundation. He wants boys and girls, but none of them over thirteen. I told him to get lost. I don't deal with kids. David Kahane, the man behind most of the menorahs sold in the world. He calls every Sunday morning after his Shabbat is over and I send over at least two Arab girls. That's all he likes. You know what sickens me is that we're all slaves to these bastards."

"And what, you'd prefer to shoot them?" Omar probably assumed Mark already had too much to drink. "You're the one who created a place for these men to go to. Something way beyond anything they could have imagined."

"This is a lie," Mark said. "The whole thing, you know, life, is a lie."

"Fine. Be a moralist. Then what?"

"I don't know, Omar. You called me." Mark had stopped nibbling.

"Now I'm confused," Omar admitted. "I was going to tell you about a whole bunch of women we have ready to work for you. They're in Turkey, with this Iraqi trader I know. Seventy-five of them. Gorgeous. From up north, Uzbekistan and places like that. I found out about it a couple days ago, and you're the first person I've come to."

"So?" Mark asked.

"If you're not interested, I'll tell someone else."

"Don't be an asshole," Mark said. "And it is all legit? No hidden issues or anything. Turkey can be iffy."

"No, I'd say about ten grand each, they're yours." Omar couldn't tell what was on Mark's mind. "But the Iraqi needs to meet you. He found out you were a Jew, and that presented a challenge."

"A challenge?"

"Yes, I mean, he will do business with you, but he wants to meet face to face." Omar seemed to be watching Mark scrunch his face together, as if he were stressed. "Can you go to Ankara? That's where it looks like this will take place."

"Moving around is getting harder and harder for me with each day. There aren't a lot of countries I can go to, but I have other papers I can use if I have to." Mark paused and darted his face around, as if he were agitated. "He's going to give me the women then?"

"The plan is for you to inspect them all. He had somebody else try and return a group of Nepali women after he was already paid. The client said they were too old. My guy lost around a million dollars on that deal. That's what worries him. You'll provide a deposit for the women and he will deliver them to you wherever you like," Omar said. "I will guarantee the whole exchange, for my usual cut."

"Fair enough. You and I both know Ramadan is approaching. I might as well be a hypocrite, too," Mark said, holding his flask raised in the air. "Ten thousand is a bargain. Let's drink to that." Mark opened the curtain and hailed the waiter. "You can have strawberry juice while I finish off this yummy vodka, you Islamic piece of shit."

"Fucking Jew."

CHAPTER SIXTY-ONE

The Most Agreeable of Sounds is
the Voice of the Loved One

"THE WAY YOUR BUTT rises into the air reminds me of an apricot," Poonah said. "It has the same curve, the thin crack at the top, even the tiny fuzzy hairs."

Poonah stood in unabashed admiration over Mary's naked body, having been preparing her all afternoon. She'd gone to Migros market, the hybrid Swiss semi-corporate generic health food conglomerate, for all the items to indulge Mary with. Almonds were soaked overnight in the room's ice bucket, then pureed in the kitchen downstairs, which she'd spread all over Mary's buttocks. Poonah minced strawberries and whisked them with egg whites and rosewater for Mary's face, with a final rinse of watercress juice. Poonah then inserted ground rosemary leaves into her vagina. Different parts of Mary were to have their own scents, such as jasmine on the breasts and saffron water on her feet. Musk was rubbed on the outside of the pubis.

Mary wanted this one to be unforgettable.

"Everyone has something going for them, a blessing," she said. "At least I have this apricot behind." She thought it came off as sarcastic.

Their suite overlooked a spectacle of an amber tree in the courtyard. It was a feeling near total serenity for Mary. The one problem was that Poonah had insisted on leaving the television on for the Family Feud Marathon. It was her favorite show. She didn't seem to care that it wasn't Mary's.

Aki sat in the other room waiting for Mary to be prepared.

"You seem lost in thought, Poonah."

"I don't know why but this is reminding me of the first time I masturbated my nephew. He was turning six."

"What do you mean?"

"We get our children ready for the future, like I'm doing for you," Poonah said. "Doing things for each other is important."

Mary didn't know people did these things.

"I would like to put my lips on you for the first and last time," Poonah said, as she pushed the top of her oily hair into Mary's privates. "You will surprise him if you go in wet."

"Let's not," Mary said. "I want to start drier."

"Are you sure?"

"This will make him erupt deeper into me," Mary answered. "You can see that, can't you?"

"That isn't my experience, but do what you like," Poonah said, her hands inside Mary's thighs, massaging her skin with the last of the almond puree. "I'm doing all this for you and Aki. You have given me so much. Saying goodbye to you will be impossible for us."

"It nearly kills me," Mary said.

Poonah rolled Mary's body around and smelled her from behind, putting her nose exactly where she'd already done an enema. "You smell like a marshmallow inside. It is so beautiful." Poonah kept her face there when she spoke. "Aki is going to lose himself when you go to him. Do you want me to get him ready, too?"

"No, I know how," Mary said, sitting at the edge of the bed. "I will serve myself to him." Mary looked at the television for a moment. She had wanted to ignore it. *Name something you buy at the last minute for Easter*, announced the host, with a voice that seemed designed for this one purpose. "And will you turn down the volume when I go in?"

Poonah seemed annoyed by the question. "But then I can't hear my show."

"Lower it as much as you can," Mary said. "I think I will go to Aki naked."

"No way," Poonah said. She looked like she'd been offended. "Trust me, wear the orange panties. Never white, you know."

"Orange?"

"Or green. And what you do, you start with your legs closed and you don't rush when you open them for him," Poonah answered. She was being pedantic again. "But you must keep the underwear on. I've tried both ways and what I learned is that men don't want a peak."

Even Aki, a blind man? Mary thought.

Mary realized this was Poonah after all. And it was Mary's moment, not Poonah's. She undressed from the hotel robe and walked with her fully erect nipples leading the way to Aki. What happened is what happens when a man and woman get into bed and are attracted to one another. They are desperate to express everything about themselves. They already know what to do to please; couple that with the ceaseless desire that we embody, and there's no stopping such creatures.

It is something that can be taken advantage of.

This was the right time in her cycle for her plan. The bed was covered with a sheer silk blanket and dark rose petals. She'd determined that this would be the first time she would force him to stay inside her through to the end.

CHAPTER SIXTY-TWO

Let's Call the Whole Thing Off

STATE OF NEW YORK

VS.   Case No. 08-CF-5094

MARK BLACK

   TRANSCRIPTION OF TAPED CONTROLLED

            PHONE CALL

            TRANSCRIBED BY:

            Will Shaheen

            LAURA SIMON REPORTING GROUP

APPEARANCES:

OMAR AMIR

MARK BLACK

CONTENTS:

MARK: You said Turkey the last time. Now it is Greece. What's next, Libya?

OMAR: Don't blame me. The Iraqi changed the plan. He doesn't feel like he can deliver from Turkey anymore. But don't worry about it.

MARK: Don't worry, huh?

OMAR: Samos is two miles from Turkey.

MARK: We're talking about a fucking island. That means boats.

OMAR: So what?

MARK: The last time we had boats involved, look what happened.

OMAR: We're talking two miles.

MARK: I've been to that area. You know how many die in those waters?

OMAR: No.

MARK: Hundreds. Bodies turn up in fishing nets.

OMAR: I didn't know that.

MARK: The water is treacherous there. Every smuggler at some point tries working that crossing. It is the obvious link to Europe.

OMAR: What do you want me to do?

MARK: Have him stay in Ankara.

OMAR: He won't, I've tried. (Pause) Can you get into Greece?

MARK: Yeah, I've the docs.

OMAR: So what's the problem?

MARK: Only one thing. I don't like when plans change. That worries me.

OMAR: Your plans changed when the boat sank.

MARK: That's apples and oranges.

OMAR: The good news is that he's giving them to you at a discount, because of the inconvenience.

MARK: He has to. I'm not bringing any cash into Greece.

OMAR: I know, we'll use banks.

MARK: I wish I didn't need those girls. Christ.

OMAR: That's a yes?

MARK: I don't have a choice. But if any of them drowns, that's his problem. I won't cover one penny of it.

OMAR: I know.

MARK: You told him that?

OMAR: I did. I'm looking out for you.

MARK: Fine. Fax me where I'm supposed to meet him. I think we should hang up.

OMAR: I'll call you if there's anything.

MARK: Okay.

OMAR: Goodbye, Mark.

(THE CALL ENDED.)

I, Will Shaheen, certify that I was authorized to and did transcribe the foregoing proceedings, and that the transcript is a true and complete record of the tape recording thereof.

CHAPTER SIXTY-THREE

There is No Evil Angel but Love

UNPLEASANT THOUGHTS HAD BEEN seizing Aki all the sleepless night, on through the morning. He stayed with Poonah, as Mary bounced around old Zürich taking care of last-minute errands. The three left the hotel together, took cabs to different places.

Poonah and Aki asked the driver of the Mercedes taxi to drop them by the lake. There was a field of grass with shaded benches, removed from the bustle of the Swiss marching to work. The weather was crappy, even by local standards, so they had their pick of places to sit. Poonah tried speaking to Aki, taking note of the seagulls or a harsh wind, but Aki would smile a smile that was incapable of hiding the pain.

As the time passed, fewer people showed up. Poonah drank tea from a thermos the hotel prepared for her. Aki, meanwhile, undid the zipper on his jacket. It was a perfect moment and yet so filled with sorrow that one had to feel for them. Aki looked like he was mourning something major in his life. He went on listening to the birds, the occasional swell and growl of lake water against the dock. He took the thermos from Poonah and spoke, "Let's go somewhere else."

"But it is so beautiful here." Poonah remained seated while Aki stood up. She'd said it as if she were hoping he'd change his mind.

"That's the problem," Aki answered. "It is too beautiful. I can't bear it."

❦

Sternen Grill
Theaterstr. 22, Zürich, ZH 8001

Aki seemed to know Mary was there before she assumed he could. Given everywhere that they'd traveled, he probably registered the unique grumble of her suitcase on the pavement. He was already on his second Pfizer. It wasn't like him to have alcohol in the morning, but his nerves needed calming.

"Finally you're here. I think Aki was losing his mind," Poonah said to Mary as she joined them at a table. "He hasn't said a word yet."

It was foggy in that little alleyway by the meeting of the trams, where some of the world's greatest sausages were being grilled. The wind had died down, but it was still bad enough that they were the only people dining.

"Aki?" Mary said.

He reached his hand forward and hugged Mary around the waist, with pure tenderness.

"I know," Mary added. Much melancholy was contained in those two words.

"We didn't have any breakfast," Poonah said. She was on a different wavelength, still speaking about her stomach. "Maybe we should order. It might cheer him up."

"I don't want anything," he said, struggling. "This is like sickness."

"I even tried getting him some sushi," Poonah said. "It is as if he left the world. I don't know what to do for him."

"Now that I'm here, maybe you'll eat," Mary said. "There's nothing we can do. We're destined to suffer for a very long time."

Mary walked over to the Arab man running the register. The Swiss must've found other jobs since the last time she'd been there, years earlier. She ordered in broken Arabic. "Three bratwursts, with the spicy mustard. And an extra roll please." It was her favorite bread in the world, after all. The Arab took her francs and she stood by the grill, eyes fixed on Aki as she waited for the food. There he was in all his glory, a mastiff of a man, with a glow to his skin even on a gloomy day such as this one. *I feel your pain worse than my own.* "And one more beer for my friend."

She made two trips to the table with the food and put the springy roll and a sausage in front of each of them.

"Got everything you needed?" Aki asked.

"Yes," Mary said, her eyes glassy from trying to keep the tears from escaping. Something about the way he asked her something so simple reminded her of the compassion he possessed, all that they'd been through together. "I have something to show you." She reached for her suitcase and unzipped the front pocket. Mary took out a plastic shopping bag and handed it to Poonah. "Take a look."

"What is it?" she asked.

"Never mind, just open it."

It was a small pink cardboard box. "Early response?" Poonah asked. The words were written in bold on the front. "Is this what I think it is?"

Mary reached forward and kissed Aki's hand. "I took the test this morning. I'm going to have your baby, Aki."

Aki's lips quivered. Words wouldn't come to him.

"It is accurate?" Poonah asked.

"I took another one as well, a different test," Mary said. "Don't worry, this is how I wanted it."

Tears fell onto the plate in front of him. "I had a feeling," Aki said. "Last night I saw it in a dream. A little girl was there and I was swinging her in the soft rain. It was a face I never saw before. But I had a special feeling for the girl."

"It is the only way I can leave." Mary looked at her sausage, and pushed the plate a few inches forward. "I thought about it more than you can imagine. I realized I had to do this. To carry you inside me when I left you."

"I understand," he said. He looked like he was trying to say more. He started on his third beer. "You have to leave, I know. It is all for those girls. It is the right thing. Mark can't have happiness built with another's pain."

"This plan would never have happened without you," Mary said. "It is everything I ever learned from you."

"Last night I was thinking about those women that drowned," he said. "And for the first time I thought maybe it is better that they did."

"Don't say that. You don't mean it," Mary said.

"It kills me to think this, but maybe there is some reason in it this way. I sacrifice myself again and again." Aki lifted his downcast eyes and looked at Mary even though he couldn't see. "They won't have to live through agony like this."

"You'll feel better soon. Don't worry," Poonah said.

She didn't comprehend the man the way Mary did.

"People stop feeling because it is convenient to," Aki said. "Everything I am is because of how I feel it, and how I see that we have to let go."

"This must be what death feels like," Mary said. "You know something has to happen, but it is the last thing we want."

"That's why I'm asking you to leave me. You need to," Aki said. "I don't know if that's the way it is only with me, but all the goodbyes in my life have been abrupt."

"You told me to do this," Mary said. "We have no choice now."

"Only if you leave can what we have stay love," Aki said. "Or I fool myself with words like that. It is my fate to be like this."

"This is temporary, Aki. Please..." Mary pleaded. "This is temporary!"

Poonah interrupted her. "That's not what he's feeling. Last night he said he knows he will never see you again."

"That's not true," she said. But she recognized that she might be lying to herself. *Even if it is true, I won't accept it.* "Imagine how we'll feel when we meet again." Mary would find him, one way or another, so long as he was alive.

Aki stayed silent and to himself.

Mary had an intuition that this was the moment to leave. She could tell that Aki couldn't handle much more. Everything had been said, and sometimes lingering masks the reality, pretending as if the parting isn't going to happen. Later, all you remember is saying goodbye, looking back in the distance, as they did after quivering in each other's arms, walking a few feet, turning around, continuing again, blowing kisses, trying to accept that life had now taken them elsewhere, apart without the other, for who knows how long. So much ends between people who were almost one after such goodbyes.

It was like this when they parted, Mary pushing her suitcase towards the Calatrava train station for her underground ride to the airport. What they each would probably realize was that their separating was the most painful and beautiful moment any of them would ever know.

CHAPTER SIXTY-FOUR

Back to Black

I T SEEMED GLOOMY TO Mark to receive an email from Omar Amir with directions on where to wait on an empty beach at midnight for the mysterious boat. So much could go wrong. In theory, it had seemed no more ominous than the usual transaction, but when it came to executing it, worry set deep into Mark. He had eaten dinner at the same taverna each of three nights, already a big fan of how Spiros, the bald but hairy proprietor, grilled the various tiny whole fish with only Greek names. He watched Spiros with discipline, hoping to mimic him the next time he was in the kitchen.

Winds so terrible he could no longer eat on the veranda, he dined by the bar instead. Mark went incognito, having the sense to tell the probing Spiros that he was interested in ancient Greek ruins. Why else would he be there? Tonight, dinner was six sardines, accompanied by small earthenware bowls of feta and wild greens drenched in olive oil, finishing off the meal. Plus two smalls bottles of cloudy ouzo—the availability of alcohol in public meant much to him.

Between courses Mark went to the back of the restaurant to call Omar, often losing reception seconds into the conversation, due to the weather.

"Are you sure they're able to cross in this wind?" Mark had a bad feeling about it. "I told you how dangerous these two miles can be. And that's in calm weather."

Omar explained that they had no choice. "The Iraqi is starting to get panicky. He paid off the Turkish Coast Guard there, but they're threatening to turn him in. They keep squeezing more and more money out of the guy. He says we have to do it tonight, or it is all off."

"I'd do it tomorrow," Mark said. "There's no goddamn rush. A day here or there makes no difference. One more goddamn day."

"Check the reports. Tomorrow and the next day are supposed to be even windier," Omar answered. "Violent storms."

Mark had to accept his fate. No one was listening to him.

He hung up, paid Spiros for dinner in cash, skipping baklava this time, and left the restaurant. Mark had rented a modest Škoda, the Czech-made vehicle, so that he wouldn't attract attention. It felt even later than it was, with all the locals long asleep, except the police. They knew Asia was across the way, and that meant trouble. Such was this business, with all kinds of exceptions to be made for getting away with the illicit. Armed with a loaded shotgun hidden in his jacket, provided by an Albanian contact and drug runner who lived on the island, he thought he was prepared for anything. He drove the mile to the beach, down a narrow road flanked by olive trees blowing madly, like people warning him of doom ahead. It was something out of Homer, this stretch of pavement, somehow horrifying. He couldn't believe someone could be so stubborn as to insist on doing business in this weather. Mark tried remaining calm, but was on edge, aware of every sound, as if the whole world was in conversation with him. Each howl of wind a threat, each rock and creak of boat to be followed by a bullet. He arrived a half-hour early, rolled up his windows and remained in the car, raising the volume on the Ottoman court music being broadcast from Turkey's shores, his hand on the gun.

❧

A FEW MINUTES AFTER midnight he saw the first sign of activity, a dot of light in the distant waters. He turned off the radio and then the car, took a deep, nervous breath to prepare to leave, assuming this was none other than the boat he was to meet. A fearful moment of silence followed before opening the door and being with the wind out there. He still had to walk to the shore itself, looking behind him as he contemplated what to do. This stretch of Samos beach was his alone tonight, a realization that shook him to the core. He climbed down some ancient marble steps in the complete darkness, the moon hidden behind clouds, trying not to fall. He'd never been so cold anywhere near the Mediterranean. He went towards the three fishermen's boats docked on the one side and where his contact would head. The noise of the sea attacked him from all directions, as he stood above the water, looking for the ship's light again without success. The captain would know better than to be too obvious. Mark was still poetic enough to see that this moment that was his destiny was unpredictable to him even days before. The same way the women from Aden who were waiting to come to shore had no idea that an emergency seconds later would cause them to jump overboard to drown. *I should not be thinking about them right now. Too late to end it now. There is a lot ahead of me tonight, and seeing their dead faces in front of me isn't going to help anything.* He'd been luckier than them from birth. But you never know who you're dealing with, and that's what the rental of a 9mm Beretta was for.

Mark pulled his hood over his head, eyes now dripped from the chill. It reminded him of what it might feel like to cry, but this was about as close as he'd get. A boat turned on its lights for a quick moment, possibly to signal something to Mark. Then nothing for thirty more minutes, he realized, checking his phone's clock more often than he should. They were late, and something might've gone wrong. Perhaps he shouldn't keep staying there and return to the car, he thought. No, he decided that was where he ought to be, for tactical reasons, in case of something shady coming up that required him to aggress.

He crouched down on the dock and gathered his body together in an effort to keep warm, ducking behind a rusted metal gate. Several times he thought about going back to his room, giving up. But then the whole deal could be called off. At that point the trip would've been a waste of everyone's time. There'd be a chance he'd lose the deposit on the girls, straining his relationship with Omar.

He had to wait.

At 1:12 A.M., to his surprise, the boat appeared, but a few meters from the dock, floating in with the engines off. It seemed to come from nowhere, as if dropped from the sky. *It couldn't have, could it?*

He figured that these people knew what they were doing after all, eluding the Greek Coast Guard.

Mark gathered himself, stood up from the silent, otherworldly state of mind he'd entered, and got ready for business of the darkest kind.

Moments later a young Turkish teenager wearing only a ripped t-shirt and cargo pants popped out from the stern and ran forward with the tow ropes, throwing them on the dock with great accuracy. He yelled something to the captain and with that the boat had completed the journey. The kid scooted over, tied the ropes, then came and shook Mark's hand. "*Merhaba*," he said. It was the standard greeting in both Turkey and Arabia. "Mark Black?" He said the name as if it were one word.

"Yes."

"Okay. Okay, Mark Black." The kid looked at Mark as if that's all he could muster in English.

A lone woman appeared on deck, gazed in the direction of Mark, and reached out for the kid's hand to grab as she jumped ashore. At first Mark had no idea what was happening, as nothing in the world was making sense, seeing Mary's silhouette here in the darkness, far from everything, where he least expected it. His mind was split in two, between revulsion and awe. He flashed on Omar, and how much she must have been paying him. It dawned on Mark that there were no women being delivered, and he would lose a ton of money. Everyone had probably been lying for Mary, and yet there was nothing more beautiful to him than seeing her at that moment. He could sense her eagerness in uniting with him, as if the past had washed itself away. *She's made this offering of herself all on her own, without asking anything of me.* He grabbed Mary's face and almost bit her lips in pleasure as he said hello with a flood of kisses and desperate embraces, those same eyes still tearing only because he was so cold.

"Wife?" the Turkish kid asked, with naïve, envious eyes that communicated one day he would want to be so lucky as Mark.

"Yes, my wife." Mark pressed her face into his chest with so much force that it seemed to him that his body missed her even more than some of the hateful thoughts that raced through his mind. He tried giving the feelings words, but couldn't. He was overcome by something he didn't understand.

Mary and Mark said goodbye to the kid and the boat, struggled together in the darkness up the steps to the black car that would take them forward to where, in so many ways, they always were.

CHAPTER SIXTY-FIVE

The Deception of Mark

MARK AND MARY SAT at the small table of their top floor room at the Hotel Oceanus in the dark saying little to one another as they finished a pot of tea. After all, each had been through so much, lately and that night. In so many ways they were above the need to communicate with words, understanding one another's needs so perfectly as to be destructive, or harmonious.

A little before five o'clock in the morning she flicked her tongue on the back of his neck. She had undressed in no time and went to the bathroom to shower. Mary stood there for longer than usual, taking deep breaths of steam, finding something like peace for the hours ahead. She figured that he couldn't mistake her shower for anything other than a prelude to what was to come. She could have been there, body covered by pajamas, on the edge of the bed, like so many other couples are, night after night, overcome by so much longing they somehow drift asleep with a feeling of emotional paralysis. In their dreams they find salvation, hoping the next day will be more gratifying. But this was Mary's life, the new one, and though to an observer the pattern was repeating itself with Mark, all that was within her being had been transformed. Yes, as she stood letting the soft hot water fall all over her body, she realized she'd achieved what she'd set out to do as she left her house on horse. Returning to him now was the acid test that demonstrated the point. But there was more to do to execute each last detail of her plan, not just shower and contemplate the nature of her new life. Desire needed to be elicited, with all its suffering. She would wait for a man no longer. Mark was in the same category as any other she'd ever known, except Aki. This was for him, all this pretending. Mary and Aki would give one another everything by never seeing one another again. Raping Mark was not out of the question. Mary sought justice in pleasure.

MARK LAID STILL IN bed, more or less towards the center, with his legs spread slightly, preparing for her in every way he could. *Who would kiss whom first and where?* At the same moment as he was desiring aspects of her, such as that first touch of the side of her buttocks, feelings of wanting her to subsume him also overcame the man. Somehow it would all get worked out. The act would occur, if it started at all. But she'd been so quiet ever since she arrived, with barely a word said to him. Not that he was much better, but she was the talkative one, at least when it came to their pairing. Hearing the water still running from the shower he lifted the blankets and reached across for the chair where he'd laid his pants and left his pistol, hiding it now in a groove under the headboard. Everything was possible when these two came together. He returned to beneath the sheets again, spreading his legs at the exact same angle as before, one that was not too wide as to be obvious, and yet not tight either, as if his plan was to sleep. The gun would be kept at an arm's distance, of course.

MARY CAME OUT OF the shower wrapped in two green towels, with nothing underneath. In her left hand was a damp hand towel. "Here. Warm yourself up for me." She tossed it his direction and sat at the edge of the bed with her back to him.

Mark took the towel and placed it on himself. She was right, it felt good, and relaxed his body. He was absorbed in gazing at her and would've given anything to know what she was thinking. What was clear to him was that he shouldn't ask. That could kill it. There was time, and though he couldn't see her face, he had the sense to recognize something powerful was happening regarding the manner with which she was offering himself to him.

She was still. So much so that she could've not been real.

A minute passed and she took the towels off her body, remaining like a statue at the edge of the bed. He watched her breath get deeper. Then she fell backwards. At first only her hair tickled him on his chest, then a playful smile on her face appeared as she landed the back of her head directly on his penis, pushing down on it. It hurt. Her breasts hadn't changed—he'd forgotten how wide her nipples were. *How is it that I remember everything about this woman and yet have never seen her nipples look just so?* Mark reached forward and placed his hands in the fold between her breasts and started pushing them apart. He craved seeing them dangling off the edge of her body. He wanted to suck on one of them.

"Make me a drink, would you, Mark?" They were her first words in quite a while.

"We don't have anything. I already looked around for that," he said.

The wind was still blowing so strong, a draft could be felt through the windows.

"I created this moment, you know." She voiced the words to the ceiling, aloud, as if it were an oration. "I lie here in total control of everything." She lifted her head as if to acknowledge his presence. "So I could kill you, or I could fuck you."

"You're asking me to pick?" Mark couldn't tell whether she was listening to him at all. He almost had the feeling that he wasn't there.

Mary let out a sigh of what he assumed was pleasure, the smallest sigh anyone could make and have it still be a sigh. She directed his hands to her enormous nipples.

Two minutes later she pulled the sheets off him, keeping her back to Mark as she mounted his body, first rubbing along the tip of him with the end of her, teasing him, her breath getting heavier.

He hadn't moved much since he'd stowed the gun.

She leaned forward and spread herself wide above him, dropping at once for him to see her taking him whole from the first moment. She lifted herself and revealed drops of blood rolling down her thighs and the side of his legs. She pumped three times, this time rougher, drawing even more blood.

Mark hadn't noticed it at first, his mind elsewhere, consumed by pleasure. He grimaced. "What's happening?"

"Lie back and enjoy me," she said, ignoring his awkwardness. "I made myself a virgin again for you."

More blood spilled from her vagina.

"What the hell has gotten into you?" He was almost yelling.

"Just enjoy me. Enjoy my first time. You're into deflowering." She took greater charge. It was rough, almost violent. "Stay in!" she said, wrapping her hand under his behind, as Mark tried to wriggle away for his climax. It was a command. She repeated it the second time as a grunt, somehow menacing in its power.

Seconds later what he experienced as pleasure was all 240 million or so microorganisms swimming in their 3.4 mm of water from his testicles, racing towards her glorious ova to coagulate.

Without a pause, Mary removed her hand from under Mark, took the towel off the bed, and went to the shower, leaving his entire midsection and a third of the bed covered in blood. "You can come in if you need to."

He jumped at the opportunity, left the bed and climbed into the narrow space to shower with her. "The strange thing that I noticed," Mark said, nibbling on her neck, "is that you smell quite a bit like Mom."

"It makes perfect sense I would."

"So you're not surprised."

"I need you to stop talking," she said. She turned and faced him. "I'm here to rub against you so you can be inside me. We're going to spend the rest of our lives doing this."

For the next three days they barely left the room, without any more blood.

March 21, 2011: *The London Daily*, **United States Extraditing National Accused of Causing the Death of Dozens of Sex Workers, by Ali McCoy.**

One man stands charged for spearheading one of the most treacherous crimes in the immigrant underground economy: human trafficking.

United States national Mark Black is believed to be in Saudi Arabia. Mounting diplomatic pressure on Saudi Arabia for cooperating with U.S. criminal investigations has occurred in multiple Congressional hearings on government reform.

From 2007 to 2011, federal prosecutors charge, Mark Black's complex network arranged for the smuggling of a minimum of 750 immigrants from their homelands to Italy, Israel and Saudi Arabia, promising them jobs, several thousand dollars a month, and free room and board. Individuals, mostly women, were sold off from countries such as Iraq, Nigeria and Uzbekistan.

The immigrants were servicing the highest end sector of the prostitution market. Included in the charges are that Mr. Black was responsible for the deaths of nearly 40 sex workers being transported to Yemen. "This tragedy is what set in motion our ability to take this in a new direction," said Chief Attorney Pabel Delgado.

None of the women who worked for him complained of violent treatment, unlike other human traffickers, making this a unique case. Mr. Black has not responded to the charges.

Trials such as this one are rare. If convicted on all counts, the defendant faces life in prison and fines exceeding ten million dollars. Should those separate murder charges concerning the drowning of the women near Aden lead to a guilty plea, the death penalty may be enforced.

Black's ventures operated under a variety of names, according to prosecutors. U.S. Attorney Joseph Bolter has said that they've only scratched the surface of these operations but have several people working abroad alongside international officials and investigators. There has been no word yet from Mr. Black's defense attorney.

According to court documents, the case began with a tip from overseas, from an anonymous source. Mr. Black has been deemed a fugitive and is considered armed and dangerous. Details about his mysterious life have yet to emerge, however.

Ali McCoy, *The London Daily*

"YOU DID THIS?" HIS face was white as stone. Emotion flooded through Mark.

The world was falling down on him.

She'd dropped the printout of the newspaper clipping on Mark's hairy chest for him to read. There was no point in hiding from it. She lugged a heavy desk chair outside and sat beside him, basking in the perfection of that island morning.

Mary feared nothing any more.

Even if he killed her they'd track him down.

Mark had already finished breakfast and had been sitting naked on a lounge chair on the balcony to get sun. She came forward to touch and soothe him, the supreme act of cunning, then refrained, letting him digest what was happening all alone.

The storm had passed.

It wasn't her job to protect him from himself and what he'd created.

"You arranged the end of me?" he asked. He'd read the article straight through, without once looking up. Only after he finished did Mark stare at her, revealing the state of his nerves. In so many ways he was a finished man.

She didn't feel a morsel of pity for him. The suffering caused by their work needed to be terminated. "How many fake passports and identities do you have at this point?" Mary had thought of everything. "I assume at least six. The Greeks think you're one person, Israel knows you by something else. So I'm not doing this for you. I'm putting an end to your business."

Mary leaned her chair back against the low railing, giving him the opportunity with one simple push to send her on towards death. *Once you're feeling eternal, there's nothing to get desperate about.* Perhaps offering him her life was a dare, even if he understood that she could help him to escape. All that mattered to her was fulfilling her sense of herself.

It was an ancient setup, played out the same way over the centuries.

"Yeah, and if they find me, I'm worse than dead." As we'd seen, Mark had a bad feeling about this whole Samos arrangement from the beginning, and by now one can only surmise that it was becoming clear to him why.

"I won't let them find you. And besides, we'll go somewhere where they can't just grab you." She had become soft, like water. It was her conviction that made it so, trusting death more than so much of what's called life. "There are extradition laws that countries must abide by. And there are countries with no regulations against consensual incest."

"Do they know all about us?" There was a harshness to his voice, as if he were capable of total and complete destruction. You couldn't miss it.

"No, they don't, but they might figure it out," Mary said. "I'm not trying to destroy you. I was putting an end to what you were doing with your workers. Meanwhile, I've set up my own network and we can start with alcohol. Yemen, Saudi Arabia."

"Only alcohol?"

"I know what I'm doing. I've learned from all your mistakes."

"Forget alcohol. I never want to see you again," he said. "I was there when you were born and I should never have trusted you, from that moment."

"And I thought I could trust my brother. But no, you have always thought of yourself. Mom told me as much."

"Yeah, sure, I'm sure Mom said that. You don't remember the love I gave you."

Mary turned her face to the horizon, reminding herself of the whole big world out there, far from his misery. "You have no choice now. You have to trust me."

"Right."

"And that means making our life better than it ever was. Besides, you have to face your responsibility now." Mary handed him the positive pregnancy test she'd shown Aki, pretending it had been opened that morning.

His face went cold, as if to say *How much can I bear?*

"We are bound together by this," she said, meeting eyes with him.

They had the same eyes, and that was still attractive to both of them.

"If you tell me to leave, then it goes against everything you've ever stood for. Children have to come before us, you said. We have to make the world right for them. We are rotten."

"So you're having this baby? I suppose you've already decided that."

"Yes, exactly. Unless you kill me."

"You must know the risks when it comes to siblings. I wonder if there's any place for that in your calculations and crazy plans."

"You can't look me in the eyes and tell me I'm crazy. I dare you to."

"So what."

"We'll get the fetus tested, make sure it is healthy in every way."

"You know, I woke up this morning and it was peaceful. You were back with me, and we were getting along. There wasn't a trouble in the world. You realize that's how my day started, staring out at this wild sea."

"No one takes that away from you." She searched for his hand. "But we're past that moment now."

She would guarantee herself to be rid of Mark before Aki's child came to the world. She had about ten months to make certain he'd be locked away, or dead.

Or it might not happen that way, and she could go somewhere with him where they could create a life. He would believe that she hadn't deceived him. She would assure him of her devotion. It was necessary to move forward in time as a unit, as beloveds, beholden to their frailty, bound by the wonder that possessed this child who would one day create her own story of how love was satisfied.

There, on that island, as the soft ocean that drowns crashed ashore, they were two with hopes of peace in a future. They glanced out across eternity knowing they will create again.

Somebody somewhere is setting out and another has left already.

No way had been invented for two to say goodbye to each other. It is the story of all happiness promised we tell as we end it.

The End